SHE BELONGED TO THEM

MARTINA MONROE
BOOK 16

H.K. CHRISTIE

Copyright © 2026 by H.K. Christie

Cover design by Odile Stamanne

First edition: March 2026

ISBN: 978-1-953268-57-0

For the everyday heroes who stand up and fight for justice.

1

LENA

ETHAN DESCRIBED the missing girl with a detached fascination that made my blood run cold. I tried to shake it off. It was just Ethan being Ethan, *I guess*. But the way he talked about the abducted girl, how he thought it happened, and what the kidnapper might be doing to her... it was disgusting. His voice had been too casual, too curious, like he was speculating about a movie plot instead of a real person.

Truth be told, I never really liked Ethan. There was something about the way he looked at me and the way he looked at other people. Like he wasn't one of us. Like he was studying us. The way we'd watch animals at a zoo, separate and detached. Sociopath-like. Major serial killer vibes. I had no idea why Jason still hung out with him.

They'd been friends since they were itty-bitty, but they were now in their twenties. It was okay to let go already. Why Jason remained friends with him was a mystery to me. Ethan had no real goals in life. He worked for his father's company, but only so his family wouldn't cut him off. Jason was different. He was in medical school and would be a doctor in a couple years.

Across the room, I locked eyes with Jason. He gave me a

playful wink. I'd never been in love before Jason, not really. Everything with him was so different, like a grown-up love. He was sweet and caring. Not just out for a good time, like so many other guys I had dated.

Tiffany flipped her long, bleached-blond hair and said, "Ethan, can we stop talking about this? It's really morbid."

"Why? Are you scared?" Ethan asked with a bit of delight in his tone.

"No. Just icked out. Maybe you should try being *less* of a creep," Tiffany retorted.

I silently thanked her. Just because Ethan's family had billions didn't mean we had to tolerate him. Yet there we were, weekend guests at his parents' cabin, deep in the woods, miles from anything. The cabin itself was impossible to criticize. Floor-to-ceiling windows. Stone fireplace. Staff who appeared with drinks before you realized your glass was empty. Still, I preferred city lights and loud bars to all this quiet.

"Well, if you don't want to talk about what's in the news," Ethan said, leaning back, eyes gleaming in the firelight, "let's play a game."

"What kind of game?" Jenna asked.

"Well, I don't know if some of you are up for it," he said. "You seemed pretty scared already. What about you, Lena? I bet you're too scared to play."

I met his stare without blinking. "You know I'm up for anything, Ethan. Give it your best shot."

Jason walked over and put his arm around my shoulders. "That's my girl."

"Okay, so here's the game. We'll gather around the fireplace and I'll tell the most disturbing story I know. You're guaranteed to be fully freaked out," he said, clearly enjoying the attention as everyone listened. "And then," he said, "afterward you have to stand outside by yourself. Whoever lasts ten *full* minutes all alone in the dark, wins."

"What do we win?" Jenna asked.

Did she really care? She was such a follower. Always just going along for the ride. I never really understood her. She was beautiful and smart; why was she so worried about what everyone else thought about her?

Jason eyed Ethan. "Do you have it?"

Ethan nodded. "Right here." He turned and went to a cabinet, opened it, and pulled out something that looked like an ancient soccer trophy that was covered in pipe cleaners and pom-poms. It had clearly been created by small children. "If you win, you get the Best Man Trophy."

"The what?" I asked.

Jason said, "It's the Best Man Trophy. If you win it, you are *the best man*. We made it when we were kids."

Ethan said, "Last one to win it keeps it. That's why I still have it. I'm the reigning champ and *best* man."

Jason turned to me. "It's highly coveted."

"I guess so," I said. "I look forward to winning it!"

Ethan said, "A girl has never won. But good luck, toots."

It was no wonder he was still single. "Not until *now*. Bring it."

The group moved from the dining room and gathered around the fireplace, sinking into the large leather sofa as the fire crackled and popped. Ethan launched into his story, describing, in vivid detail, a serial killer who hunted in the woods, capturing and carving up victims. He spoke calmly, almost reverently, as if savoring every word. The killer, he said, was finally stopped by a local FBI agent. Something prickled at the back of my neck.

Ethan continued. "And my friends, the punchline is, it's not just a story. It all happened here. In the very woods surrounding us *right now*."

Tiffany and I shared a glance before I realized I'd heard the story before. "I think I read about that. How do you know all those details?" They certainly weren't in any of the news reports I had read.

"My family's friends with the locals. We got all the details. Apparently, that FBI agent still lives here." He scanned us one by one. "So now that you know serial killers have roamed these woods, who wants to be first to stand outside? Blindfolded. In the dark. Fifteen feet from the house. All alone on the edge of the woods."

My heart thumped once.

"You make it ten minutes," he continued, "you win the trophy, or perhaps something even better."

Jason fidgeted. "Lena, why don't you go first? I know what an adrenaline junky you are."

It was child's play. I didn't know why anyone would be scared. According to Ethan's own story and the news articles I read, the killer was caught. There was nothing to worry about. But I sure would like to rub the win in Ethan's face. I said, "Sure. Let's do this."

Jason helped me up. Ethan held up a black satin handkerchief and carefully tied it around my eyes.

"Jason will lead you outside. You ready, Jason?"

"I am."

"Ooohs" and "aaahs" rose from the group.

"I can't wait until that trophy's in my possession," I said as Jason led me toward the front door. The door creaked open, and cool night air brushed my skin as I stepped outside.

"Are you sure you're okay?" Jason asked quietly.

"Piece of cake," I said. "Go ahead. Close the door. Start the timer."

He kissed me on the cheek and whispered, "I love you. See you soon."

My heart fluttered. "Love you, too."

Grinning, I paced fifteen feet from the house, as instructed. Twigs cracked under my shoes. I heard birds flutter and brief rustlings, probably squirrels or other small animals moving through the brush. The sound of the door shutting made me think of Jason. He was so sweet and so gorgeous, and he was mine.

As I inhaled the air, it smelled like pine and earth. There was literally nothing scary about it. I couldn't wait to win so I could taunt the trophy in Ethan's smug little face. I began counting in my head, trying to make the ten minutes pass faster. I was on the number 1-9-7 when I heard it.

A creak, like a large branch shifting.

"Jason?" I called. "Is that you?"

No response.

"Ethan?"

Footsteps grew closer.

They weren't coming from the house. They were coming from the woods. It was all probably a setup. Ethan probably planned for one of his friends to come out there to freak me out. *Nice try.* It wasn't working.

As the person approached, I could smell their aftershave. It was musky. Probably male. "I know you're there. And I'm not scared of you."

The figure moved closer. I could feel their breath on my neck, and a chill crept down my spine. I thought, *Well played, Ethan.* He was so sick to set it up, but I wasn't falling for it.

A deep voice said, "Well, then, that's your first mistake."

My smile vanished.

Before I could react, a large gloved hand clamped over my mouth, and everything went dark.

2

MARTINA

WITH A RIGHT HOOK and a jab to the midsection, I imagined my opponent falling to the ground, vowing to never hurt anyone ever again. He'd ride the pain, but that wasn't what I wanted. I didn't want pain. I wanted justice.

I spun into a roundhouse kick to the side. *Just one more.* Maybe another, and then another. The heavy bag jolted under the impact, the thud echoing against the gym walls. I grabbed the bag with both hands and bowed my head as sweat dripped from my temples and stung my eyes. My breath sawed in and out of my lungs, the air tasting like sweat and chalk.

The gym was the only place I could stomp out the memories of the last year. The man who abducted my daughter, he'd gotten more than a few theoretical punches. I'd nearly sprained my finger in one particular session. I exhaled long and shaky, trying to slow my pulse.

"Looks like you could use some water."

I glanced over my shoulder and saw Selena, a towel wrapped around her neck. She handed me a bottle. I nodded and took it. "Thanks."

"You're hitting it pretty hard," she said. "Maybe too hard?"

Selena, my stepdaughter, could always sense when something was bothering me. Which apparently, as of lately, I'd been wearing those emotions on my sleeve. "I'll be all right."

My muscles quivered with fatigue. I wasn't as young as I used to be, but I needed to stay fit and vigilant. I wasn't taking any new cases, not until my therapist thought I could handle one without spiraling or losing control again. Not until the nightmares stopped. I leaned against the wall.

Selena stepped closer. "Bad night?"

"Are you saying I *don't* look like a glamorous movie star?"

She smirked. "I just know you, Martina. And I know when you're going a little harder at the bag than usual."

"It helps with frustration." *And anger*, I thought.

"Everyone is safe now," Selena reassured me gently.

For a second, I couldn't look at her, not when I knew she could see straight through me. "I know. I just... I always wanted to protect her. And I couldn't."

Those facts didn't just disappear when the threat had been eliminated. That loss of control and safety lingered; longer than I cared for.

"She seems like she's doing really well, Martina."

Zoey, my daughter, had been abducted last year and would bear the scars for a lifetime. But Selena was right. Zoey was coping better than any of us expected. She was a tough young woman who had gotten married shortly after her rescue and was thriving in her third year of veterinarian school.

"Maybe a new case would help," Selena offered.

"I'm not taking any cases right now. Just administrative stuff. I need a break." And I hated that it was true. I wanted to keep going, but I knew if I didn't take a break, someone could get hurt. Like me, or my friends and family, or someone who crossed me on a bad day.

"I think you've more than earned it, Martina."

"I guess."

"You guess?" Selena raised a brow as she took a sip from her water bottle.

"Maybe I'm getting too old for this."

"You're not old."

I was nearing fifty. I felt pretty old. Or maybe it was just life. I'd seen so much loss, heartbreak, and injustice. Some mornings my joints agreed with me before my mind did. I'd been a private investigator and security consultant most of my adult life. I'd tried to find balance, to make it all seem worth it, but sometimes the silver lining felt impossible to find.

"I think you're doing pretty well. And everyone needs a break every once in a while. Somebody very wise once told me that."

Selena loved to turn my own advice around on me. I looked at her and wiped my forehead with the back of my sleeve. "True."

The gym door banged open, breaking the silence. Vincent hurried inside. He wasn't in gym clothes, just in his typical jeans, T-shirt, and hoodie. His hair was mussed, as usual.

"What's up?" I asked.

"There is a client upstairs, and he's insisting that you're the only person who can help him."

"Did you tell him I'm not taking any cases right now?" My entire staff was instructed to defer new clients to either Stavros, if he was in the office, or another senior investigator.

"I did, but he insists."

"Well, there have been others in the last few months who insisted too, and we turned them down. We have plenty of capable investigators, both you and Selena included. They don't need me."

"He's refusing to take no for an answer, Martina," Vincent said. "And he's... I don't know. Maybe you should at least meet with him."

"I'm in no condition to meet a client," I snapped, harsher than intended. Vincent flinched slightly. He didn't deserve that. He was just the messenger. "I guess I could be upstairs in twenty minutes," I said, softening my tone. "Where is he now?"

"Talking to Stavros."

"Stavros is here?" Stavros, my semi-retired business partner, usually only came into the office on Thursdays and Fridays.

"He is. Apparently this guy called the office first and couldn't reach you, so he asked for Stavros. They called him at home and he drove in. Stavros is entertaining him while he waits for you."

I shook my head. "Why would Stavros do that?"

Vincent lifted a shoulder.

"I'll shower and head upstairs and then I'll let this person down gently." Sometimes, if you want something done, you just have to do it yourself.

"Cool," Vincent said, but there was a knowing look in his eyes. One that said this client wasn't going to easily take no for an answer.

Which, to be honest, made me curious. Who was this guy who had enough influence to bring Stavros into the office? I knew I shouldn't take on anything potentially dangerous. But darn it, it had already piqued my interest by the fact Stavros felt compelled to come in on his day off. It didn't mean I'd take the case. It just meant I'd hear him out and assign him to our most capable investigator, and then I'd move on.

As I turned toward the locker room, I tried to release the thoughts of a new case from my mind. Some pushy client who expected our firm to be at their beck and call was the last thing I needed in my life. Nor did I need to put myself or anyone close to me in danger. But as I pushed open the locker room door, a cold flicker of something ominous crawled up my spine.

3
———

MARTINA

STRUTTING THROUGH THE OFFICE AREA, past rows of cubicles, my mind swirled with curiosity about the case. Who was this person who insisted I attend this meeting? If Stavros was involved, it had to be either someone he respected, owed a favor to, or was personally tied to. It made me fear I wouldn't be able to walk away from it, even if I wanted to. But I had to stick to my guns. *No new cases.* My health and my family had to come first.

As it was, my name had been splashed all over the news after a serial killer contacted me during the holidays. In the end, it was heartbreak all around with the small exception that I'd met two new friends, Kate, a homicide detective, and Natalie, a crime reporter, who had quickly felt like family.

If I were to take a new case, I needed one that was uplifting, not tragic or bittersweet like so many. We'd had life-affirming cases in the past, but it seemed so long ago. In those cases, we'd reunited families and brought justice. I could really use some good vibes like those. Not a case where I questioned whether bringing the bad guy to justice was enough, or even the right thing to do. Shaking off the thought, I approached my office and halted.

Stavros and a man I'd never seen before were standing inside my office. I had an open-door policy, but come on, I wasn't even in there. It felt like they were invading my space. Who was this guy? I plastered on a smile and waved. "Stavros. Good to see you."

"Hi, Martina. Thanks for making the time to meet with us."

I gave him a look like I knew I didn't really have a choice. "Of course." I turned to the stranger. "And you are?"

He wore what I guessed was a very expensive suit. The fabric was luxurious enough that a ridiculous part of me wanted to touch it. His eyes were a dazzling blue, his skin flawless, but sadness and fear filled those eyes. My gut stirred.

"My name is Joe," he said. "And I presume you're Ms. Monroe?" He extended his hand.

I shook it. "Yes. Please call me Martina. Why don't you two have a seat?"

I gestured at the two visitor chairs, subtly moving Stavros away from my desk chair. They sat, and I hurried around the corner to take my seat. I gave Stavros a look, prompting him to begin.

"Martina, you've just met Joseph Sapphire. As you know, he's requested our help. I think we should hear him out." He turned to the man. "Go on and tell Martina what you told me."

Joe nodded. "My daughter, Lena, she's twenty-three. She went away this past weekend with friends to Red Rose County. But she disappeared. There's no trace of her."

"What were the circumstances of her disappearance?"

"Lena and her friends were staying at a friend's family home in the woods. I guess she went outside on Saturday night. I'm not sure why. It's unclear why she'd go out at night alone. They said she was only gone a few minutes, but when they went to check on her, she was just gone. They didn't see or hear anything unusual, other than the fact she wasn't there."

"Did they say why she went outside?"

"No, but she was with her boyfriend and three other friends. Maybe she and Jason had a fight, or she wasn't getting her way. They told me they don't know why she did."

That's odd. Surely *someone* knew why she went outside. The story didn't sit right with me. "Did they look for her?"

"They did. All four of them, and some of the staff, took flashlights and looked for a while."

Staff? "How long is a while?"

"A few hours."

And they just gave up? "When was this?"

"She disappeared Saturday night. I didn't find out until this morning."

It was Monday. "Why didn't they tell you she was gone until this morning?"

"Lena is full of life and is smart and ambitious, but also a bit of a free spirit, prone to taking off with only a moment's notice. And that group is big into pranks, games, and dares. Her friends figured she was just trying to get attention or playing a prank on them. They're in their twenties, but really they're still children. Her boyfriend, Jason, told me he wasn't worried about her disappearance until they called me to see if I'd heard from her." His voice broke. "She's my baby girl. And she's missing. I know you can relate to that."

He knew about Zoey's abduction. He'd done his homework *on me*. That was a little unnerving. "Is that consistent with Lena's behavior?"

He gave a sad nod. "Sometimes if the 'vibe' isn't right, she'll just leave. The woods isn't her thing. She's a city girl."

"What made you decide to seek a private investigator as opposed to just letting law enforcement handle the case?"

"I'm going to be blunt with you, Ms. Monroe—"

"Please call me Martina."

"Martina, I don't have much faith the police will do anything. She's an adult, and when I spoke with them, they advised me to wait to hear from her. If a few days passed and she still hadn't turned up to let them know. I can't wait around any longer."

There really wasn't anything pointing to foul play, yet Joe was obviously worried. "Have you done any investigating on your own?"

"My assistant checked her social media. She hasn't posted. I've tried calling her, but there's no answer. I checked our cellphone records—she's on our plan—and there has been no activity since early Saturday. I think maybe the answers are in Red Rose County. I haven't had a chance to go up there myself. But I figured we could bring in the best, and your reputation precedes you. Money is no object. Please understand that *all I want* is to bring Lena home."

"Do you have the address of where she was last seen?"

"I do. And I have the names of all the friends she was with."

My eyes met his. The sadness and fear radiating off him was palpable. I understood why he'd come to me. I knew what it was like to have a daughter go missing. But something was off. Perhaps Lena's friends knew more than they'd told her father. "Do you know if she has her phone with her?"

Voice trembling, he said, "It wasn't at the house, according to her friends. They brought back her suitcase. It wasn't inside. I'm really worried."

"I understand." I'd be worried if I didn't know where Zoey or Selena were, even if they were known to take off last minute. Despite the fact that both were adults, one married and in veterinary school and the other a private investigator working in our office.

He met my gaze. "So you'll do it? You'll find Lena?"

"Our firm is more than happy to help."

"I need you, Martina. I need *you* to find her."

I sat back, arms crossing my chest. "From our conversation, I'm assuming you know my daughter was abducted last year. And you may have read about my involvement in a case where there was a series of killings around Christmas. It's been a hard year for my family. I'm not taking any cases right now. But we have many highly capable investigators—the best of the best. One of which used to work for the CoCo County Sheriff's Department. He's excellent. And Selena Bailey is another solid choice. They've both found missing persons before." I would have offered up Hirsch too, if he wasn't fully retired now. As a former homicide detective, and my partner, he was the best investigator I'd ever worked with, but also one of the most cautious. He had a wife and a young daughter to think of. They were both threatened last year, and he was done taking chances with their lives. I understood, and respected, his decision.

"It must be you, Martina." His tone hardened. "You."

Why? Was he simply a man who was used to calling the shots and he wanted me to find his daughter? I shook my head. "I'm so sorry for what you're going through. Truly. But you must understand what my family went through last year. I can't take your case."

Stavros tilted his head. "Martina, may I speak with you outside?"

I gave Joe a tight-lipped smile. "Of course." I nodded at him. "Please excuse us."

Stavros and I slipped out, and I shut the door behind us. "I can't take this case, Stavros."

"Look, I hear you. And I agree, you shouldn't take on anything dangerous. But chances are Lena's off on an extended holiday. And in case the name Joseph Sapphire didn't ring a bell, he's one of the top CEOs in Silicon Valley. He's worth *a lot* of money. Which means his daughter has means too."

Why did that matter? Just because Lena's family was wealthy didn't make her case any more important. "So?"

"So she could've hopped on a helicopter from Red Rose County, gone to the nearest airport, and flown to Europe without telling anyone. You heard him. She's carefree and spontaneous. Into pranks. We just need to track her movements. It could be an easy case that we can solve in a day or two."

Stavros may be right. I glanced through the office window. Joe sat bowed forward, his hands tugging at his hair.

"Can I at least think about it?"

"Yes, but think quick."

My stomach growled. "Give me thirty minutes to grab a bite to eat and I'll give you my answer."

Stavros nodded.

We stepped back inside.

Joseph's eyes lit up with hope. "You'll do it? You'll take the case?"

"For all the reasons I stated, I need time to think about this." I lifted my hands. "I'm going to grab lunch. I'll be back in thirty minutes."

Joe gave me a sheepish grin. "Of course."

"In the meantime," Stavros added, "we'll have the team start pulling preliminary data."

"Thank you, Martina. Thank you, Stavros."

I grabbed my backpack, shook Joe's hand, and stepped out. I couldn't sit in that office a second longer with him staring at me like I was his last chance.

I needed something hearty. Something healthy. A salad, avocado, and maybe a treat. I took the elevator down and headed to my car in the garage.

As soon as I slipped inside the vehicle, I let out a breath and sat still for a moment before I pulled up a guided meditation on my phone. Maybe clarity would show up if I invited it. A few minutes in, a sharp knock on my window made my heart jump and my eyes flew open. Joseph Sapphire stood outside my car window.

I opened the door and climbed out. "What is it?"

"I'm sorry," he said. "I know you need lunch. I know you need to take care of yourself and your family. But I need you to find her, Martina. I am begging you. My daughter's life is on the line."

Something stirred inside me. "Do you have reason to believe she may have met with foul play?"

"Just a father's instinct. *Please.*"

Well, I'd give him props for caring so fiercely. Maybe some of his instincts were right, but not likely. Still, I found it weird that he showed up at my car door. How did he even know which car I drove? Did he follow me?

Something felt off. But if he truly wasn't going to leave me alone... I leaned against my car and sighed. "I'll take the case and I will help you find your daughter."

"Thank you, Martina."

I nodded, but a nagging flicker in my gut made me question if I'd made the right decision.

4

LENA

OUR EYES LOCKED as he entered carrying a tray of food. He wore a mask. It was one of those old-school knit black ski masks and all his clothes were black, too. I could only see his dark, brown eyes and peach-colored lips. My body tensed as he placed the tray on the bolted-down table next to me.

My chair was also bolted to the floor. When I first arrived, I tried to lift it, to use as a potential weapon, but all I managed to do was practically dislocate my arm. It was a massive fail. At least I could walk around, as far as the chain around my ankle let me, and there was a mattress on the floor that wasn't totally uncomfortable. The room itself was grim with cement walls and only a tiny window that let some natural light in. It smelled of dirt, urine, and disinfectant. A gross combination.

Since I'd been taken, drugged, and chained up in the room, I hadn't been hurt. Not physically anyhow. He'd just kept me there, like a prisoner. At first, I wondered if this was an elaborate joke orchestrated by Ethan. But from what I could tell from the sunlight emitted through the window at the top of the far wall, it had been *two days*. Ethan knew there would be serious consequences for keeping me captive for that long. He was a jerk, but he wasn't *that* stupid.

But if it wasn't Ethan, why hadn't this guy hurt me or do whatever people do when they abduct someone? Surely, my disappearance was in the news, like that other girl who had gone missing. The one Ethan had been talking about. Had that other girl been killed? From what I remembered they hadn't found her yet. Would they find her? Would they find *me*?

I supposed it was a good thing this guy was wearing a mask. I couldn't identify him, which likely meant he hadn't planned to kill me. I'd watched nearly every true crime series out there, I knew the rules. I had even tried to use that fact to my advantage and had explained to him I couldn't identify him so he could just let me go. It hadn't worked. I then explained my family had money and they'd pay whatever he wanted. That was a no-go, too.

I looked over at my meal. A sandwich, an apple, and a bottle of water. It was the same as before.

He stood there, staring at me. It was unnerving. "Do you want to watch me eat?"

He didn't say a word. Just continued to stand there, motionless.

The truth was, he only came in three times a day and brought me food each time. My stomach grumbled, and I picked up the sandwich and took a bite. "Not bad," I said, trying to get some sort of reaction out of him. "You make good sandwiches. Do you work at a deli?"

No reply. The creep just stared like he was some kind of weird kidnapping robot.

I'd figured out pretty quickly there was a camera in the room. The red blinking light was a dead giveaway. Maybe he just liked to watch people in captivity. What would he do when he was bored of me?

I took another bite.

And he continued to stare.

Finally, I huffed and looked straight into his eyes. Swallowing the fear that was growing by the hour, I said, "What do you want with me? Like, what's your deal?"

His lips were mostly covered by the mask, but I saw what looked like a smirk or a small smile.

"You already know I can't identify you," I said. "Why don't you just tell me what's going on? Like I said, my family has money. You want money? You got it. You want me to sit here and eat? Fine. I don't care. But people are looking for me. And if you want to get out of this alive, you should let me go. My family will stop at nothing to get me back."

To my surprise, he stepped closer.

My body went rigid, and I instantly regretted my threats.

"I have no doubt," he said calmly, "that your family will do whatever it takes to get you back. Don't worry about that."

Was that supposed to be reassuring?

"So... what? You want something from my family?" I pressed. "Look, I'll tell them you treated me well. I've been fed. I've been hydrated. I don't love the bucket in the corner, but it works."

I glanced at it, grimacing. At least there was toilet paper. The smell was my biggest gripe, aside from the chains, but he did empty it each day. That was something.

"Who are you?" I asked. "What do you get out of this? Are you one of my dad's rivals? Some other tech company trying to steal secrets? Is this corporate espionage?"

He smirked. "You're so naïve."

There was something about the way he said it that made my skin crawl. "How long are you going to keep me here?"

"As long as it takes, *Lena*."

The way he said my name, it was like he hated me. Almost familiar.

My stomach dropped. "Do I know you?"

Before I could get an answer, his hand was around my throat. My head slammed back against the wall, pain exploding behind my eyes.

"You don't know me," he hissed, "but I know you. And if you want to survive, you'll keep your stupid mouth shut and do as I say. Do you understand?"

I nodded, gasping for air.

He released me. I choked, the sandwich still clutched in my hand. My appetite was gone.

"I'll do whatever you want," I croaked.

"Good," he said. "Now finish your sandwich."

I looked down at it. My hands were shaking, but I ate. And as I chewed, I thought about my life. I'd had a lot of time to think over the last two days. But the biggest question that played on repeat was, why hadn't anyone found me yet?

5

MARTINA

IN AWE, I parked my car in front of the stunning Sapphire home. Hidden behind the gates and lush landscaping, the walls were a creamy stucco with a red-tiled roof. If I had to guess, I'd say it had to be at least 10,000 square feet and on at least an acre of land. It looked like a palace you'd find in France or Italy, not in the Bay Area, at least not where I lived.

Parked on the street, I headed toward the gate and into the garden with its paver paths, calming fountain, and colorful foliage. I had a hard time believing anyone would run away from a place like this. But things weren't always as they seemed.

Before I could even make my way to the front door, it opened. Joe Sapphire stood there with a hopeful expression. Since we'd met a few hours earlier, my team had dug up everything they could on Lena. I was about to wave and meet Joe, when my phone buzzed. A quick glance at the screen caught my attention. Lifting a finger to let him know I'd be a minute, I turned away and answered, worried something serious had happened. Usually Kate texted; a call was usually reserved for emergencies.

"Hi, Kate. How are you doing?"

"Doing well, Martina. I was just calling to see if you wanted to grab dinner with Natalie and me. I know it's kind of short notice, but Natalie's really excited. She's making progress on the book and wants to share a few chapters with you."

"That's exciting," I said. "Hopefully I can wrap up here in a few hours. I'm working a new case."

"I thought you weren't taking any cases?"

Detective Kate Maddox and I had only met a few months ago, but there was something about her and Natalie. They were friends but had bonded like sisters, and now there was a bond between the three of us, too. Maybe it was the shared hostage situation that tied us together. Or maybe it was more than that.

"We're hoping it's just a simple runaway, or she's off taking a trip. It wouldn't be the first time."

"Stats?" Kate asked.

I gave her a quick rundown on the situation, before I explained, "I'm at their house now to learn more about her. I'll have to text you later."

"Hopefully you can make it tonight, and good luck on the case. Let me know if you need any help."

With thanks, I ended the call, feeling a mix of pride and concern. Kate worked far too much, but also never hesitated to lend a helping hand. And I was so happy to hear Natalie was working on her book, telling the story of how she'd come face-to-face with a serial killer and survived. A crime reporter by trade, she'd gotten too close to the story and became part of it. My husband, Charlie, had convinced her to write a book about the experience. She hadn't wasted any time. It had only been a few months since the ordeal, but maybe it was healing for her. I hoped so.

With a steady exhale, I turned my attention back to the house and headed toward the front door. Joe met me on the porch and ushered me inside. The house was expansive and immaculate. Oil paintings lined the walls. Oversized white furniture sat untouched, the kind that would never survive in my house. Between the dog and my coffee habit, it wouldn't stand a chance. We also didn't have a cleaning staff. "You have a lovely home."

"Thank you. It's been in my wife's family for generations. Alice's great-grandparents had it built in the 1920s. They raised her grandmother here, and then Alice's father, and now we've raised our children here."

"That's incredible." That kind of inheritance was hard to imagine. No one had ever handed me a mansion, or the kind of wealth—and obligations—that came with it.

Joe tipped his head. "Can I get you something to drink?"

"Water would be appreciated."

Before he could move, a woman stepped forward. Gray dress. Hair pulled back. White apron.

"A water for Miss Martina Monroe," Joe said. "And a Perrier for me."

"Still or bubbly?" she asked.

"Still," I said. I'd never been asked that in someone's home.

"Before I show you Lena's room, can I answer any questions?"

"Have you received any messages regarding her disappearance?"

He shifted his weight. "No. And I know coming from money puts a target on us. But I don't think that's what this is."

"Why not?"

"It's been two days, with no demands."

"Sometimes they wait," I said. "Let the fear build."

"Well, I can give you a list of associates. Past dealings. But no one stands out."

"That will be helpful."

The woman returned with a bottle of Evian for me and Joe's Perrier in a shiny green bottle.

"Would you like to see Lena's room first, or speak with my wife?"

"Lena's room," I said. "Unless this is a good time to speak with her. I understand she's not well."

His wife was bedridden with stage four breast cancer. Now, their only daughter was missing. I wondered if the weight of her mother's illness had pushed Lena to leave. A dying mother. A house heavy with grief. Anyone might want a break from that, at least for a little while.

He led me down the hall and stopped. "This is Lena's room." He opened the door. The room was large and carefully styled. Teals, blues, and purples. Everything in its place. "It's clean."

"Lena's always been tidy," Joe said. "I'll check on Alice and leave you to it."

I searched quickly. A desk, a TV console, and a bookshelf were the only furniture aside from a bench, the bed, and night-stands. All surfaces had either decorative figurines ranging from animals to abstract art pieces and a few framed photographs.

I checked every nook and cranny. The mattress, the desk, nightstand, and TV console drawers. There weren't any hidden panels or secret journals. Only a paper day planner with social activities penned inside. Nothing terribly interesting. Dinner and drinks events. Jason's name came up more than once. Tiffany and Jenna's, too. Including the weekend at Ethan's house in Red Rose County.

The closet was enormous. Clothing was arranged by color. Shoes lining the walls on shelving. An island of drawers in the center. Jewelry. Socks. Nothing unusual. Back in the bedroom, I stopped. It wasn't what I saw, it was what I didn't. *A computer.*

Back to the desk, I stood looking for any dust or imprints of a desktop, or charging cables. There were none. She likely had a laptop.

Footsteps approached, and I picked up the framed photograph of Lena and a young man with dark hair and bright green eyes. "Is this Jason?"

Joe's face fell flat. "Yes."

"Not a fan?"

"He's fine," Joe said with hesitation. "He's smart and serious with a plan for his life."

"And Lena fits into that plan?"

Joe shrugged slightly. "He's in medical school and wants to be married by the time he's finished with residency. At thirty he wants kids and a wife at home."

"That's not Lena?"

"No," he said with a slight shake of the head.

"How long have you known him?"

"Ten years or so. They went to the same high school and were in the same friend group. They started dating about a year ago."

"Where's her computer?"

Joe glanced around. "Maybe in the study. Or the theater. She sometimes has her computer propped on her lap while watching movies."

"I'd like to find it," I said. "May I hold on to this planner?"

"Of course." He smiles in a sad way. "She wanted an 'old school' planner. Prefers paper to electronics. Likes to take a digital break, as she says. She only reads paperback novels, no e-readers or audiobooks for her."

I smiled faintly.

"Let me introduce you to my wife," he said. "And I'll see if I can locate the laptop."

"Thank you."

Joe led me down the hallway. Staff members passed us

quietly, moving with purpose. Our only pause was for Joe to request a search for the laptop. As we continued, I said, "And your sons?"

"They're both in Europe right now. One's in France, the other in Italy, on holiday with their families. They're a bit older than Lena, both in their thirties."

"She was a surprise?"

"She was. What a blessing, though. Daughters are special," he added. "I don't have to tell you that, do I?"

"No," I said, and meant it. I was blessed with a biological and a bonus daughter. We continued down the hall and I admired the paintings. The home resembled an art gallery or museum.

"Have you reached out to your sons to see if they'd heard from Lena?"

"They were the first people I called. They haven't."

We reached the bedroom. The faint beeping of medical equipment grew louder as Joe opened the door.

An adjustable bed was in the center of the room. A woman lay propped against pillows, a tube running from her arm. The light from the windows behind her highlighted her pale skin and her hair, which was a mixture of blonde and gray. She lifted her hand weakly in a small wave as we entered.

"Alice," Joe said gently. "This is Martina."

She nodded in recognition. "It's very nice to meet you."

"You too. I won't take up too much time. I just have a few questions for you about Lena."

Her eyes fluttered shut. "You have to find her," she whispered. "You have to."

"I will do everything I can," I promised. "When was the last time you spoke with her?"

"She came into my room before she left for the weekend with Jason and her friends. And she called to check on me early on Saturday."

"How was the conversation? Did you argue or was she troubled by anything?"

"She didn't want to leave me," she said. "I'm not well, as you can see. But she told me she'd only be a few hours away and that she'd come back instantly if I needed her."

That didn't fit with a runaway or prank. Lena and her mother were close, and from the looks of Alice Sapphire, I'd guess she didn't have a lot of time left. Would a daughter who claimed she'd return instantly if needed run off without anyone knowing where she was or how to reach her?

"Did you hear from her, other than early on Saturday, while she was in Red Rose County?"

She looked away. "She called me when she arrived on Saturday. I haven't heard from her since."

"Can you think of anyone who might want to hurt her?"

She glanced at Joe and then back at me. "No."

An uneasy feeling slid through me. "And how do you feel about Jason?"

"He's a lovely young man," she said. "I don't know if he's right for Lena, but he's kind."

"And her friends?"

"Ethan. Jenna. Tiffany," she said. "Thick as thieves since they were teenagers. All are from good families."

"Is there anything else you can tell me that could help me find her?"

She shook her head slowly. "No. I just beg you, please find her. I don't have much time. I need her back here."

"I'll do everything I can."

Her eyes closed again, her breathing evening out as if she were drifting to sleep. I glanced at Joe. His head was bowed, the weight of his wife's illness and his daughter's disappearance pressing down on him.

Up until I'd met her mother, I'd believed the most likely

scenario was that Lena had run away. But after speaking to Alice, and hearing how reluctant Lena had been to leave her side, even for a few hours, I began to believe something else entirely. Something had happened to Lena Sapphire. She hadn't left on her own. Everything inside me told me I needed to do whatever it took to find her, and bring her home.

6

MARTINA

EVERYTHING in me was screaming that Lena hadn't just ran off on holiday. The details of Lena's disappearance in Red Rose County felt incomplete. Despite what Lena's father told me, somebody had to have known why Lena went outside alone, and I had a feeling that person would be her boyfriend, Jason.

Jason Turnbull fidgeted in his chair, his knee bouncing under the small café table. The cafe was quiet at this late hour. Only a few patrons getting treats or a latte. We'd agreed on the location due to the cafe's proximity to Jason's medical school.

He wouldn't look at me, not at first. "Thank you for meeting with me, Jason." I'd much rather have been having dinner with Natalie and Kate, but something inside me told me this conversation couldn't wait.

"Of course. I'm really worried about Lena."

"So am I."

He glanced up, met my eyes for half a second, then looked away. "I just want her to come back."

"That's what we all want," I said. "So let's start at the beginning. Tell me about your relationship with Lena. How long have you been together?"

He took a breath, staring out the window like he might find the right answer there. "We've known each other forever. Friends first. Then last year we were at Jenna's house." His mouth twitched. "I don't know. Maybe I'd had too much to drink, or she had. She kissed me on the cheek. Just playing around. But our eyes met and—" He shook his head. "It sounds stupid."

"It doesn't," I assured him.

"We're opposites," he continued. "I'm structured. I plan things. Lena, she just lives. No real plans. Not that she isn't smart or ambitious. She is. She just doesn't want to decide her whole life yet."

"Opposites attract."

"Yeah," he muttered.

"And you've been together about a year?"

He nodded. "Almost."

"Any problems?"

"No." He said it too fast. Then corrected himself. "I mean, nothing serious. We're good. We're happy."

"You're exclusive?"

"Yes."

Eyeing him, I said, "Are you sure? Is it possible Lena was seeing someone else?"

"No. That's not Lena." His voice wavered. "People think she's flighty. A party girl. But she's loyal. She wouldn't do that. Not to me."

Unfortunately, I think most people think that about their partners, but only about a third of them are right. "Are you in love with her?"

His answer came softer. "Yeah. I am."

"And you haven't heard from her since Saturday night?"

He shook his head, his fingers tightening around his coffee cup.

"Tell me about that night," I said. "Start from the beginning."

He exhaled sharply. "She went outside and—"

"What happened before that?" I interrupted.

"We were inside just talking and drinking. Ethan was telling stories. Stuff about a serial killer who'd been in the area." His jaw tightened. "Trying to scare everyone."

"And Lena?"

"She just rolled her eyes at him."

"When did she go outside?"

"About nine."

"Why did she go outside by herself?"

He shrugged, "I don't know," but didn't look at me. Jason stared down at his hands now, fingers twisting together.

He was obviously lying. "Jason, I need the truth. If we're going to find Lena, you need to tell me everything."

His chest rose and fell. His fair skin flushed pink. "Fine. It was a setup."

I held still. "Explain."

"It was a dare," he said, his voice so quiet I could barely hear it.

"A dare that would lead to her kidnapping?"

"No, not like that."

"Then like what?"

He looked around the café, lowering his voice. "If I tell you, can you promise not tell anyone about this?"

"That depends on what you say next." My gut clenched. "Go on."

He swallowed hard. "Ethan told stories about the serial killer in Red Rose County. Then we dared her to stay outside in the dark for ten minutes." His voice cracked. "I knew she'd do it. She never backs down."

"So she went outside to prove him wrong."

"Yes."

Staring at him as he avoided my gaze, I said, "But that wasn't the real dare."

Jason finally looked at me. "No."

"What was it?"

"The dare was to get Lena alone," Jason said, then paused and glanced around the café again, as if someone might be listening. "So I could propose, as a prank. Ethan dared me."

I straightened in my seat and took a slow sip of my coffee. It was bitter and burnt, it had probably been sitting on the burner too long.

"We had lights set up," he continued. "Fairy lights. I was supposed to turn them on once she'd been outside long enough. When I went to flip the switch, the lights came on... but Lena wasn't there. She was gone."

I lowered my cup carefully. "So what you're telling me," I said evenly, "is that you dared Lena to go outside in the dark, after scaring her with stories about a serial killer, so you could *fake* propose to her."

"I know it sounds really stupid now." Jason winced. "We're kind of into pranks. Our group is just like that," he rushed on. "Ethan dared me to do it. He knows I love Lena more than anything. I mean, I want to get married. But it was supposed to be a joke at first, and then I was going to let her in on it. There's no way she'd want to get married right now. I don't think. I don't know." He dragged a hand down his face. "Please don't tell anyone. I'd be humiliated."

I looked at him, this young man in medical school, someone who would one day have people's lives in his hands, was more afraid of embarrassment than of telling the full truth about his missing girlfriend. "And you looked for Lena?"

"Yes. Everyone did. The staff. All of us."

"How long was she outside?"

"About six minutes." He swallowed. "It was the plan all

along. Six minutes, lights go on and then I'd do the fake proposal. It was supposed to be funny."

"You weren't worried she'd take the proposal seriously? And then be devastated when you told her it was a joke?"

His eyes widened. "Oh my. I didn't even think of that." He shook his head. "If she had... I guess I could've said it was a promise ring." He let out a hollow laugh. "That was so dumb. Why do I let Ethan talk me into this stuff?"

Unbelievable. Why indeed. "How long did you search for her?"

"A few hours. Maybe three. We had flashlights. The staff helped. Everyone was out there looking." He hesitated. "The girls were scared. Ethan had really freaked them out with those stories. Then Lena was missing. I thought maybe she ran off to scare us back."

"When did you realize that wasn't the case?"

"Something didn't feel right, but I told myself it was so like her. Lena's kind of a daredevil. Ethan's always pushing her." He swallowed again. "But she wasn't answering her texts. She hadn't posted anything on socials. And when she didn't show up by Monday, when we were heading back to the Bay Area, I called her dad. Her mom's really sick and there's no way Lena wouldn't check in with her. When he said they hadn't heard from Lena, that's when I got really worried."

"So that's when you reported her missing?"

"I think her dad did. I wanted to call the police, but Ethan said it wasn't a good idea."

My body shifted. "Why not?"

"He doesn't like talking to cops."

Red flag raised. "Why?"

Jason hesitated. "I don't know. He's just... like that."

"Like what?" Who were these people? A fake proposal? Not

wanting to report her missing to the police? I certainly hoped Selena and Zoey's friends had more sense than this group.

"Kind of weird," he said. "He's fascinated by serial killers. Likes scaring people. Living on the fringe." He shook his head. "Which is crazy, because he's loaded. Like, really loaded. With a corporate gig."

"Do you think Ethan and Lena could have planned this as a hoax?"

"No. No way. Not a chance."

I slid my card across the table. "If you think of anything else, anything at all, call me."

He nodded.

As I left the café, I couldn't stop thinking about what Jason had told me. If this was how the studious one behaved what were the others like? Joe had said they were like kids, despite being in their twenties. But then I thought back to Ethan's refusal to involve law enforcement. His fixation on serial killers. The way he'd pushed Lena outside alone, into the dark. If she'd been taken, her kidnapper had to have known she was going to be out there. One of the staff? Ethan? All of them? None of them? One thing I knew for sure was that I needed to talk to Ethan, the man who set up the prank, as soon as possible.

7

THE ARCHITECT

SHE WAS STARTING to lose her cool. Was it because she finally realized she was powerless in this situation? Yes. Lena Sapphire, you have *no power*. You have no control. And you will obey.

She stared at me as she shoved the sandwich into her mouth. She was quite striking with her father's sparkling blue eyes, her natural blonde hair falling almost to her waist. So young. So naïve. But if I was being honest, I was beginning to tire of her. This whole thing was taking far too long.

"This sandwich is great," she said casually. "You know, if this whole kidnapping-people-and-keeping-them-hostage thing doesn't work out for you, maybe you should open your own café. You could have a really bright future."

So smug. So certain of herself. Her confusion about who held the power here needed to be corrected. "That's not my fate. I know my fate. What is your fate, Lena?"

She dropped the sandwich onto the plate and looked straight into my eyes. "Well, if you don't kill me, I suppose I'll go back to my privileged, carefree life. As for you..." She tilted her head. "You'll probably live in your mother's basement. Is that where we are right now? Your mom's basement?"

I said nothing.

"What's the matter?" she continued. "Did girls make fun of you in school? Is that why you took me? Who else have you taken? What have you done with them? What's your plan? Do you even have one?"

I didn't know what game she thought she was playing. But it was time to teach her a lesson. I walked to the table, picked up her half-eaten breakfast, and left the room without a word. After I set the tray outside the door, I returned with a present. She stared at me. "I wasn't done."

"Oh, you're done."

Her bravado faltered, giving way to something else.

"What do you *think* you're doing? Do you think you can talk to me like that and get away with it? The fate of your life rests in the palm of my hands, and you speak to me like I'm some common man-child." I stepped closer to her. "You clearly have an issue with respect. So I'm going to teach you that while you're here. How does that sound, Lena?"

No remarks. No jokes. No teasing. No attempts to belittle me now.

From my back pocket, I pulled out a lighter, stepped back and held the object by its chain. The flame flickered as I waved it back and forth over the object. I watched her face drain of color. She knew exactly what I was about to do. The implication was clear. This would be a reminder that would last her a lifetime.

Her eyes widened.

I smiled.

"You don't have to do that," she cried. "I'm sorry. I promise... I'm sure you're very talented and very smart. I'm sorry. I'll do whatever you want. I'll be... I'll be nice. I swear."

"Lena, I believe you. But sometimes in life we need reminders. And what's better than something that will always be with you?"

She leapt from the chair, but the chain around her ankle allowed her only a few frantic steps.

"Where are you going to run?" I asked. "You can't get very far. And if you resist, this will be much, much worse." She collapsed onto the mattress, nodding as tears streamed down her cheeks.

If I didn't know better, I'd say Lena was already learning the lesson. Perhaps she was intelligent after all. Now she would always remember. She belonged to me. *She belonged to us.*

I left the room without a word, the chain clutched in my hand. I removed my mask, raked my fingers through my hair, and walked down the hallway.

"Did you do it?" he asked.

"I did. Perhaps she'll be a bit more humble now."

"You don't think that was taking it too far?"

I shook my head. "No. I think it was just far enough." I had guts and integrity. I wasn't a follower who simply did what I was told. I wasn't like the *others.*

He said, "It's been three days. This wasn't supposed to take this long."

"I know," I agreed.

"Maybe we need to up the stakes."

I considered that. "I have something in mind. Something I think will get us exactly what we want."

8

MARTINA

HE SAT THERE with the confidence of a king. "Thank you so much for coming down to the office, Ethan. I really appreciate it."

"No problem," he said. "Anything to help find Lena."

There was very little emotion behind his words. He was good-looking in an all-American kind of way, with his dirty blond hair and perfect smile. But there was a darkness in him, as if kindness was something that hadn't come naturally, and he'd never learned to speak it fluently. "Were you and Lena close?"

"No," he said. "Same friend circle, that's all."

"Did you get along with her?"

"Mostly," he said after a pause. "We're very different. She's a bit flighty for my taste. A little silly." He said it as if he was far superior to her.

From what I knew of Lena's background, she'd earned excellent grades in both high school and college. She played sports and worked hard. Lena also liked to have a good time and was fortunate enough to be able to whenever she wanted. She was young and had the whole world at her feet. And I needed to find her before her future was taken away.

"You're friends with Jason," I said. "Her boyfriend."

He remained stoic, showing little emotion. "Friends since we were kids. We're practically brothers."

"It must be difficult to see him so upset about Lena."

With no emotion, he said, "It is."

He certainly didn't act like it. "Can you walk me through the events on Saturday leading up to Lena's disappearance? From the moment you arrived in Red Rose County to when you realized Lena was missing."

He nodded and began to speak. His story matched Jason's exactly. *Too* exact. The way he delivered it, smooth and rehearsed, made me believe he and Jason had spoken, and had compared notes. His version was similar to what Jenna and Tiffany told me when we spoke earlier too. Like Jason, they too were genuinely concerned for Lena. But other than that knowledge, nothing had been gained from speaking to the two women as they appeared completely unaware of the true game Jason and Ethan had set up.

Jason cared about Lena. Her friends cared about her. Her parents cared. It was obvious Ethan didn't.

When he finished, I asked, "And when you realized she was missing, did you call the police?"

"No, I thought it was better to speak with her family first. We wouldn't want them to find out about her disappearance on the news, right?"

He was slick. I'd give him that. "I understand notifying her family," I said, "but you were in Red Rose County. You could've gone directly to the sheriff's department after speaking with her parents. Or had them come out to the house to take the report."

"Honestly, I didn't think it was my place to do so. I was sure her family would take care of everything, and they have."

"Is there anything else you can tell me about Lena, or that night, that could help us find her?"

"I can't think of anything else," he said. "But my family and I will be praying for her."

I highly doubted that. I didn't like Ethan. It wasn't just his personality, it was the way he spoke, the way he carried himself, and the way he was convinced he was getting one over on everyone in the room. As if we couldn't see through the thin veil of concern he'd draped over himself. Narcissist. Sociopath. I wasn't a mental health professional. I couldn't diagnose. All I knew was that he gave me the creeps. And from everything I'd heard about him, he was, in fact, a creep.

"Where do you work, Ethan?"

"At Buck Industries."

Of course he did. "That's your father's company," I said. "You work for him?" Something flickered across his face, irritation, maybe. An Achilles' heel perhaps. "You know," I said, "if there's anything you're not telling me about Lena's disappearance, anything at all, I will find out. And when I do, I won't hesitate to make it public. The news. Social media. I imagine it would make it into the business section too. I can see it now, 'Son of the CEO of Buck Industries refuses to cooperate in the search for missing Lena Sapphire.'"

He smirked. "I assure you, if anything else had happened that day, I would tell you. Now, if there's nothing else, I have prior engagements."

Probably heading back to work, or to a two-martini lunch. "That'll be all, Ethan," I said. "Have a good day."

"You too, Miss Monroe."

After escorting him out of the office, I felt like I had slime on my skin. I met up with Selena at her cubicle. "How did it go?"

"As expected," I said. "Same story as the others."

"Do you think he could be involved?"

"I don't know," I said honestly. "But somebody knows something. It's too coincidental. From what I understand, the house in Red Rose County is relatively remote. Somebody didn't just walk by or drive past and pick her up. Someone was planning on her, or someone else, being outside that night. We need to know everyone who knew Lena would be in Red Rose County at that house on Saturday."

"Well, we know her parents knew and the four friends with her knew. Maybe she told someone else, or they did."

"We need to find out." I paused. "Did you hear back from Red Rose County?" Hopefully they had done a decent job investigating Lena's disappearance. It was possible they'd have some useful information that could help us find her.

"I left a message last night. I'm waiting on a callback from a Deputy Brady Tanner."

"All right," I said. "Let's keep pulling backgrounds on everyone she knows. Friends, extended circles. You okay doing more interviews?"

"Yep," Selena said. "I'm ready. I've got a list started for the extended friend circle, and business associates of her father. Vincent's going to help, too. We'll be sure to find out who knew she was going to be up in the mountains."

"Perfect."

Just then, the desk phone on Selena's cubicle lit up. "Oh. Let's see who this is." She answered while I stood there, my mind racing.

I had a very wealthy client with a missing daughter. A wealthy circle of friends whose initial stories had sounded fragmented, almost deceitful. Now they were identical. Polished. As if they'd been rehearsed. Were they covering something up? I glanced back at Selena. She was nodding slowly, her brow furrowed.

"Are you sure?" she asked into the phone. "Okay. Thank you very much."

She hung up and looked at me. "Well," she said, "that's interesting."

"What is it?"

"That was Deputy Brady Tanner from the Red Rose County Sheriff's Department. Guess who was never reported missing in Red Rose County?"

My stomach dropped. "Lena Sapphire."

"Exactly."

"That doesn't make any sense," I said. "I thought her father told me he reported her missing." Had I been mistaken? With a nod, I said, "Looks like I'm paying Joseph Sapphire another visit."

"Good luck. I'll keep working with Vincent on the interview list."

"Thanks." As I walked back to my office, I shook my head. How was I supposed to help a client who wasn't being truthful with me? If they were hiding the lack of missing persons report, what else were they hiding? And why ask for my help at all if they weren't going to tell me everything I needed to do the job?

9

VAL

LIFE WAS PEACEFUL, I thought as I stared out the window of my new home and smiled. As much as I missed living with my mom, there was something that didn't feel quite right about living in my childhood bedroom at nearly fifty years old. Not to mention, I was engaged to be married. Brady and I wanted to build a home and a life together.

Our romance, in some ways, felt like a whirlwind. In other ways, it felt like a long time coming, like he'd always been mine, even when he wasn't. We met as kids and were great friends all through high school, but we lost touch after we both got married and started families with other people. And then, wouldn't you know it, we hit our mid-forties and both ended up back in our hometown. Reunited with a romantic twist.

"Is the tea ready yet?" Julie asked.

"Not quite." I turned to see my mother's friend standing in the kitchen doorway, her arms crossed, a playful impatience in her eyes.

Although I didn't live at home with my mom anymore, I still saw her and her friends nearly every day. Her friends were basically aunties at this point. They visited my new home, or I went over to Mom's. Honestly, I didn't have a whole lot else to do since I retired from the FBI and I hadn't worked any cases with the Red Rose County Sheriff's Department in over a year.

I'd taken to decorating our new house and spending time with my mom and her friends and with my friends. I still got all the juicy updates in the county from Lucy and Sally, both of whom worked at the sheriff's department. My two besties, as the kids say. Lucy was a researcher, and Sally the county medical examiner. And to be honest, when we're together I felt a pang of jealousy when they spoke about work. It was meaningful and important.

The kettle sounded, its sharp whistle cutting through my thoughts. I pulled down mugs for Julie, my mom, and myself. Look at me, in the middle of the day, drinking tea.

I carried a tray of teacups into the living room, the porcelain clinking softly. As I set it down, a thought flickered through my mind: *Is this really me?* Former FBI agent Val Costa, serving tea on a tray in the new home my fiancé and I just bought? I think my mother was right. I needed a hobby. *Or something.*

I set down the tray. My mom picked up her cup first, then Julie and I followed suit.

"Well," Mom said, taking a careful sip, "looks like you're settling in nicely."

"Yes. It's cozy. Not that I don't miss being home with you."

She gave me a knowing smile. I could never pull anything over on her. She was the former sheriff of Red Rose County up until she had retired. It was kind of a pain in the rear never being able to lie to your mother and get away with it, especially as a teenager.

"I'm sure you're very much enjoying your alone time with Brady," she said.

"I am. Lots of hiking. Lots of nature."

Julie looked at my mom, then back at me. "Oh, come on. You're bored to tears."

"I am not," I said, a little too defensively.

My mom shot me a sharp look. "Who do you think you're talking to?"

I sighed. "What am I supposed to do? Rejoin the FBI? I don't want to work at the sheriff's department. I could open a shop? A bookstore?"

My mom burst out laughing, like I'd just told the funniest joke she'd ever heard. Once she'd settled down, she said, "You know you could always start an investigation firm. You might not have a lot of business at first, but you'd be great at it. You'd get to choose your own hours and be your own boss. A lot of ex-law enforcement people do it. Or maybe you could be some kind of security consultant."

"I don't know," I said, but I'd be lying if I hadn't thought about it before. "We'll see. I think it's probably good that I take a break for a little while."

Mom nodded, her expression softening. "I'll say this, you've had quite the eventful few years. And as much as I know you're itching to do something, maybe start small."

Julie leaned in. "I agree with Elizabeth. Maybe you could start with a small case. It doesn't have to be the murder spree of the century, like you used to take on. Nothing complicated, or dangerous serial killer stuff. Maybe a missing person or someone looking for a long-lost relative. Just something to keep you busy that won't put you in the crosshairs of a deranged killer."

Again. "It's something to think about."

Brady, and the sheriff, had mentioned more than once that I was more than welcome to take on a full-time position at the sheriff's department, but I wasn't sure that was the right fit for me. Not that my fiancé, Deputy Brady Tanner of the Red Rose

County Sheriff's Department, wouldn't love that. He not only enjoyed being my life partner, but had enjoyed partnering on cases as well. In those investigations I was just a consultant, not an employee of the county. And as much as I enjoyed being with him, I wasn't sure I wanted to work with him, live with him, and do *everything* with him. After all, absence does make the heart grow fonder.

"Okay," my mom said gently. "I'm sure you'll figure it out. You're too young to not be doing *anything*."

It did feel a little early in life to be giving up on work entirely. If I didn't find something to do, I was likely to take up gardening or baking, or worse, *turn into my mother*.

A soft chime sounded from the front door as the lock disengaged, followed by the muted click of the security system. Brady must be home. That was odd. He didn't usually come home during the day.

The door opened and Brady walked in, still in full uniform. He gave my mom and Julie a warm smile. "Ladies," he said, tipping his head slightly. "How are you doing?"

"Doing well, thank you, Brady," Julie said. "Good to see you."

"You too."

I stood and leaned in to give him a quick kiss on the lips. We were still in that stage, where the second one of us walked through the door, we had to kiss. It was silly. It was romantic. And I liked it.

"What brings you home?" I asked. "We just made tea. Want a cup?"

"No, thank you. Actually..." he said, his tone shifting just slightly. "Val, I was hoping to talk to you."

He glanced at Julie and my mom. "Sorry, Julie and Elizabeth, I didn't know you were going to be here."

"Oh, by all means," my mother said with a wave of her hand. "Take her away, Brady."

"Excuse us," I said, standing.

"Of course," Julie said with a knowing smile. "Go along now."

I swear, even before Brady and I got together, those two, and their friend Diane, were all over us about being in a relationship. Maybe I protested too much at first, but everyone around us quickly decided Brady and I were meant to be together. Maybe not when we were kids, but at this phase of our lives, definitely.

Inside the kitchen, Brady pulled me in by the hips and kissed me again.

"Oh," I said, laughing as I pulled back. "Is that why you came home? That's what you wanted to talk about?"

"No, but I couldn't resist," he said, stepping back and leaning against the counter. His expression shifted, the playful warmth replaced by something more serious. "So... we found a body today."

"A body?" I echoed.

"Yes. It doesn't appear to be an accidental death. It looks like the person had been restrained. Maybe held for a period of time."

I felt the familiar tightening in my chest. "A new case," I said slowly. "And you want my help?"

"I mean, I know you're technically on a break," he said, watching my face carefully. "But if you wanted to take on a case, we could definitely use the one-and-only Special Agent Val Costa."

I raised an eyebrow. "Former FBI Special Agent Val Costa."

He smiled. "Former FBI Special Agent Val Costa *extraordinaire*. The sheriff was actually the first to bring it up. At the scene, he said, 'I think we need Val.' And I agree."

I hesitated for only a moment. "I'm not really doing anything else. The house is pretty much done. So... yeah. Okay."

Relief flickered across his face. "I thought so." He said with a small boyish smile I couldn't resist. He continued, "The body was discovered today. The scene has been preserved, so if you want to come down now and take a look before they remove it, now's a good time."

Was it bad that I could feel that old adrenaline rush of a new case, and I kind of loved it? "Let me tell Mom and Julie. I'm sure they won't mind."

"I'm sure it won't be a problem," he said, giving me a knowing look. Those two were always pushing me toward Brady and toward solving cases. But something in Brady's expression made me pause. "Is there something else?"

He nodded. "It's a little strange. Could be a coincidence, but I got a call from a private investigator's office yesterday. They were asking about a missing person report supposedly submitted by the woman's father, but it turns out no missing person report was ever filed."

My pulse picked up. "That is odd."

"Yeah," he said. "Right after I got off the phone with them this morning, I got the alert that a body was found."

That couldn't be a coincidence. "You think they're connected?"

"I don't know, but I think we're about to find out."

10

MARTINA

FURIOUS WITH JOSEPH SAPPHIRE, I drove straight to his office. I needed to know why he hadn't reported his daughter missing with local law enforcement. That was a crucial step in any missing person's case. If something tragic had happened to Lena, if she'd died or had an accident, she could end up as a Jane Doe if she didn't have identification on her. But with her photo in a missing persons database, or even just on law enforcement's radar, there would be a record that a woman had gone missing in that area. This was outrageous.

Standing in front of the reception desk of an office building in Menlo Park, I said, "I need to see Joseph Sapphire. My name is Martina Monroe."

"Do you have an appointment?" the receptionist asked, her fingers hovering over the keyboard.

"No, but this is important. It's regarding his daughter. I need to speak with him immediately."

"I'll let him know you're here."

Why do people do this? Why hire me to find your daughter, but you didn't even report her missing? It didn't make any sense.

I spiraled through every possible reason he might not have done it, or why he'd led me to believe he had.

Then the receptionist looked up. "You can see him now. He's just down the hall."

"Thank you," I said, already moving. I walked until I saw his name on the door. It was open.

"Martina," Joe said, rising from his chair. "Have you found her already?"

"No." I quietly closed the door behind me and approached his desk. "I haven't found Lena. And neither has local law enforcement."

He opened his mouth to speak, but I didn't let him.

"Do you want to know why they haven't found Lena?"

His brow furrowed.

"Because you never filed a missing person report in Red Rose County."

His face fell. "No. I didn't."

Blood boiled through my veins. "Why not? You told me you spoke to law enforcement."

His shoulders sagged, the fight draining out of him. "I spoke with a friend of mine in law enforcement," he said. "He told me that since she's an adult, there were no signs of foul play, and given her past behavior, they likely wouldn't do anything. So... I didn't file the report."

I felt my jaw tighten. "Did your friend explain how important it is to file a missing person report? Because it is." I fumed, "What if her body showed up in the morgue? What if she hit her head and had amnesia, and she didn't know who she was? Having her listed as a missing person could help identify her. Not only that, it would mean there are more people looking for her. It could help bring her back home!"

Silence filled the room. He squeezed his eyes shut, as if replaying everything he'd done, or failed to do. When he opened them again, I saw regret and grief. "You're right. I hadn't thought of that. I'll do it right away."

But he didn't reach for the phone.

I cleared my throat. "Is there anything else you haven't shared with me about Lena's disappearance?"

"No," he said quickly. "There's nothing else."

I watched him carefully, filing his response away. "Who knew she was going to be in Red Rose County?"

"Her friends knew. Her mother knew. I'm not sure who else she told." He rubbed his temples, the movement slow and tired.

"They planned to come back on Monday, which is typically a workday. Was there anyone she'd need to notify that she wouldn't be around on Monday?"

"Lena doesn't work. She's not part of any volunteer organizations. She says she's just having fun before she settles down. That's how she puts it." There was hesitation there. A pause that lingered just a little too long. "If I'm being completely honest," he went on, "I was hoping we'd be able to find her quickly. That *you* would be able to find her and put an end to this. Based on my position here, if I report her missing and the news gets hold of it, it could turn into a total circus."

I met his gaze. "But if her face is all over the news, it could help us find her. Maybe somebody saw something. Maybe someone knows where she is." I leaned forward slightly. "That's one of the actions I was going to recommend we take. We need to put her face out there. What if she really is overseas on holiday? Someone could recognize her, and we could end this. Everyone would be reunited, safe and sound."

He nodded slowly. "You're right. Let me speak with our in-house counsel. We'll draft a statement. We have media contacts. We can hold a press conference."

I studied him then. A CEO. A powerful man. And yet, sitting there, he looked consumed by the tragedies in his life, his wife's illness and his daughter's disappearance. Maybe he wasn't thinking clearly. Maybe I needed to dial back my judgment. He had a lot on his plate. Or he was hiding something.

"My firm can help with all of that," I said. "If you'd like, we can set up a hotline. We can coordinate with the media. It doesn't have to all fall on you."

"That would be much appreciated, Martina. I'm sorry I misled you. Sometimes…it all just feels like too much."

The sadness in his voice was unmistakable. Now I felt like a jerk for storming in there guns blazing, metaphorically speaking. Maybe he wasn't hiding anything, rather he was overwhelmed. Understandably so. "Life can feel that way sometimes, but asking for help takes strength. You asked my firm for help, and we will do everything we can to find Lena. We'll handle the media. We'll continue to interview friends, family, and the staff in Red Rose County. We'll talk to everyone." I held his gaze. "We're going to find out what happened to Lena. I guarantee it."

As I said it, I thought of Hirsch. My closest friend and retired homicide detective. He used to get so annoyed when we worked together on a case for the CoCo County's sheriff's department and I promised we would find a missing person. He used to tell me that in law enforcement, you didn't do that. You didn't make promises you couldn't keep. But I'd explained to him they weren't false promises. I would find them. He'd usually followed up with a, "Sometimes you don't get to predict the ending." He was wise and had been on the job a long time, but I usually found exactly what I was looking for. And I knew in my gut I would discover the truth, and I *would* find Lena. Hopefully, I wasn't too late.

11

VAL

WELL, that was *not* what I was expecting. Staring down at the body, I couldn't help but think, *How was it just now discovered?* The trail was a busy one. On any given day, it received a steady stream of hikers, runners, and dog walkers. The body was impossible to miss, and once you saw it, it would haunt you for a lifetime.

I glanced over at Sally, one of my closest friends and the county medical examiner. She stood a little farther back than usual, her posture rigid, hands clasped tight in front of her as she scanned the scene. "What can you tell me?"

"Adult female. Beyond that, I'm cautious. Age range is broad, definitely not a minor. Race is hard to say at this point."

"What do you estimate for time of death?"

She crouched slowly, her bright red hair falling forward. Her eyes moved over the body, the soil, the clothing, but when they reached the wrists, she hesitated. No doubt, she was recalling her own captivity. Those were the type of scars that never healed, not completely. I would know.

"Well," she said. "I don't want to overstate it. At these temperatures, and exposure outdoors could suggest weeks. But a confined, hotter environment, like a trunk, can accelerate decomposition dramatically, making it only days."

"If she was out here in the elements, how was she not discovered before today? This is a popular trail. Dozens of hikers use it every day."

Sally shifted her weight, angling herself so she didn't have to look directly at the victim's hands. "I don't think she's been here that long. I think she was placed here. It's possible she was buried and placed here. Burial muddies the waters further. Soil affects heat transfer and limits insect access. If she was moved, the time of death won't be so straightforward."

I knelt for a closer look. Dirt was packed into the victim's clothes, ground deep into seams and folds, not the kind you picked up from lying on a trail overnight.

"It's odd. When Brady told me there was a body, I assumed it was fresh."

Sally glanced down at the body. "The autopsy will tell us more."

Her gaze drifted again, to the wrists. The rope restraints were still there. I saw it then, the way Sally's shoulders drew inward, the way her breathing shallowed just slightly.

"Any theories on cause of death?"

"Nothing obvious, but it's hard to tell at a glance based on the state of decomp. I'll know more after I perform the autopsy."

I stood, brushing dirt from my knee, and turned to Brady. "How many missing persons do you have in Red Rose County that match her description?"

"None."

A victim who hadn't been reported missing. Buried, or at least concealed, then dug up and placed on a trail where there was no doubt she'd be found.

The sheriff approached, scanning the area. "What do you think, Val?"

Meeting his gaze, I said, "It's peculiar."

"That's why you're the first person we called."

I glanced back at Sally. She'd taken a step away from the body now, her arms folded tightly across her chest, eyes fixed on the trees.

"This isn't a typical disposal," I said. "If anything, it feels deliberate."

"A message?" Brady asked.

"Maybe," I said. "I just don't know what the message is yet." There were several possibilities. It could be the killer had a change of heart and wanted the family to know the woman's fate. Or the perpetrator wanted credit for the kill. But if that were the case, I'd expect more victims, which would mean we'd have another serial killer in Red Rose County.

Or it was something we wouldn't understand without more messages. Unfortunately, more messages meant more victims.

The sheriff stood with his hands on his hips, staring down at the body like he was trying to will it into explaining itself. He looked at me. "What kind of killer does this?"

I took a slow breath, letting my eyes track the restraints, the placement, and the trail beyond. "Not a reactive one," I said. "Not someone who snapped or panicked."

Brady frowned. "Not a crime of passion."

"No," I said. "This person planned. Waited. Chose when and where she'd be found."

The sheriff crossed his arms. "Serial?"

"Maybe." I crouched again, pointing at the bindings on the wrists. "This isn't about speed or body count. It's about control. Someone who wants to hold a victim, restrict them, and be the ultimate decider of what happens next."

Sally shifted behind me. I felt it more than saw it.

"This kind of offender is comfortable with waiting. They don't need immediate gratification."

"So what do they want?" the sheriff asked.

"Ownership," I said. "And narrative control. They want to decide when we found her and when we start asking questions."

Brady glanced down the trail. "You think they wanted her found."

"Yes," I said. "Just not right away."

The sheriff exhaled slowly. "So what are we dealing with?"

I stood, meeting his eyes. "Someone organized. Patient. Someone who understands how investigations work, or at least how they start."

"Is this person likely to kill again or have killed before?"

I didn't hesitate. "Yes."

He nodded once, grim. "This doesn't feel like the end."

"No, it doesn't." To Brady, I said. "You said someone called today asking about a missing person report that was never filed."

He nodded.

"When did that person go missing?"

"Just a few days ago."

"Did they give you details about the missing person?"

"Only a name. Asked what we'd found so far. But there was no investigation because there was no report."

"Do you have the contact information?"

"Yes. A private investigator named Selena Bailey from Drakos Monroe Security & Investigations down in the Bay Area."

The sheriff looked at me. "Do you think it could be connected?"

"I don't know," I said honestly. "But the timing feels awfully coincidental."

Or it was something else entirely. I looked back at the body, at the restraints and the staging, and couldn't help but feel a sense of foreboding.

12

MARTINA

Joe Sapphire was sympathetic and the grief in his voice sounded real. His plea to the community, to call the tip line if anyone had seen Lena or knew where she was, felt genuine. He talked about how much her family loved her and missed her, and how her mother didn't have much time left.

Even I was nearly moved to tears listening to him. I just hoped the press conference did the trick and it would help bring Lena home. The camera light clicked off, the faint whir of equipment powering down filling the silence. Joe walked toward me, rubbing his hands together like he didn't know what to do with them.

"How did I do?"

"You did very well."

He let out a breath. "Now what do I do? I feel like I should be doing more."

"We pray. And my team will keep working to find her. Finding her laptop may give us more answers." He'd finally found it in her suitcase. The tech team was working on getting into it while we held the press conference.

I continued, "I'll submit the missing persons report today

and see if we can get some help from law enforcement in Red Rose County. And we still have leads to follow and people to interview. I'll let you know if there are any updates."

"Thank you, Martina."

"You're welcome. That's what we do at Drakos Monroe. We help find people nobody else can find."

He gave me a look I couldn't quite read. Maybe it was hope or fear, or maybe both. "I hope so. I really do." Then he turned and walked out of the conference room.

The way he said it struck me in the gut. It was almost apologetic. Could he somehow be involved in his daughter's disappearance? Or knew more than he was telling me? I inhaled and let out a slow breath, trying to center myself. The press conference was just one thing off the list. Now I needed to get ready for our trip up to Red Rose County.

We needed to check out the property where Lena was last seen and to question the staff who worked at Ethan Buck's cabin, and anyone who had been in the vicinity that day. Somebody had to have seen something. Or heard something. Rumors had a way of surfacing when you knew how to listen. And, of course, we still needed to file an official missing person's report. Joe was supposed to have done it yesterday, but he'd been so overwhelmed that I'd offered to handle it for him.

Vincent, one of our top investigators, approached. We'd first worked together at the CoCo County Sheriff's Department back when I was contracting with them to solve cold cases. He'd been young and cocky then, sharp-edged, and restless. He'd matured quite a bit since, but he was still the same old Vincent. He was always ready with a grin, a sharp remark, and an instinct for uncovering even the tiniest clue.

"Boy, that was a tough one," he said.

"Yes. Have you and Selena made any progress?" It was a rhetorical question. I already knew the answer. Despite

Vincent's growing family, he was still a workaholic, like most of us. We tried to keep each other in check, to make sure we took weekends off and actually went home for dinner. But sometimes a case, a special case, consumed us and no one quit working until the truth came out.

"We have all the names of the staff working at the Bucks' cabin the weekend she disappeared," he said. "We've lined up interviews for later this afternoon."

"Excellent."

"Are you sure you don't want any company?"

"Selena is checking to see if she can make the trip with me. Otherwise, I'll be fine."

"Okay. I'll keep calling and try to get information over the phone, to see if there's anything anyone remembers. Maybe we can give you some clues on who to zero in on once you're up there."

"I appreciate it, Vincent."

"Of course. I'll let you know if I find anything."

"I appreciate that."

I headed back toward my office. Halfway there, a strange feeling settled over me. I couldn't name it. It wasn't pulling me in any one direction, just the sense that something bigger was unfolding, something I couldn't see yet. By the time I reached my office door, I'd refocused on the facts of the case and the long to-do list. Seated, I picked up the receiver of my phone and dialed the Red Rose County Sheriff's Department.

"Yes, how may I direct your call?"

"I'd like to make a missing person's report."

There was a pause on the other end.

"Okay. I'll transfer you to Deputy Tanner. One moment please."

"Thank you."

Deputy Tanner kept me waiting for nearly three minutes. It

didn't sound like much, but when you're on hold, time stretches. My mind drifted. Did Red Rose County have a lot of missing persons? Who was Deputy Tanner? Was he competent? Could he actually help us find Lena?

A low voice came on the line. "This is Deputy Tanner."

"Yes, hello, Deputy Tanner. My name is Martina Monroe, and..." I went on to explain that I'd been hired by the family, the details of Lena's disappearance on Saturday night, and how I'd like to get the missing person's report filed.

After a pause, he said, "I spoke with Selena Bailey from your firm yesterday. Is this the same missing person?"

That was a good sign he had remembered. It meant he hadn't brushed it off, and it was weighing on his mind. "Yes, it is."

"May I ask why the report took four days to file?"

I explained the friend group along with their history of pranks, and her father's initial hesitation to involve law enforcement.

"And you're sure she's only been missing since Saturday?"

Am I sure? Not one hundred percent. Was it possible her friends hadn't been truthful? Could Lena have been missing longer? "As far as I know. Why do you ask?"

"A body was discovered yesterday."

The words landed hard. Had we been too late? "Does it match Lena's description?"

"It appears to be a woman, but time of death hasn't been determined yet. We won't know age and manner of death or any other characteristics until the autopsy is complete."

The uneasy feeling I'd shaken off earlier came rushing back. "When is the autopsy scheduled for?"

"It should be completed later today."

That was good news. They must not get many dead bodies or it was looking like a suspicious death to get the autopsy scheduled so quickly. "I'm planning to drive up from the Bay Area today," I said. "We'd like to interview the staff and anyone who was near the property while Lena and her friends were visiting. I'd also like to speak with you in person about the case. Would that be okay with you?"

"Of course, we can discuss Lena's disappearance further," he said. "But as far as the body we found, it's an active investigation, Miss Monroe, and therefor there will be details I can't discuss with you."

"I understand." But I'd try my darnedest to change his mind and get him to share all relevant details, including the results of the autopsy. Until then, I'd pray the body wasn't Lena.

After a brief pause, he said, "Miss Monroe, I've heard of your firm and you. I used to work at SFPD before coming back up to Red Rose County a few years ago. Any insights you have will be welcome and appreciated."

Good. "I look forward to meeting you."

We exchanged information, and I ended the call. Leaning back in my desk chair, I contemplated the conversation. They'd found the body of a woman yesterday. Lena had been missing four days. If the body was Lena, it would be tragic. If it wasn't her, it could mean something bigger. Red Rose County had an active serial killer a year ago. Was it possible they had another?

I walked over to Selena's cubicle and filled her in on the details. Her eyes widened. "Are you sure only I should come with you?"

"You don't think we can handle it?"

"I'm just saying," she said, "bodies are showing up. Backup is always a good thing, right, Martina?"

She said it in that familiar way, like she was handing my own advice back to me. Selena had a habit of doing that. "It's only a three-hour drive. The two of us will go. If things start to look hairy and it looks like we need backup, we can ask the sheriff's department for help or we'll call in our own team."

Selena cocked her head. "It's an awfully strange coincidence, don't you think?"

Unfortunately, the likelihood it wasn't Lena was small. "Yes, I do."

Then she smiled, a twinkle in her eye. "And you know what Hirsch always says about coincidences?"

It made me happy that she'd gotten to know Hirsch and his sayings. "He doesn't believe in them, and neither do I."

13

MARTINA

THE SCENERY UP to Red Rose County was stunning. I was surprised I'd never visited before. The towering redwood trees, the rolling hills, the way nature seemed to close in around the highway and then open back up again. The drive brought Deputy Tanner back to mind. He'd mentioned working at SFPD. It had been years since Hirsch worked there, but maybe they'd crossed paths. On the phone, Deputy Tanner sounded a bit younger than Hirsch, but it couldn't hurt to check. I turned to Selena. "I'm going to call Hirsch and see if he's ever heard of Deputy Tanner."

She nodded, and I put the call on hands-free. He answered right away. "Hey, Martina."

"Hey."

"What's up?"

"Well, Selena and I are headed up to Red Rose County to work a missing person's case. We're meeting with a Deputy Brady Tanner. He says he used to work at SFPD. Ever heard of him?"

"Boy," Hirsch said, "it's been quite a while since I worked there. But the name sounds familiar. I could call an old pal at

SFPD and see what I can find out. Any idea how long ago he worked there?"

"Maybe a few years. I'm not sure. I just want to know who we're working with, and who we're letting work with us." My first impression was Deputy Tanner was competent, but a little evidence would be nice.

"Fair enough," he said. "What's the case?"

After I gave him the short version including the discovery of the body, he said, "All right," he said. "I'll make a call."

"Thanks, and hey, how are you doing? How's the new hobby?" He was still in physical therapy since he'd taken a bullet the previous year. He hadn't bounced back quite as quick as he'd liked.

He chuckled. "Well, I can tell you one thing about pickleball, it makes you feel young. I'm the youngest one out there. My partner yesterday was eighty years old."

I laughed. "Pickleball is great for you, Hirsch."

"I mean, it's fun," he said. "And it's nice being outside, moving around. I'll have to get you and Charlie out on the court sometime."

Since the shooting last year, Hirsch had stepped back from work with strong urging from his wife and daughter. We'd both tried to keep danger away from ourselves, but tough cases tended to have a way of finding us.

"Definitely."

After ending the call, Selena said, "You know, pickleball isn't just for old people. It's a whole movement now. Young people and old people. Everyone plays."

That surprised me. "Have you played?"

"I played a game at the gym the other day. They have an indoor court. It was fun." She cocked her head. "But you don't get to punch or hit anything. I still prefer kickboxing and the heavy bag."

Understandably. Boxing was a great way to work up a sweat and get out any frustrations. But fun was okay, too. "Might be nice to have a little balance."

"True. Plus you can hit the ball pretty hard with a racket," she said, grinning.

An hour later, we arrived at the sheriff's station. As we parked, I scanned the surroundings. Peaceful. My phone buzzed just as I was getting out of the car. "What did you find?"

"Brady Tanner worked robbery, then major crimes," Hirsch said. "Not homicide. But he's solid. Good police."

"That's good to know. Any idea why he left SFPD?"

"Divorce," he said. "Moved back to his hometown."

"Got it. Thanks, Hirsch."

"Good luck."

I slipped my phone into my pocket and looked back at the station. Whatever was happening here, we were already walking straight into it.

Selena and I made our way into the sheriff's station. Once inside, we provided identification and were asked to wait. The building smelled faintly of coffee and old paper. The kind of place where not much happened on most days. We took seats along the wall.

It wasn't long before a man in a brown uniform approached us, accompanied by a woman wearing black slacks and a dark sweater. Her shoulder-length hair framed her face neatly, her posture confident and alert.

"Miss Monroe?" the deputy said.

Selena and I stood. Extending my hand, I said, "Call me Martina. And this is my associate, Selena Bailey."

The deputy smiled easily and had a firm handshake. He was rugged, late forties, the kind of man who looked like he belonged outdoors. "Nice to meet you," he said. "I'm Brady

Tanner. And this is my associate—" He hesitated, then stepped slightly aside. "This is Val Costa, retired FBI."

Selena's eyes widened. "Oh," she said, unable to stop herself. "I read about you in the paper. You're the profiler who worked that serial killer case."

Val nodded once. "That's me. Call me Val."

I interjected Selena's fan girling, and said, "It's nice to meet you, Val."

"Likewise."

"Why don't you come back to a conference room," Brady said, "and we can talk."

An FBI profiler? I followed them down the hallway, my thoughts racing. Why bring in a profiler for the discovery of a single body?

We sat, Selena and I across from Brady and Val, each of us quietly assessing the others. Selena looked downright delighted. I made a mental note to ask her later just how much research she'd done on Val Costa.

"When we found the body," Brady began, "I remembered your call about the missing person. We immediately wondered if the two were connected." He leaned back slightly. "We don't get many missing persons here. And when we do, it's usually short-term and relatively innocent. Like someone gets lost on a trail, or wanders off and can't find their way back. That sort of thing. Someone vanishing and not being reported for days? That's unusual."

I nodded.

"And then the body showed up," he continued. "That's when we started to think something might be going on. That's why we brought in Val."

As if Selena couldn't help herself, her eyes lit up and said, "I've read about your career, Miss Costa," she said. "Really impressive. Martina and I have worked with the FBI before, but not directly with a profiler. This is so cool."

Val returned a small, polite smile. "I appreciate that. I'm retired now. I only consult when the sheriff's department asks. Brady's been telling me about Drakos Monroe Security & Investigations and your track record. It's impressive."

She glanced at Brady, then back to us. "That's why I suggested to the sheriff that we work together. Normally, with an open investigation, we're limited in what we can share. But we'd like to bring you in, with the expectation the details stay between us. My understanding is that you've worked closely with law enforcement in the past and therefore you understand confidentiality and discretion."

"We do. We won't share any unauthorized information outside the team."

Val's expression was serious. "Good." She eyed the deputy, and then continued. "The autopsy is in progress, but we believe we have a homicide. And based on my profile of the individual responsible, this isn't someone who's a one-and-done. I'm concerned that our perpetrator isn't finished killing." She folded her hands on the table. "With your skills, and the fact that the family has hired you, I think between your team and the Red Rose County Sheriff's Department, we can prevent more bodies from turning up on our trails."

I hadn't been expecting that, but was happy to hear it. If I were in her position, I would have suggested the same thing. "Agreed."

Val continued, "Sounds like we're all ready to stop this guy from hurting anyone else."

There were nods all around.

Brady leaned forward. "Let's get started."

14

MARTINA

THE REALIZATION that I was knee deep in a homicide case hit me hard. I wasn't supposed to have taken *any* cases. Everything inside of me was screaming this was going to be a complicated and dangerous case. Being away from home, I didn't know the territory and would have to rely on a team I'd just met. Based on Selena's reaction to Val, it sounded like she was highly skilled and someone we'd want on the team. And according to Hirsch's contact, Brady had a good reputation at the SFPD. Despite all that, something felt... dark. Like this case was a big one. An ugly one. Not a happy ending kind of case. *Please, Lord, let me be wrong.*

Selena said, "Why don't we tell you everything we know about Lena and then you can discuss the homicide. We can draw similarities and angles to explore first."

Val eyed her with interest. "Sounds good."

I said, "Lena Sapphire, aged twenty-three, went missing from Ethan Buck's family cabin four days ago. Since then, she's had no cell phone activity and no new social media posts. We checked her laptop and cell phone data for any clues to where she could have gone, or if there was anyone suspicious in her life. So far it hasn't given us anything to go on. We held a press conference this morning hoping to get her face out there, and we set up a hotline for any tips."

"You've interviewed the people she was with Saturday night?" Brady asked.

"Yes, at first they were a little cagey, but eventually their stories aligned."

"Eventually?" Val questioned.

I explained the fake engagement prank, and the distress of her boyfriend along with the strange behavior from Ethan Buck. Val wrinkled her brow. "That's weird."

"Agreed!" Selena said.

"Have you done background checks on the friends and parents?" Val asked.

Selena explained, "Vincent and I finished them all. No criminal backgrounds for any of them. All met at private schools and remained friends after."

Val looked at me. "What's your take on the friends and family? Anyone we should look at closer."

"Ethan Buck."

"Why?" she asked, but I had a feeling she knew why and was testing me.

"He set up the prank. It was almost as if the kidnapping was set up for her to be taken at that very moment. The boyfriend and friends are distraught. Ethan's not."

Selena added, "And it was at his family's house."

Brady said, "We can head over there later. They probably have security cameras."

"We have interviews set up with the staff for this afternoon."

"The Bucks own quite a bit of Red Rose County," Val said, and then paused. "Brady and I grew up here. We know most people, at least by reputation."

"Do you think they'll cooperate?"

She cocked an eyebrow. "It wouldn't look good if they didn't."

"So, they will."

Val nodded. "Anything else that can help?"

"That's it. We're hoping visiting the Buck home will give us more to work with."

"Agreed."

Brady said, "Are we ready to discuss the homicide?"

"Yes." Val looked down at the folder in front of her. She didn't open it right away. Instead, she studied the tabletop, as if arranging her thoughts before letting anyone else see them. "I want to be clear," she said. "What we're about to tell you is preliminary. The autopsy isn't complete and we don't have cause of death yet."

That's interesting they don't know cause of death considering they think it's a homicide. I would have assumed it was obvious. "Understood."

Val continued, "The body was found on a popular trail yesterday afternoon. It was discovered by a hiker, who called it in. The body is in an advanced stage of decomposition, but it's a woman. Time of death and cause of death is uncertain, due to the state of the body. Different environmental factors can effect time of death. It could be a few days to a few weeks according to our ME, so it could be Lena. We believe it's a homicide because she still had restraints on her wrists. There was also soil embedded in her clothing, that makes us believe she'd been held captive, killed, and buried before she was dug up and placed on the trail yesterday."

This case just got stranger.

Val said, "That's not accidental. Whoever did this wanted the body found, but not immediately."

Selena said, "That's staging."

Val nodded. "Yes. But this person isn't theatrical. They're controlled and methodical."

My stomach sank.

"Inexperienced killers tend to panic," Val said. "They rush disposal. They overcorrect. This individual didn't."

With a sickening realization, I said, "They were comfortable leaving a body behind."

"Yes, and that tells me something else," Val went on. "This isn't their first time. This wasn't opportunistic. This wasn't a crime of sudden rage. The location suggests familiarity. Not just with the terrain but with how long it would take for someone to stumble across her."

Selena said, "You're saying they planned for the discovery."

"Not only that. They planned for the *timing* of the discovery."

Val shifted her gaze to Selena. "If Lena Sapphire disappeared Saturday night, and this woman was held captive, killed, buried, and then left on a trail... four days isn't a lot of time for all of that to happen. And looking at the photo of Lena with her long blonde hair, I don't think it's her. The victim has dark hair."

Val eyed Brady. He nodded. She continued, "If I'm right, then we may not be dealing with a single event. If the two are connected, we're dealing with something much worse."

My chest tightened.

"If Lena's disappearance is connected to the body we found," Val added, "then she isn't missing because of chance. She might have been selected by our killer."

That was not good news for Lena. "Any idea for what reason?"

Val folded her hands again, calm as ever. "That's unclear. But I don't think this killer is done. And if they escalate, it won't be with warning. They might escalate quietly, by shortening the time between acts."

A serial killer.

Selena said, "Could it be a copycat?"

Val shook her head. "I don't think so. The MO and the scene

is very different from previous killers I've studied. This one is puzzling. I would swear it wasn't their first time. But we've only found one body. And now have one missing person. There is an unpredictability about this situation. I have a feeling we're not dealing with a textbook killer. This one has written their own rules." She met my eyes. "And that's why I'm worried about Lena. I think we need to act smart and fast."

Selena and I exchanged glances. The message was clear, Val was worried, and so were we.

15

MARTINA

THE DRIVEWAY UP to the Buck Cabin, as they called it, wasn't what I'd imagined at all. This wasn't a cabin. It was a large home, hidden among towering trees high in the hills. Stunning. Massive. The kind of place where people could disappear without anyone noticing. With plenty of places surrounding it for a perpetrator to lie in wait.

At the top of the long driveway, I stepped out of the car and scanned the property. Val and Brady stood near the sheriff's county vehicle, both already alert, their posture telling me they were doing the same thing I was, studying the area and trying to picture how it happened.

"The property manager is waiting for us," I said as I approached them.

Val nodded, and I led them toward the front of the house, carefully surveying the surroundings as we walked. There were paths wide enough for picnic tables, but beyond that, dense forest wrapped itself tightly around the property, the trees hovering on all sides.

I stopped near the front door. The spot where Lena had disappeared. Stepping back beneath the trellis, I noticed the fairy lights woven through it. Unlit now in the daylight, but I could picture how they would glow softly in the evening. And behind it all was dense forest. Anyone could've been waiting there in the bushes, watching for the right moment to grab Lena.

But how would they get away?

The property wasn't right off a main road. You had to drive the entire length of the driveway just to reach the house. I turned to Brady and Val. "Is there another way to access the property from here?"

Brady said, "There's probably a trailhead nearby. Let me check." He pulled out his phone and started tapping and scrolling. After a moment, he nodded. "There's a trail about two hundred yards from here. Small parking area, or at least a turnout where someone could park." He walked over and showed me the screen. A detailed map appeared with trails, terrain, and nearby homes. "It's common for homes like this," Brady added. "Sometimes it's by design. People like being able to go for a hike without having to drive anywhere. Looks like it starts over there." He pointed to a spot about twenty-five feet away near the driveway. A small clearing, showing a narrow trail.

I walked over and took a look at the trail that had a canopy of trees shading the path. If you weren't looking, you might not realize it was a trail. I didn't see any signs of disturbance or drag marks. "Someone could've parked at the trailhead, hidden in the woods, grabbed Lena or forced her at gunpoint, headed back down the trail, gotten into their car, and driven away."

"Or drugged her and carried her down the trail," Val added.

Brady said, "On a trail like this, I'd guess they would have to have dragged her or there was a second perpetrator."

Could there be two kidnappers? Looking over at Val, I said, "Two kidnappers?"

She stood still for a few moments, obviously contemplating. "It's possible. If our killer and kidnapper are one and the same, it would make sense. Our killer placed the body on the trail. That wouldn't have been easy for one person."

There were likely two killers.

"It's pretty quiet out here," I said. "Do you think if a car engine started up, even two hundred yards away, you'd hear it from the house?"

"They might," Brady said. "If they were outside. But if they were inside, probably not. Especially with a group of young people that were likely talking and maybe had music on. This place is big. It probably insulates most noise."

That made sense, and the kidnappers probably would've known that. But the same thought twisted in another direction. If the trailhead was that close, Lena could've snuck away herself. Maybe she met someone. Someone she trusted. Someone who turned out not to have very good intentions. The Sapphires had granted us permission to Lena's cellphone records. We didn't find any new contacts or any indication she'd been planning a getaway, and it hadn't been used since Lena disappeared. That made it unlikely she'd left on her own accord.

As we walked back to the front door, Val stopped and pointed up toward the corner of the house. "They have security cameras."

"At a place like this, I figured they would," Brady said.

"I just hope they captured what we're looking for," I said.

I knocked, and a moment later the door opened. A man in his fifties stood there, dressed neatly in slacks and a button-down shirt. His posture was polite but guarded.

"Hi, I'm Martina Monroe," I said. "I have an appointment to interview the staff about Lena's disappearance."

His eyes flicked briefly over my shoulder. I stepped aside slightly. "And this is Deputy Brady Tanner and Val Costa with the sheriff's department and my associate Selena Bailey. We're all working together to find Lena."

"Of course," he said. "I'm Jerome Dumphy, the property manager. Please, come in."

The inside of the house was just as grand as the exterior, but instead of rustic charm, it leaned modern with white walls broken up by red brick accents, plush furniture throughout, and a massive fireplace dominating the far wall. Everything felt expensive. "I take care of the home when the Bucks aren't visiting," Jerome said as he led us further inside. "I've gathered the staff in the living room for you to question. Mr. And Mrs. Buck instructed us to answer all questions." He paused, likely reading my expression. "We all have signed NDAs to not discuss our work here, but they have granted permission for us to speak freely."

Giving an understanding nod, I said, "I appreciate that."

With that we walked down the hallway, our footsteps muffled by thick rugs. Two people sat on the sofa, hands folded, waiting.

"This is Delaney," Jerome said. "She's our chef. And this is Porter he's in charge of hospitality, housekeeping, and groundskeeping."

"Basically anything they want, I get it done," Porter said with an easy smile.

"What does that entail?" I asked.

He shrugged. "For example, they wanted fairy lights installed on the terrace before they arrived. I went out, bought them, and installed them."

I nodded, filing it away. *So it was premeditated*, I thought. Whatever this was, it had been planned before they arrived.

"Okay," I said. "Selena and I will speak with you, Porter. Brady and Val would you like to talk with Delaney?"

Val said, "Perfect."

"Please, come with me," I said to Porter. We stepped away from the others, giving us some privacy. "Can you tell me exactly who was here this weekend?"

"The group of friends. Jenna Bakewell, Tiffany Gordan, Ethan Buck, Jason Turnbull, and Lena Sapphire. Plus Delaney and myself. No one else was on the property, and no one else was expected."

"Before the group arrived," I asked, "did you notice anyone near the property who shouldn't have been? A hiker off trail? Unfamiliar cars near the driveway?"

"No," he said. "Everything was very quiet."

"When did they request the fairy lights?"

"Ethan called the day before, on Friday, asking for them."

"Did he say why?"

"No. I didn't ask."

"Any other special requests for the weekend?"

"He put in a catering request with Delaney," Porter said. "I was on call in case they wanted takeout instead of home-cooked food. I made sure the guest rooms were ready and helped with luggage." He hesitated. "Oh, and one more thing. A little unusual, but not the first time it's been requested."

I waited.

"Ethan requested that I turn off the security cameras for the weekend."

Selena and I exchanged a look. "You said it wasn't the first time he'd requested that. Do you know why he'd want the cameras off?"

"Usually for privacy. Usually when it's Ethan or his brother with his friends. I always assumed they don't want their parents knowing what they're up to."

"What were they usually up to?" Selena asked.

He shrugged. "We're instructed to stay in our rooms when we're not needed."

"Lena went missing around nine p.m. Saturday night," I said. "Do you recall hearing anything? A car engine? A scream? Shouting? Anything unusual?"

"No," he said. "At nine, I was in my room watching television. That's where I was the majority of the evening."

A detail we couldn't verify. "Anything else you can tell us that might help us find Lena?"

He shook his head.

"Thank you for your time," I said.

As we stepped back toward the others, Jerome reappeared, his hands clasped in front of him. "Everything going well?"

I forced a polite smile, but my mind was already racing. "Yes. I have one more question for you," I said. "We were told the security cameras weren't on that weekend. Porter turned them off. Are there any other cameras, ones that Porter or the family might not have thought to disable?"

Jerome shook his head. "Unfortunately, no."

It was a long shot. "Do you mind giving us a tour of the house? Show us where Lena was staying?"

He motioned toward Porter. "Porter will have to show you. He's the one who prepared the house that day."

"Great. Thank you."

Porter led us through the house, room by room. When we reached the bedroom Lena had stayed in, I asked if it had been cleaned. "Yes. The rooms are cleaned daily while the guests are here."

There was nothing in the room that pointed to what might have happened to her. Nothing out of place. Nothing broken. Nothing screaming for attention. Porter escorted us back downstairs, and Val and Brady stood off to the side, speaking quietly. I waved as we approached.

"I think we're done here," Brady said.

We thanked Jerome and Porter once more and stepped

outside, pacing off the fifteen steps from the front door, the same spot where Lena had been abducted.

I stopped and said, "Ethan requested the fairy lights the day before. He also requested the security cameras to be turned off."

Val raised an eyebrow. "I think I'd like to interview Ethan."

"Yes, an additional conversation is certainly warranted," I said. "Did you learn anything from the chef?"

"Other than the fact that, despite being young, they had extravagant tastes and expected very high-quality meals. But nothing unusual. She didn't hear anything that night. At the time Lena disappeared, she was in her room listening to a podcast."

Selena crossed her arms. "No security footage. Remote location, but easy access in and out, two hundred yards away. A prank planned well in advance. And we have one guy who made all of it possible."

Thinking back to conversations with Ethan and Jason, I said, "You'd think for such an elaborate prank they'd want it caught on camera."

"I'd think so," Selena said.

Val eyed me. "Ethan could be the key. Or Ethan and Jason together. We need eyes on them, and another conversation ASAP."

My money was on Ethan. He gave me an icky vibe during our first meeting. He may not have abducted Lena, but I had a feeling he knew a lot more than he'd told us. Ethan hadn't just planned a prank. He had created an *opportunity*. The question was whether or not it was intentional.

16

VAL

ALL OF MY experience told me this was a calculated, carefully planned abduction. Lena had been selected for a reason, which made me believe we were dealing with an organized killer or killers, but unlike others I've studied. Yes, this person was methodical. They planned. But I don't think they abducted for sheer, sick pleasure. There might have been pleasure in it, but most killers knew better than to abduct a high-profile victim. Someone with means. Unless, of course, it was a ransom kidnapping. And I didn't think that's what this was. There had been no ransom demands. Unless money wasn't what the kidnapper wanted. Maybe Lena's family had something else, something far more valuable than cash. Something that couldn't be delivered easily, the way money could.

I'd been suspicious from the beginning, especially when they hadn't immediately filed a missing-person report. I wanted to interview the family myself. Something about this case felt off and nothing fit a pattern I'd seen before.

And then there was the homicide. My experience told me it wasn't Lena, unless the killer died her hair. Not entirely out of the question. I sure wished the autopsy was complete. I'd like confirmation I was on the right track. Because if the two cases were connected, and I believed they were, then the body left on the trail wasn't accidental. They wanted us to find it. They wanted us to know the cases were linked. That had to be the reason for the timing. Not much else made sense.

Red Rose County didn't see many homicides. Not really. Aside from a cluster a few years back, violent crime like this was rare.

Turning to Martina and Selena, I said, "Come on. Let's head back to the station. We should start making calls and setting up interviews. I want to re-interview everyone." I paused. "And I don't want you to think this is about distrust. You did solid initial interviews. We just have more information now."

Martina nodded immediately. "Of course. You might pick up details we didn't."

Brady and I headed toward his SUV. As we walked, I watched Martina out of the corner of my eye. She was clearly used to being in charge, but seemed like she'd be reasonable to work with.

I meant it when I said we could solve this together. More minds were better than fewer. We needed every perspective we could get. Maybe she'd see something from a different angle, one I wouldn't. That thought alone told me how strange this case was.

Inside the vehicle, Brady was mid-sentence when I glanced down to look at the buzzing phone in my lap. "It's Sally," I said, already answering. "Hi, Sally. What's up?"

Sally's voice came through professional, but heavier than usual. "I finished the autopsy on our homicide victim."

"What did you learn?"

"Definitely homicide," she said. "She did not slit her own throat. The neck injury is sharp-force trauma, clean and deliberate."

I nodded at Brady. Confirmation, though neither of us had doubted it.

Sally continued. "Even with the level of decomposition, I can deduce that the positioning of the bindings on her wrists and the impressions on the remaining tissue are consistent with her being bound for a prolonged period, not just at the time of death."

That distinction mattered.

"But there's more," she said. "I found a burn on the back of her shoulder."

"Cigarette burn?" A lot of killers liked to torture their victims in this manner.

"No, it's larger than a cigarette burn. Several centimeters across. The edges are irregular, but there's a discernible pattern. This wasn't incidental contact with heat."

"Like a brand?"

"Possibly," she said. "At the very least, it was intentional. The depth of the burn and the tissue response indicate it happened while she was alive."

I exhaled slowly.

"I also confirmed she had been buried before being placed on the trail," Sally added. "There's soil embedded in areas that don't match the surface environment where she was found. Fine particulate matter in her hair and clothing, compression patterns along the back, and insect activity that suggests delayed exposure. In my opinion, she was buried, or at least concealed underground, for a period of time before being moved."

Buried. Then displayed. "Time of death?"

"I estimate she's been dead for ten to fourteen days."

It wasn't Lena.

"And there's more."

More? Please be something we can use.

"We have an identification. She's a thirty-year-old teacher

named Teresa McDonald from Concord, California. She was reported missing three weeks ago."

The timeline locked into place with a sickening clarity. "Which means she was likely held for at least a week before she was killed."

"I'd say so." Sally hesitated. "I hope this isn't starting again."

Sally and I had been through a lot in the past few years. And neither of us wanted another serial killer in our town. "I think this is different. But, keep your guard up. Between me and you, I think the kidnapping is connected to the homicide. I don't know the connection or why the victims were chosen. Until I do, everyone needs to stay alert."

"Understood. How is it working with the PI?"

"I think she's used to being in charge," I said. "But so far, she seems competent. And if these cases are connected, I have no doubt well figure it out."

Sally sighed quietly. "I hope so."

The call ended and the silence inside the vehicle felt heavy. Held captive for a week. Dead for two weeks. Buried, then unburied and placed on a trail for us to find. Lena had been gone four days. If the killer had a pattern, that meant we may have some time to save her, but not a lot. We needed to act fast. Lena's life may depend on it.

17

LENA

CURLED UP ON THE MATTRESS, I began to wonder if this nightmare would ever end. Was anyone ever going to come for me? Was I really on my own? *I need a way out.*

Maybe I could make them believe I was compliant. Let them think I'd given up. I could go along with it, for now. Maybe then I'd find a way to escape. I forced myself to look around the room again, really look. High up near the ceiling was a narrow window I couldn't reach. The chair was bolted down. So was the table. There was no way to climb up there, even if I wasn't chained to the wall.

Unless... I could somehow break free of the chain, then I could poke holes in the wall and use them to climb up, like a rock climber? Not that I'd ever done anything like that but I'd seen a movie once that featured climbing. You just need to find places for your hands and feet and then just... climb up. *I think.*

The thought barely had time to form before I noticed the red blinking light in the corner. The camera. A reminder I was being monitored. Surely, if they saw me trying to escape, they'd come rushing in. They'd catch me and then punish me. No thanks. I had to be smarter than that. I needed to gain their trust.

Somehow convince them I wasn't a problem and then get them to let me out of here, even just for a moment.

The door opened. Out of instinct, I sat up straight, my heart dropping into my stomach. The masked man was back. But he wasn't alone. And he wasn't empty-handed.

I gasped.

They had another victim.

The man being dragged in was unconscious. Hopefully not dead, just drugged. Probably the same way they'd drugged me. It was the only explanation that made sense. One minute I'd been outside the house. The next, I had woken up here. But who was this guy? And where were they going to put him?

I didn't say anything because I knew better than that. I didn't like punishments, and I definitely didn't want another one. They carried him over to the mattress and placed him down beside me.

I scooted away, my back pressing against the cold wall. Not because he was a threat, he wasn't even awake, but still. He was a stranger. Why couldn't he have his own room? Who was this person?

"How are you doing, Lena?" one of them asked casually, like this was some normal check-in.

I wanted to scream, "How do you think I'm doing? I'm a prisoner!" Instead, I said, "I'm fine."

"You've got yourself a roommate now. Lucky you." He tilted his head. "I'm going to have to apologize for the noise, but, well, we can't just let him move freely in here, can we?"

He glanced up at the windows.

"Wouldn't want him getting any ideas, would we?"

Of course not, I thought. My eyes flicked to the table. There was still only one chair.

"Don't worry," the masked man said, the one with the dark

eyes, the one who'd been in my room before. "I'm hoping this will all be over very soon. Aren't you hoping the same?"

I nodded.

The other man removed a black backpack and unzipped it. Chains clinked together as he pulled them out, followed by a drill. He went to work quickly and silently, securing the restraints to the wall.

The drill was loud and unnerving. Soon, the man was chained by one ankle and one wrist. It happened so quick, it was obvious this wasn't the masked man's first time installing restraints. How many others had there been? I didn't know, but suddenly I was grateful I'd only been attached at the ankle.

"I hope you two get along," the masked man said. "If not, you'll be punished."

A chill slid down my spine.

I nodded again.

The two men turned and walked out of the room without another word.

It was creepy, like they were robots. Efficient. Emotionless. Refocusing, I stared down at the man who now shared my predicament. I couldn't help but wonder who he was, or why he'd been chosen. And not just that. Why had *I* been chosen?

A few hours later, I sat cross-legged on the mattress, staring at the man lying beside me. He was covered in bruises and there were small cuts along his cheek and knuckles. He must've fought them when they took him. At least I hadn't been beaten up. I mean, I wasn't sure that would've made things all *that* much worse than my current situation. I hadn't been hurt other than the burn. Branded. Like I was a cow.

But the man was right, I'd learned my lesson. I needed a different tactic if I was going to get out of here. If only they would tell me what they wanted and I would tell them how to get it.

They were clearly planning something. And this guy, this stranger chained beside me, felt like part of it. I'd read stories like this. Two people held captive. Forced to do things. I swallowed hard, my stomach twisting. Please don't let that be our story.

The man was bigger than me. Hopefully stronger too, so he could help us get free. He groaned softly, and I watched him carefully as his eyes fluttered open. They were bright blue, like mine. He lifted a hand to his head, wincing, and the chain clinked loudly. He looked down. Not just at his wrist, but his ankle, too. He cursed, and I jumped.

His gaze snapped to me, startled, clearly not expecting to find someone else in the room.

I gave a small, cautious wave. "Hi."

"Where am I?" His voice was deep.

"Honestly, I don't know. They took me, I think it's been four days." I hesitated. "I'm Lena."

He pushed himself into a sitting position, chains scraping against the wall. Once settled, he glanced around the room. His face distorting at his new reality. He turned back to me. "I'm Derek."

"What happened to you?"

"I was doing work on a house, leveling an exterior door, and then there was this man... then another one. I thought—" He shook his head slowly. "Something happened. I don't remember. And now I'm here." He looked at me.

"They didn't say anything to you?"

"Not that I remember." He eyed me. "Have you tried to escape?"

"There's a camera," I said, pointing. "The window's too high." My voice faltered. "We could work together, maybe, but the camera..." I trailed off, defeated.

He studied it for a moment. "Do they feed you?"

"Yeah. It's not bad. They've actually treated me... okay. Other than chaining me up and the burn."

"That's...weird. They haven't—" He stopped himself. "You know."

I shook my head. "No. Nothing like that. But they burned me. Branded me with something, I think. But other than that, no violence, not really. Just being held captive." Although there was the time he grabbed me by the throat, but that startled me more than hurt me.

"Has anyone else been here?" he asked. "Chained up with you?"

"No." I frowned. "They installed the chains while you were here."

He lifted his brows. "That's strange."

Then his expression shifted. "Oh," he said quietly. "But that's a clue. It means they hadn't planned to have another person in here. But then they chose to."

I wasn't sure how that helped us. "Maybe you're right. But why do you think they took you?"

He shrugged, the chains shifting softly. "I have no idea. How about you?"

I shook my head. "My family has money. I assumed it was for ransom. At first, I thought it was my jerk of a friend, not really a friend, but... kind of playing a joke." I let out a shaky breath. "But then I realized it couldn't be him. I have no idea who took me or why. I just get this feeling they're planning something. I don't know what."

"And you have no idea who took you?"

"No idea. They wear masks. I thought it was just one guy at first. Then the second one came in, with you, and then they chained you up and left."

"You said you've been here four days?"

"Yeah."

He looked around the room again, really taking it in this time. "I don't think this is going to end well for us."

My breath seized.

He bowed his head, staring at the floor. I could see the weight of it settling on him, the same way it had settled on me days ago. I couldn't let him give up. I couldn't let either of us.

"No," I said firmly.

He looked over at me.

"Whatever it takes, we have to figure out how to get out of here. At least—" I faltered, then forced a small smile. "At least we're not alone. I mean..." What did I mean? I hugged my knees to my chest. I'm usually someone who's always chatting with someone somewhere. Social media, friends, and family. I'm always with someone. And then suddenly, it was just me. All by myself. I exhaled softly. "I've been here so long I was starting to go a little nutty. I considered creating some imaginary friends."

He nodded as if he understood what I was going through, even though I know he didn't.

"I was staring at you earlier, wondering if you were real," I admitted. "But you're talking back, so I'm gonna go ahead and guess that you are."

He lowered his head. "As much as I can't believe this is happening, it is. I'm real. This is real." The chains rattled as he shifted again, restless. "How long have I been here?"

"It was light out when they brought you in, and it's dark now."

He eyed the window.

"I think we should come up with a plan," I said. "There are two of them, maybe more. I've only seen two." The realization sent a chill up my spine. Could there be more than two?

"And they've given you no indication of who they are or what they want?" he asked again, stunned.

I shook my head. I'd had days to sit with the fear, to turn it over and over until it dulled at the edges. He had just woken up after being beaten, kidnapped, and drugged. His shock was fresh.

"No. Not at all."

He bowed his head, and then he started to cry.

The sound cracked something open inside me. My throat tightened. If he gave up, I would give up too. I reached out and put my hand on his shoulder. "Don't cry. We'll figure this out."

He wiped his eyes with one hand, breathing hard. "There has to be a way out of here," he said. "We're going to figure it out. Okay?"

"Okay." I glanced up at the camera. "But we shouldn't act like we're planning anything. The camera." I turned my body away from him and lowered my head, angling myself so they couldn't see my lips move. "We can't let them think we're conspiring," I whispered.

"Agreed," he said. "Let's figure out how to loosen these chains. If we can do that, we've got a fighting chance."

Why hadn't I thought of that? I'd given up somewhere along the way, convinced they could overpower me, that I'd never reach the window. All of it was true. But this man had something I'd lost. Confidence. We might actually get out of here. I closed my eyes and whispered a prayer to the God I hadn't prayed to since I was a little girl, kneeling for my First Holy Communion. *Please, God, if you're listening. Please let me out of here safe and sound so I can see my mother, my father, my brothers, and Jason. I'll do anything.*

The door creaked open. I snapped my eyes open just as one of them stepped inside, carrying food. There was only one of them. The one with the dark eyes, the same one who always came in alone. "Dinner time," he said.

He walked over and set a sandwich down in front of Derek,

along with a bag of chips. Then he looked at me. "Lena, you can eat at the table."

I nodded.

He placed my food on the small metal table. I didn't look at Derek as I walked over. We ate in silence, the room filled only with the sound of chewing. I took a bite of the sandwich, chewing even though my mouth had gone dry. It tasted fine. Too normal for a place like this. That's when it hit me. They weren't rushing. They fed us. Emptied the bucket. Let us talk. Let us hope. If this were about ransom, surely this would be over by now. If it were about punishment, they wouldn't be so careful. I glanced at the camera, then at the door where he'd disappeared, my pulse hammering in my ears. Whatever they were planning, they didn't need us yet. And that scared me more than anything else.

My gut was screaming at me now, louder than ever. This could be far worse than I'd imagined. Derek and I needed to get out of there. We needed a plan. *And fast.*

18

MARTINA

PART of me couldn't believe what Val was telling me. Another part of me knew it fit perfectly. The homicide victim was from the Bay Area and found in Red Rose County. Lena was from the Bay Area and abducted in Red Rose County. The connection was too significant to ignore. Red Rose County wasn't particularly large. At least it didn't feel that way with its small-town feel where everyone knew everyone. There were no coincidences here. We had someone killing and abducting with ties to both places. I knew exactly one person who fit.

"I think we need to head back to the Bay Area," I said to Val and the team. "Question Teresa McDonald's family. Find out everything we can about her disappearance. See if there's any connections to Lena or similarities in her abduction."

Val said, "That's exactly what I was thinking. I don't think we're being told the whole story by Lena's friends or the family. Something doesn't add up. They know more than they're saying. Why don't you two re-interview Lena's pals, especially Ethan and Jason. Push a little. Let them know what we found and let them know we think there's a connection. It might scare them into opening up."

Not that I thought I needed instruction, but I agreed and said, "Do you think they're involved?"

"I'm not sure. After you talk to the friends again and we compare notes, I'll want to meet them myself."

Thinking back to my conversation with Ethan, I recalled his cool demeanor and what Jason said about Ethan's fascination with scaring people. And how Jenna and Tiffany claimed Ethan was always kind of a creep, but that he was harmless. Maybe he was, maybe he wasn't. "It's possible Lena wasn't abducted," I said. "One of them could have killed her, and the abduction story is a cover. Possibly an accidental death?"

Val met my eyes. "Maybe. But since we also have a homicide victim, I think it's more likely a planned abduction, unless one of her friends is our killer, which we can't rule out at this point."

That had my mind spinning. Could Ethan be a serial killer? Anything was possible. He had the means, the opportunity, and possibly a motive if was really as into the macabre like his friends claimed. Val had good instincts. It was almost as if she could see things others couldn't. Not that I hadn't had the same uneasy feeling about the family and friends, and that it felt like information was being withheld.

"Why don't we head back to the Bay Area tomorrow?" Val said. "It's getting late. I'll interview Teresa McDonald's family and friends, make the notifications. After you've both met with Lena's friends again, we'll compare notes. See what stands out." She paused. "And I think we should push hard on the father. It could be that Lena was chosen for a reason. The kidnappers may want something, maybe not cash. Maybe blackmail. Revenge. I don't know. But something tells me the identities of these victims mean something. I just don't know what yet. I'll know more after I've spoken with Teresa McDonald's friends, family, and coworkers."

As much as I agreed with Val, I didn't love being told what to do. Selena and I exchanged a glance before she said, "I think dividing and conquering makes sense. When will we have a copy of the autopsy report?"

"It could be a few weeks before it's finalized," Val said. "But if you want to see the body, Sally, Dr. Edison, can show us."

I thought about what Val had already told us. "I'd like to see the body. Especially the burn mark."

Selena chimed in. "So would I. It could help to know if it was intentional, or if there's something else that gives us a clue about what happened to her." Selena quieted and then said, "And what might happen to Lena."

Val said, "The medical examiner is just down the hall in the other building. Let's go."

AFTER INTRODUCTIONS with the medical examiner, we stood over the body and examined the burn. "Could it be from a stun gun?" Selena asked.

Dr. Edison shook her head. "I don't think so. Stun guns typically leave paired contact marks. Two distinct points with consistent spacing. This is a single focal burn, several centimeters across, with deeper heat penetration. There's no electrical patterning. No satellite burns. No evidence of arcing."

She gestured just above the skin with a gloved finger. "This looks more like prolonged contact with a heated object than a brief electrical discharge."

Selena leaned over the body. "It almost looks like a rose."

Val tipped her head toward the mark. "Kind of. What do you think, Martina?"

I studied it again. The edges weren't clean, but there was a symmetry to it. "I can see it as a possibility."

"It could be significant," Val said.

I pulled out my phone and took a photo. I hated doing it, taking pictures of a deceased young woman who didn't deserve to be seen that way. It felt like a violation, but if it brought her killer to justice, it was necessary. "Any sign of sexual assault?"

Dr. Edison said, "Not that I can see."

That's a little odd for this type of crime. "Did you find anything else unusual about the body?"

"Other than the fact that we believe she was buried for a period of time before being dug up and placed on the trail," Dr. Edison said. "Not really."

So strange.

"Any other questions?" Dr. Edison asked.

Selena shook her head. "No. I think I've seen enough."

"Me too," I said. "Thank you, Dr. Edison. It was good to meet you."

"You too," she said as she removed her gloves.

I glanced at the clock. It was getting late. We still hadn't eaten. "Selena and I are going to grab dinner," I said. "Then we'll stay here tonight and head back to the Bay Area first thing in the morning."

After goodbyes were exchanged along with recommendations for food and lodging, Selena and I headed out.

"So," I said as we pulled onto the road, "what do you think of the case?"

Selena sighed. "I think it's a lot more dangerous than we originally anticipated."

"I think so too. We'll get more team members on it. I've got a bad feeling about this one."

"Me too."

After driving a few minutes, I glanced in the rearview mirror. "Do you remember seeing that car behind us when we left the sheriff's station?"

Selena frowned. "I'm not sure."

At the next light, I turned left, heading down a street lined with shops and restaurants. The car stayed behind us. I made a right turn into a parking lot, looped through, then pulled back onto the road. The car reappeared. Selena said, "I think someone's following us."

"I do too."

I eased to the curb and killed the engine. We sat idle as a four-door sedan rolled past us, slowly. I caught the driver's profile. He was male and wearing a baseball cap that was pulled low, obscuring any distinguishing features. And as the car drove past, I was surprised to see it didn't have license plates. It was sketchy as all get out. If my gut wasn't tingling before, it was scratching at me now. For a long moment, neither of us spoke. Then Selena said, "I think we should talk to Val and then head back tonight."

"Agreed."

19

THE ARCHITECT

STANDING in front of the group, I couldn't help but be disgusted with all of them. And with myself for ever believing they were strong and powerful. *Special.* Oh, how wrong I'd been. Perhaps they'd once been that way, but was no longer. But I knew I could make it that way again. And I would. With confidence, I said, "It appears our message was received. Things are proceeding as expected."

"Are you certain?" she asked.

"Yes."

A pause. The faint sound of fabric shifting, a chair adjusting. Eying me with skepticism, she said, "Do we have a timeline?"

"I will have this concluded by the end of the week."

The other smirked. "For the entirety of what you've proposed?"

With my chin held high, I said, "You'll have your result by the end of the week."

She said, "The three of you have yet to deliver. It should have been done by now."

Yes, it had taken longer than planned, but I had a remedy.

She needed to believe I could do it. "I assure you, I'll have it done by the end of the week."

The second architect seated to my right said, "This is our greatest challenge yet. It stands to reason there will be additional requirements and time needed."

She said, "Fine. The best architect will prevail."

I felt the corner of my mouth lift. That was my belief as well. And I was *the best*. Everything was aligning. The threads tightening, and paths narrowing. With the additional assistance now in place, the design was no longer theoretical.

My phone buzzed softly against the table. I didn't look at it. Interruptions were not tolerated here.

"All right," she said. "I expect a progress report in forty-eight hours."

The three of us inclined our heads.

"You're dismissed."

We exited together, the door closing behind us with a sharp click. Only then did I check my phone. A message from one of my helpers.

"We need to meet. Our Ladybug has crawled home. We will maintain observation."

I stared at the screen longer than necessary. Frustration stirred inside of me. Why had she gone back? This was proving to be more of a challenge than I'd expected. But difficulty had never discouraged me before. Quite the opposite.

If the first message hadn't been sufficient, then another would be. This one would be clearer. This one would move pieces that couldn't be returned to their original positions. She would step where I needed her to step. And when she did, the rest would take care of itself.

20

VAL

WE WERE APPROACHING the home of Teresa "Terry" McDonald's parents, the schoolteacher we'd found in Red Rose County. As the house came into view, I started rehearsing what I would say, what Brady would say. Death notifications were the worst part of being in law enforcement. The only thing worse than telling a family their loved one passed was when families asked questions and I didn't have answers. At that point, all I could tell them was that their daughter had been killed and we didn't know who did it or why. We couldn't tell them what we feared, that a deranged killer or killers were on the loose and they had already taken another victim.

Martina and Selena had been followed after leaving the sheriff's station. A car with no license plates. I didn't blame them for driving straight home, even with the long distance. Martina's place, by her own admission, was fortified with security cameras, sensors, and probably an arsenal to match. Still, the fact that it had happened at all bothered me.

Something was brewing in Red Rose County, and I didn't like it. It had been over a year since our last murder. I'd thought that it had been a once-in-a-lifetime event. Something we'd endured and then moved past. I'd let myself believe we lived in a safe place again. A community where everyone knew one another. Where people looked out for each other.

Sally was worried.

So was I.

It felt like it was starting all over again.

"Up there," Brady said, nodding toward a house on the left.

I parked in front of it and took a deep breath, gripping the steering wheel for a second longer than necessary.

"You okay?" Brady asked.

"I don't like any of this."

"Neither do I. I've got a bad feeling about this one."

"So do I," I admitted. "Something feels off. Like there's something big we're missing—something that should be glaring us right in the face."

The truth was harder to admit, even to myself. But I was starting to wonder if I'd lost my touch. As someone who had a twenty-year career with the FBI, I should have known the peace and quiet wouldn't last. I'd let my guard down and gotten too comfortable. Now the threat was back. A different threat, but a threat all the same.

He reached for my hand. "We've got this. Together, we can handle anything."

I smiled despite myself.

"I love you," he said.

"I love you too."

But as we stepped out of the car and headed toward the front door, the weight settled in my chest. We had each other. That part was solid. That part was good. But we were about to walk into this house and ruin a family's life forever.

We made our way up to the front door. Brady knocked. He stood beside me in his deputy's uniform, broad-shouldered and calm, the kind of presence that instantly signaled authority. I couldn't help but think how alarming the sight of us would be to a family whose daughter had been missing for three weeks.

The door opened.

A woman in her late fifties stood there, pale skin stretched tight, eyes already heavy with grief, as if she'd been living in anticipation of this moment. "Yes?" she asked. "Can I help you?"

"My name is Deputy Tanner," Brady said gently. "This is my associate, Val Costa. We're with the Red Rose County Sheriff's Department. We're here to talk to you about Teresa."

The woman swayed slightly, as if the words had knocked the breath out of her. Tears welled immediately. "Oh," she whispered. "Oh, no…"

"May we come in?" he asked.

She nodded and called out. "George."

George was her husband of more than thirty years, and Teresa's father.

Footsteps sounded on the stairs. A man appeared moments later, his face creased with confusion that quickly turned to fear as he took in Brady's uniform. "What's going on?"

She turned to him, her hands trembling. "The police are here."

We sat in the living room, the air thick and still. She introduced us to her husband and then, his face collapsed.

Brady spoke quietly. "We found Teresa. I'm so sorry, but she's gone."

The words landed with devastating finality.

They clung to each other as Mrs. McDonald cried, her sobs deep and unrestrained. We gave them a moment. When they finally looked back at us, their faces were hollow. "How… how did this happen?" Mr. McDonald asked. "Where did you find her?"

"In Red Rose County," Brady said. "Did your daughter know anyone in Red Rose County?"

"Not that I know of," Mrs. McDonald said. "You'd have to ask her friends, I suppose. But as far as I know, she'd never been there."

"May we ask you a few more questions about your daughter?" I asked.

They nodded, brows furrowed.

"We spoke with the CoCo County Sheriff's Department about Teresa's disappearance," I said. "From what we can tell, she went to work at the elementary school, then returned home. Her car was found parked in the driveway of her home in Concord. After that, she was never seen again."

"That's right," Mrs. McDonald said softly. "She was supposed to come over that evening. We were going shopping together, it was her sister's birthday. We wanted to pick out a gift." Her voice trembled. "I kept calling her. She didn't answer. So we went to the house. Her car was in the driveway, but no one answered the door." She swallowed hard. "I got nervous. A mother's intuition, I guess."

I understood that instinct all too well. My son was across the country at MIT about to finish his sophomore year. I was proud of him, but I hated he was so far away. Too far away for me to protect him.

"And according to the missing-person report," Brady said, "coworkers and friends didn't indicate she had any enemies. Nothing unusual happened leading up to her disappearance."

"No," Mr. McDonald said, shaking his head. "Nothing. Terry was... she was a good person. She didn't have a mean bone in her body."

I watched their faces closely. Grief. Shock. Confusion. And underneath it all was a terrible, aching absence.

George continued. "She taught third grade. She wasn't dating anyone. The kids loved her." His voice cracked. "We loved her. I can't believe she's gone."

I let the silence settle before continuing. "And where did Terry go to school? Was it here in Concord?"

"Yes," Mrs. McDonald said. "She was born here. Raised here."

"And college?"

"UC Santa Cruz," George said. "She majored in psychology."

"And her teaching credential?"

"Sacramento State University."

I nodded, jotting it down. "Did she have any ex-boyfriends?" I asked.

Mrs. McDonald seemed to calm slightly, focusing now. "She's had boyfriends, sure. A few lasted a year or two. But nothing in the last few years."

"How were those relationships?" I asked. "Did they end amicably?"

"Yes," she said. "One was from high school. Another right after college. But that was years ago. I think she liked being single. She liked to travel and just have fun."

"Where did she like to travel to?"

"All over," Mrs. McDonald said. "As a teacher, she had summers off. Sometimes we traveled with her. We've been on cruises together. We went to the Mediterranean last year." She smiled faintly, then bowed her head. "That was... that was so much fun."

"Did Terry ever meet anyone on her trips?" I asked. "Someone she stayed in touch with?"

"She met people," George said. "She was very outgoing. But no one we ever met."

"And she had a lot of friends?" I asked.

"Oh yes," Mrs. McDonald said. "We knew most of them. Everyone would come over to the house for parties, even as adults."

Her voice wavered. "Becky... her sister is going to be devastated."

Rebecca McDonald, I thought. Younger by three years.

"Would you like us to help notify her?" I asked.

"No—no," Mrs. McDonald said. "We'll call her. Oh gosh. We should call her right now." She looked at me. "Would you want to talk to her too? I know the other detectives did."

"Yes," I said. "That would be very helpful."

She stood abruptly and disappeared down the hallway. When she returned, she held her phone tightly in her hand. She sat back down, glanced at her husband, and nodded.

I looked away as she made the call, but I could hear as she cried into the phone telling her daughter that Terry had been found.

After everyone had composed themselves as best they could, I spoke again. "Do you have photographs from Terry's trips? Anything we could look at?"

"Oh yes," Mrs. McDonald said. "Terry and I loved to scrapbook. After every trip, we made one together. It was kind of our thing." She gave a small, apologetic smile. "I know scrapbooking isn't really cool anymore, but we loved it." She returned a few minutes later with a stack of photo albums.

She sat beside me on the sofa, flipping through pages, pointing out places they'd been. Smiling faces. Sunlit landmarks. A family frozen in happier moments. I wasn't looking at the smiles. I was looking at the background. Faces. Strangers. Anyone who might not belong.

But there was nothing. I pulled out my phone and made notes of locations, dates, timelines. Maybe something would overlap with Lena's circle. If we could find the connection, we could find the killer.

Thirty minutes later, Terry's sister arrived. We asked her the same questions, and her answers confirmed everything her parents had told us. Before we left, I handed them my card and gave them space to grieve together. As we were walking out, her sister stopped us.

"You're going to find who did this, right?"

"Yes," I said. "We are."

With tears in her eyes, she said, "Why would they do this to her?"

"I don't know, but if you think of anything or of anyone who acted strange, showed too much interest, or wouldn't leave her alone, please call us."

"I can't think of anyone, but maybe talk to her coworkers."

"We will."

As we turned to leave, she added, "What if it wasn't someone she knew? What if it was a stranger?"

"We'll find them."

Outside the house, I took a deep breath. We had more information, but not enough.

Next stop was the school. Coworkers. Students. Anyone who might have noticed something off in the days and weeks leading up to her abduction. Everything inside me was telling me we didn't have much time. And wherever Lena was, she was running out of it.

21

MARTINA

I SAT at the conference table with four members of our team, the hum of computers and shuffling papers filled the room. "I just got off the phone with Val," I said. "She wants background checks on everyone in Lena's circle including school records, employment, friendships, travel. Everything."

A few eyebrows went up. "We've already pulled most of that," Vincent said. "But travel over the last ten years?"

"It seems like a lot," I said. "But Val thinks it could be useful."

We were trying to find any connection between Lena and Teresa McDonald. If there was one, it wasn't obvious. So we were going to widen the net, cast it further than we had so far, and see what surfaced. Val and I were in agreement on one thing. We didn't think we had much time left to find Lena.

"All right," I continued. "Ethan is coming in today for a second interview. Jason's in class, so we'll have to catch him on campus later."

"What about Joe Sapphire?" Stavros asked.

"Val and Brady plan to interview him later today." I looked around the table. "Everyone's got their assignments. Travel histories for friends and family along with dates, locations, hotels, anything you can find. Let's move."

I dismissed the team and had just reached for my coffee when my phone rang. Surprised by the caller, I answered. "Hi, Natalie."

"Hi, Martina."

"What's going on?"

"Well," she said, "I'm writing an article about Lena Sapphire's disappearance. I know your firm is handling the investigation, and that you were up in Red Rose County. Is there any way I can get a full interview for the piece? Are there any leads?"

I exhaled slowly.

"And I also read there was a body found in Red Rose County," she added. "Was it Lena?"

"I'm sorry, Natalie," I said carefully. "I can't tell you much right now. I can confirm that a body was found in Red Rose County, but it was not Lena. We're still actively searching for her and working closely with the sheriff's department."

"So you're working together?"

"Yes."

"How are things looking?" she asked. "Off the record."

"Strange," I said. "Very strange. But we'll figure it out. We have a lot of people working on this. That's about all I can tell you right now."

"Okay," she said. "I'll let you go. We'll have to catch up soon. Maybe dinner, when you have time."

"Will do," I said. "Talk to you later, Natalie." I ended the call and stared at my phone for a moment.

Natalie was a crime reporter and good at her job. I was honestly surprised she hadn't called sooner. Maybe the press conference had satisfied her for now. Or maybe she was just waiting for the right moment. Either way, she knew better than to expect too many off-the-record details.

I walked back to my office and the moment I sat down, my phone lit up. I picked up the receiver. "Hello?"

"Ethan Buck is here," our receptionist said.

"I'll meet him in Conference Room One. Thank you." I ended the call and stopped for coffee before the meeting.

Selena had already beaten me to the machine. "How are you doing?" she asked.

"I'm fine. Not thrilled about last night, but I feel safe here. I think we're better off staying put."

"But what if we have to go back?" Selena said. "Maybe we bring some muscle. I mean—more than just us. Our own detail."

"That's a good idea. Ethan's here, do you want to sit in?"

Her eyes lit up. "Absolutely."

I figured.

Coffee in hand, Selena and I headed toward Conference Room One. I had questions for Ethan Buck. And he'd better have answers.

When we entered, he was already seated, leaned back in his chair, arms loose at his sides, smugness written all over him. Beside him sat a man in a suit. Family resemblance, maybe. More likely a lawyer. "Ethan," I said. "Thank you for coming down."

"This is Selena," I added. "My associate."

He nodded. "Of course. Anything to help find Lena."

"And who's accompanying you?" I asked.

"Oh," he said casually, "this is my lawyer. He's just here to advise me, in the event I need advising."

The tone rubbed me the wrong way. He slid a business card across the table. "James Hiddleston."

I glanced at it and nodded. "Nice to meet you."

The receptionist had already set water and coffee on the table. I took a seat.

"So," I said, "there have been some developments in Lena's disappearance. We went out to Red Rose County and spoke to the staff at your home." I paused. "A few things stood out. One was that your staff was instructed to turn off the security cameras before you and your friends arrived. And the second was that the fairy lights were installed ahead of time for the prank."

Ethan seemed unfazed. "That's correct."

"Why didn't you want the security cameras on?"

"Because it was just me and my friends," he said. "We were there to relax and have fun, not have cameras watching us."

"But the cameras are on the outside of the house," Selena said.

Ethan licked his lips. "We like to party outside. It's... nature. Feels primal, you know?"

Selena didn't respond.

"And the fairy lights?" I asked.

"The prank was planned ahead of time," Ethan said. "Jason and I have had a rivalry forever. He was getting serious with Lena." He smirked. "I told him, why don't you propose to her? I dare you."

"And he took the bet?" I asked.

"We devised the plan together," Ethan said. "It was going to be epic."

"And you didn't want to capture it on film?" Selena said. "I would think you would, if it was going to be so *epic*."

Ethan shrugged. "You know, I didn't really think about it. Probably should have. In hindsight, we would've seen who took her."

I leaned forward slightly. "Do you think somebody took her, Ethan?"

"I mean, where else could she have gone? I suppose she could've gone down the trail, reached the trailhead, met someone, and left. Do you think she did that?"

"I don't think that's what happened," I said. "But it's possible. We don't know yet."

Ethan nodded, but something about him put me on edge. I assessed every movement, every shift in posture, and every glance toward his lawyer.

Selena jumped in before I could redirect. "You know, Ethan, it seems like you set this whole thing up."

Ethan's brows lifted.

"You arranged for Lena to be outside in the dark. You arranged for the security cameras to be turned off. You planned the fairy lights. I think you orchestrated her kidnapping and I want to know why."

Ethan chuckled. "Interesting theory, little girl."

I turned sharply toward Selena. Her eyes widened, cheeks flushing red. Calling her little girl was not a good move, it was one of her pet peeves. It stemmed from the fact she was petite and, truthfully, looked more like a teen than early twenties. She'd been mistaken for younger, for as long as I had known her.

"I don't think it's just a theory, little boy," Selena shot back. "I think you're working with someone. What I don't understand is why. Why set Lena up to be abducted?"

She stood now, arms crossed. "Were you jealous that Jason had a girlfriend? Are you in love with Jason?" She tilted her head. "Oh, maybe that's it. You were jealous of Lena, so you took her out of the picture."

Ethan scoffed. "You're crazy."

"Then who are you helping? Or did you have someone take her so you could have her all for yourself?" Selena didn't let up.

"We know about your fascination with serial killers. True crime. From all accounts you're a *creep*."

Out of my seat, I stepped toward her, placing my hand on her arm. "Selena, let's take a breath."

She shot me a look that said she absolutely did not want to calm down, but after a beat, she sat back down. I refocused on Ethan. His lawyer cleared his throat. "If you brought my client in here just to harass him, we're done."

Ethan raised a hand. "No, no, it's fine." He smiled thinly. "I'm not threatened by this little girl. I'll set the record straight."

Selena glared at Ethan.

"I am not in love with Jason," Ethan said with amusement in his eyes. "I was not jealous of Lena. And I had nothing to do with her disappearance."

I leaned forward. "How about Teresa McDonald? Have you ever heard of her?"

The smile slid off his face. "Who?" he said, rather unconvincingly.

"Teresa McDonald," I repeated. "Did you know her?"

He looked away. "Never heard of her."

"She was murdered and found in Red Rose County, about a mile from your family's home."

"I don't know anything about that," he said quickly, pushing back his chair. "I'm very busy. I need to get going. If you have any more questions, you can direct them to my lawyer."

Before he could stand fully, I said, "If we find any connection between you and Teresa McDonald, you're going to need a whole team of lawyers." I held his gaze. "I will find out if you do. Mark my words."

Ethan swallowed. I'd touched on something. The question was, what? Did he know Teresa McDonald? Had he killed her?

22

MARTINA

Selena and I sat quietly while Ethan and his lawyer briskly exited the conference room. The door clicked shut behind them, leaving the air feeling suddenly heavier, like something unfinished had been left behind.

"What do you think of that?" Selena asked.

"I think he knew Teresa McDonald. Did you see the look on his face when I asked him about her? He said he didn't, but—"

Selena looked at me, her eyes narrowing. "Wait. Wasn't the statement from Jenna and Tiffany that he'd been talking about a girl who had gone missing? That he was using it to scare everyone out at the house, talking about what they were probably doing to her?"

"That's right."

"Do you think he was talking about Teresa McDonald?"

"That's a very good question," I said. "She's not the only missing person, but it would help to know."

"All right. I'll call them right now."

Selena picked up the folder that had been sitting in front of me, flipped it open, and immediately started dialing on her cell phone. She was never one to wait around, or delegate, so I let her work while my thoughts drifted back to Ethan. Something else clicked into place. I still hadn't followed up with Jason. Did he know the cameras were off? He'd been in class earlier, but he might be out by now.

I stepped outside the conference room and called Jason, and he answered right away. That, at least, felt like a good sign. "Jason, this is Martina Monroe."

"Hi, Martina. Have you found Lena yet?"

"No," I said. "But I have a few follow-up questions. We went out to the house in Red Rose County and spoke with the staff. Were you aware that the surveillance cameras were off?"

There was a pause. "I didn't even know there were security cameras."

"There were. Ethan requested they be turned off."

"Why would he do that?"

"I don't know. He also had the fairy lights put up before you arrived. Did you know about the prank ahead of time?"

"Yeah, we talked about it. I knew he had the staff put them up."

"Okay. And just one more question for you, Jason. Do you recall the conversation you were having before Lena went outside, the one about the missing person?"

"Oh. Yeah. We were talking about that serial killer in the county."

"But before that, Jenna and Tiffany told us you were talking about a missing girl. Do you recall who it was?"

He hesitated, just barely. "Vaguely. I mean... I don't know. Maybe Ethan was talking about it. I guess it was on the news."

"Do you recall hearing the name Teresa McDonald?"

"Sounds familiar, but I don't remember."

I didn't have him face-to-face to read his body language, but my gut told me he was being truthful. "Okay. Thank you, Jason. We'll be in touch."

"Are there any new leads on Lena?"

"No. I'm afraid not. But I'll keep you posted."

"You'll call me if you do?"

"Of course."

I ended the call and turned my attention back to the conference room, where Selena had the phone pressed to her ear, pacing slowly as she listened.

Jason couldn't remember the name of the missing person. Maybe the girls could. Everything so far pointed to Ethan acting strange and suspicious, but strange behavior wasn't evidence. It didn't make him a kidnapper or a conspirator.

I stepped inside just as Selena ended the call, a slow smile spreading across her face. "Guess who Ethan was going *on and on* about the night Lena disappeared?"

I stopped short. "Teresa McDonald."

"Exactly. He just lied to us. Makes you wonder what else he's lying about, doesn't it?"

"It sure does."

Selena's voice dropped, quieter now, more serious. "Do you think Val will be able to do a profile on Ethan? See if he could've done this, or planned it? Or maybe he's a killer too. Maybe he killed Teresa McDonald, and that's why he was talking about what was probably happening to her."

I watched her as she spoke, the words tumbling out faster now. "He kept saying she was probably being held captive, that they were torturing her. Who says that unless it's something you know is happening, or something you're doing yourself? He's got money. People with a lot of money think they can get away with pretty much anything they want." She stopped abruptly, catching herself, then added, more grounded, "What if this is all just a game to Ethan?"

"We need to dig deeper on him."

Selena agreed.

"I want to know everything about him. Who he talks to, who he's friends with, his past. I think we need surveillance. I'll put a team on him."

"Or I could tail him," she offered.

"No," I said. "We'll get a team. We need you doing interviews, liaising with Val and Brady. Plus, we have a whole slew of information to check. Can you work with Vincent instead?"

She looked deflated for a moment, but Selena doing whatever she wanted, including putting herself in danger, wasn't happening on my watch. We'd been followed the night before. I wasn't about to make her a target. I'd already had one daughter kidnapped. I wasn't risking a second.

"I'd also like you to stay with me and your dad while this is going on," I said. "At least for now."

With defiance, she countered. "I'm more than capable of taking care of myself, Martina."

"I know you are. But we were both followed last night. Why don't you stay with your dad and me tonight?"

She let out a long breath and rolled her eyes. "Okay. I can stay with you guys. But only if Dad is cooking."

"He will." All I had to do was let him know his daughter was coming over, and he'd start preparing his famous lasagna.

"Fine. I'm going to try to catch up with Vincent. See if he's learned anything new." She smiled, fake, but affectionate, and headed out.

She acted like she couldn't stand me mothering her, but I knew she appreciated it. Maybe not today. Maybe not even tomorrow. But one day. She was my bonus daughter, and I loved her like my own. I couldn't bear the thought of anything happening to her. Not to mention what it would do to my husband, Charlie. Selena had grown more cautious over the years. Just not enough for my liking. Before I even made it to my office, my phone rang. *Val.* "How did your interview with Ethan go?"

I explained what happened and how we'd caught him in a lie.

"Well, isn't that something," Val said. "Not surprising, though. He's connected to this somehow. We'll find the link. I'm about to head over to Lena's parents' house. Do you want to meet me, or are you okay with me going in alone?"

"You go ahead," I said. "I want to see what he says when I'm not there."

"Okay. Maybe we catch up later tonight?"

"Sounds good. Thanks, Val."

Something Selena had said stuck with me. Was this a game to Ethan? Lena's father had mentioned early on that the group was into games and pranks. And with Ethan's wealth, practically unlimited, he could've orchestrated all of this. Every detail. Every misdirection. Did that mean Lena wasn't in danger? Or did it mean we had a serial predator on our hands? One with money, a twisted imagination, and an expensive lawyer to keep the law at bay? All my instincts told me Ethan was at the heart of this. The question wasn't if he was involved. It was how.

23

LENA

THE LIGHT from the window illuminated our space. On the mattress, I turned to Derek, trying to figure him out. He'd been a gentleman when he slept next to me on the mattress. I didn't really expect anything else. But, honestly, I didn't know anything about him. We hadn't talked much after dinner. He just sat there, staring out like he was somewhere else entirely. Or maybe he was coming up with a plan.

"Are you okay?" I asked.

Derek turned to me. "I think I figured out a way to get out of here."

My heart skipped a beat. "You did?"

"I've been thinking about how the bolts are attached to the wall." He glanced toward the wall, where the chains attached to the plate on the concrete. "I think I can undo the bolt to get free. It's not that solid of a job. If I can loosen it, I can be free to attack them when they come in. Take them by surprise. That is, if there's only one of them. I can overpower one. And when I do, we *run*."

It sounded good, but I was skeptical. "Do you really think it'll be that easy?"

"It has to be." He studied the bolts again. "I know how to build things. I know how to take things apart. I don't think it'll be that difficult. It'll just take time."

I leaned closer, afraid to let myself believe him. "You're sure?"

"I've thought about it all day, I'll loosen the screws. And when he comes in with a meal, I'll break free and attack."

A bloom of hope filled my chest. "What do you need me to do?"

"When he comes in, you distract them. But first, I need to free my wrist and then I can loosen the ankle chains."

I hesitated, glancing up at the camera. "What if they see?"

"We'll talk facing each other to hide my hands." He gave me a faint smile. "They won't know."

We'd have to work together. Trust each other. "Okay," I said. "Let's do it."

"Get closer. Face me. Turn slightly so your back's to the camera."

I did as he said, but I didn't understand how he planned to loosen a screw with nothing but his fingers, until he slipped his hand into his pocket.

He pulled something out slowly. A coin.

"Sometimes a quarter isn't just a quarter," he said, smiling.

"That'll really work?"

"It will."

"So, where are you from, Lena?" he asked as he worked.

"Palo Alto."

"How'd you end up here?"

"I was in the mountains with my boyfriend and some friends." My voice shook. "I went outside alone. Trying to prove I wasn't scared. I was on the edge of the forest where a serial killer had been."

He shook his head. "How old are you?"

"Twenty-three. You?"

"Same." He smirked. "But I'm certainly not from Palo Alto."

"Where are you from?"

"Modesto. I'm a handyman by trade, just like my old man. And it seems that my job training is coming in pretty handy."

A handyman? It didn't fit with what I'd assumed. I always thought they took me for a reason like my family's money, or connections, but it didn't sound like Derek had that. "Why do you think they took you?"

"No idea."

After a few minutes, I said, "Any luck?"

"Not yet," he said, still working. "But I'll get there."

We kept talking. About our lives. Our pasts. We couldn't have been more different. Private schools versus public. Country music versus Pop. Racing cars versus charity galas. The more I learned, the less sense it made. A cold feeling settled in my gut. A sense of something worse coming.

Footsteps outside the door. I froze. The lock turned slowly, deliberately, like they wanted us to hear it. My breath caught as the door creaked inward. They didn't speak.

One of them crossed the room in three long strides and grabbed my arm, fingers digging in hard. I stumbled back.

The other one went straight for Derek.

"No," I said, my voice thin. "Please—"

The man in front of Derek paused. Just for a second. "You're coming with us. Fight, you die. Understand?"

Derek nodded.

The chain rattled as it was unhooked. The man twisted Derek's arm behind his back, forcing him forward while the other had a gun aimed right at him.

Derek met my eyes as they dragged him away. There was no panic there, only a look of failure and loss of hope. The door slammed shut behind them.

As I stood alone, my arm aching where he'd grabbed me,

staring at the empty space where Derek had been. They had interrupted the plan. Did they know? What would they do to Derek? Was I next? I dropped my head and realized, they hadn't only taken Derek, they'd stolen my hope.

24

VAL

STANDING at the front door of the Sapphire home, I wondered what we would discover inside, about them and what theories they might have regarding why their daughter had been taken. The most obvious motive was money. Except, as far as we knew, there hadn't been any ransom demand. And if Lena's disappearance was related to Teresa McDonald, it didn't fit. Teresa's family wasn't poor, but they certainly didn't have the kind of money that would justify a kidnapping for ransom. Not that we could tell, anyway. We were still waiting on background reports. Maybe they lived simply and saved every penny. But even if that were true, how would anyone know?

Before I could contemplate it further, the door opened. To my surprise, it was Mr. Sapphire himself.

"Good afternoon, Mr. Sapphire," I said. "We spoke on the phone. I'm Val Costa, and this is Deputy Brady Tanner."

"Yes, of course," he said, stepping aside. "Please, come in."

We followed him into the stately home, its grandeur immediately apparent. Everything gleamed with polished floors, soaring ceilings, and carefully curated elegance. Like an art museum. Not my taste. I preferred contemporary and modern. Not ultra-modern, but comfortable and clean.

Mr. Sapphire moved with the practiced politeness of someone used to hosting. "Can I get either of you something to drink? And please, call me Joe."

From everything I could see, he was grieving. A man clinging to the hope that we would find his daughter. But grief didn't mean honesty. It didn't mean he'd told us everything. "I'd love a coffee, if you don't mind," Brady said.

"Absolutely." Mr. Sapphire turned toward the hallway. "Dolores?"

A woman in a neat uniform appeared almost instantly.

"Dolores, please get us coffee. How do you take it, Deputy?"

"Just black is fine."

"Same for me," I added.

"And I'll have one as well. Thank you, Dolores."

"Yes, sir," she said, already turning away.

"We'll set ourselves up in the blue room," Mr. Sapphire said.

"Of course, sir."

She hurried off, and Mr. Sapphire led us down the hall and into the aptly named Blue Room. Robin's egg-colored walls framed a deep blue sofa accented with gold trim. Regal. The room smelled faintly of lemon polish and something floral, understated but expensive.

"I was surprised to hear that we have an FBI agent working the case," Mr. Sapphire said as we settled in.

"Former FBI," I corrected.

"What did you do while you were at the FBI?" he asked.

"I was a profiler."

"Excellent," he said, nodding. His lips pressed into a tight smile, as if the word profiler wasn't entirely good news to him.

I explained that I'd worked with the Red Rose County Sheriff's Department before, helping solve missing persons cases and murders in the area. He nodded again, said he understood, but there was something else behind his eyes. Worry. Maybe fear.

"Well," he said, folding his hands together, "I appreciate any help we can get finding Lena. I'm assuming Martina has filled you in on the case."

"Of course," I said. "But sometimes when I re-interview family and friends, people remember things they forgot the first time around." I decided to come right out with it. "Before I ask additional questions," I said, "is there anything else you can tell us about your daughter's disappearance that might help us find her?"

Joe Sapphire stared at his hands. "I can't think of anything."

"You weren't contacted by anyone after she was taken?

He swallowed and shook his head.

If I didn't know any better, I'd say he was lying. "Because if you had," I continued, keeping my voice even, "it could help us get her back, even if you didn't comply with whatever demands were made."

He said nothing.

"I've worked kidnappings before," I went on. "It's not a secret that you have considerable means. That alone could make your daughter a target. She's been missing five days now. That's a long time for a kidnapping involving ransom."

Silence stretched between us.

I leaned back slightly, changing tactics. "I've been thinking about this as if it were my own child. I have a son a little younger than Lena. Harrison is currently studying at MIT. He's far from home, so I tried to put myself in your shoes. In your wife's shoes." I paused, watching him carefully. "And I thought, if it's not money the kidnappers want, what else could they want? Something that would take longer to arrange. Another kind of demand. Something unusual. Can you think of anything someone might want from your family in exchange for Lena's safety?"

He held my gaze. "There's nothing I have that they'd want."

The way he said it stuck with me. Nothing *he* had.

"What about someone from your company?" I asked. "Or perhaps your wife?"

His shoulders sagged. "My wife is very ill. She doesn't have much time left." His voice cracked. "She wants to see her daughter again before she goes. And I'm sure Lena would want to see her mother too."

The room felt heavier after that. "And you're sure," I said quietly, "that no one has contacted you about Lena's disappearance?"

"I'm sure."

Dolores returned then, carrying a tray of pristine white china. The cups were delicate, with thin gold rims. She set them down carefully and left without a word. "Pretty," I said absently as I picked up my cup and took a sip. Good coffee. Better than what they had at the station, that was for sure. I set the cup down and met Joe's eyes. "There's something else I need to tell you. It may be difficult to hear."

He tensed instantly.

"There's been a murder," I said. "A body was found in Red Rose County. The victim was from the Bay Area. There are some details at the scene that make us believe it may be connected to Lena's disappearance."

He gasped, one hand gripping the arm of the chair.

Did he just now realize Lena could be in danger? "That's why it's so important we hear everything you know about what happened to her."

"I don't know what happened to her."

"Are you friendly with the Buck family?" I asked. "Ethan Buck's parents?"

"We see them sometimes at the club. We're not close friends. More like acquaintances. Our families have been in the area a long time. My wife's family, actually."

I nodded. "We learned that before going up to the cabin, Ethan Buck requested that the security cameras around the house be turned off."

"Ethan did?" His expression shifted, this time, genuine surprise. "I didn't know that."

"Yes," I said. "We spoke to Ethan. He confirmed it. He said he sometimes does that when he goes up there with friends."

Joe's expression went flat.

"Do you know Ethan well?"

"Since they were kids."

"Do you like him?"

He shrugged. "I don't know him very well. He and Lena weren't close. I got the impression she wasn't fond of him. But he was sort of part of the group, you know."

"And you don't have regular contact with his parents? At parties or events?"

"My wife might be able to answer some of these questions," he said. "She knows them better than I do."

"I'd like to talk to her," I said, as I stood and set my coffee cup down, a little disappointed I didn't get to finish it. It was quite good. But speaking with the wife was more important.

Joe stood up, and Brady and I followed him upstairs.

When we stepped into her room, I was surprised by what he meant by very ill. He hadn't exaggerated when he said she didn't have much time. The room was dim, the curtains partially drawn, the air tinged with antiseptic and something medicinal. Machines hummed and beeped beside the bed.

I approached her bedside, Brady beside me.

"Darling," Joe said gently, "we have visitors. This is former FBI agent Val Costa, a profiler, and Deputy Brady Tanner from the Red Rose County Sheriff's Department. They have some questions."

Despite her condition, her eyes followed us, sharp and assessing. Her body was failing her, but her mind appeared very much intact. "Thank you for coming," she said. "I presume you're helping find Lena."

"Yes, ma'am," I said. "That's what we're trying to do."

"Good."

Joe said, "They have some questions about the Bucks."

Mrs. Sapphire's eyebrows lifted ever so slightly.

"Yes," I said. "How well do you know the Bucks? Are you close friends? Have you known them long?"

"I don't think they had anything to do with this," she said abruptly.

"How long have you known the Bucks?" I asked again.

"Most of my life. They grew up in town, like I did. Our families knew each other."

"How often do you see them?"

"Not much since the cancer spread and I spend most of my days here."

"And before?"

She exhaled slowly. "Maybe every few weeks or so. There's always a charity event or a dinner party."

"And how well do you know their son, Ethan?"

"He's a good kid," she said. "Works for his father."

"Good kid" was not how anyone had described Ethan Buck until this moment. "He's someone you would trust with your daughter's life?"

Her head snapped toward Joe, then back to me. "What do you mean by that? Did Ethan do something to her?"

"We're not sure, but we do know that he turned off the security cameras at the Red Rose County house before they arrived. That made it quite easy for someone to abduct Lena without leaving evidence. If the cameras had been on, it would have been captured."

"Did he say why?"

"He said he likes privacy," I said. "It wasn't the first time."

She nodded slowly. "Kids," she said, attempting a light tone, but it didn't quite land. Something was being concealed. Whether by medication or intention, I couldn't yet tell.

"Do you have any reason to believe Ethan Buck would want to hurt your daughter? Perhaps as part of a game or a prank? I've heard the group is into that kind of thing."

"That's absurd," Mrs. Sapphire said sharply. "Ethan wouldn't do that. She's been gone five days. Their pranks don't last that long."

"So you do know about their pranks?"

"Yes," she said, irritation creeping into her voice.

I let the silence settle before continuing. "Has anybody contacted you about Lena's abduction?"

"What do you mean?"

"Making demands for a ransom. Say, pay us five million and we'll return your daughter."

She shook her head.

"What about something else other than money?" I pressed. "Something that might take longer to arrange. Intellectual property. Anything someone might want badly enough to take Lena."

"No."

"Is there anyone who'd want to hurt you or your family? A business deal gone wrong? They could have taken Lena as a way of hurting you."

"No, of course not. But I wish you'd find her soon. It's been five days." Her eyes flicked to Joe. "I'm not so sure this contract with Martina Monroe is working out," she said, venom suddenly sharp in her voice. The polite woman of the house was *gone*.

"I'm sure Martina is doing her best," Joe said.

"Well, perhaps her best isn't good enough," Mrs. Sapphire snapped. "It's been five days. You've got the FBI, the sheriff's department, and this Martina Monroe all looking for her, and nobody has found her. You *need* to find my daughter."

My thoughts were swirling now. Something was off here, I just didn't know what yet. "Is there anything else you can think of that might help us find Lena before it's too late?"

"Too late?" Mrs. Sapphire echoed.

"Yes," I said. "We recently found a body in Red Rose County. We believe it may be connected to Lena's case."

Her eyes narrowed. "Well then why aren't you back in Red Rose County investigating it?"

"Because the victim was from the Bay Area and we needed to notify the family."

She nodded once, absorbing that.

I exchanged a look with Brady. He gave a small nod and stepped in. "Did you know anyone named Teresa, or Terry, McDonald?"

"Never heard of her," Mrs. Sapphire said immediately.

Joe shook his head as well.

There was deep sadness etched into his face, the kind that settled into the lines around a person's eyes. But sadness didn't mean he was telling us everything. "Well," I said, "thank you very much, Mrs. Sapphire. This has been helpful."

She shut her eyes and turned her head away, the conversation clearly over.

Outside, Joe walked us to the porch. I stopped and turned to face him. "Whatever you're not telling us, we're going to find out," I said. "*I'm* going to find out. Do you understand what I'm saying, Mr. Sapphire?"

His blue eyes fixed upon mine. "Just find Lena."

The look he gave me wasn't contempt. It wasn't anger. It was something close to pleading. It was *fear*. Was he afraid for Lena or of something or someone else?

He wanted to find his daughter. Of that, I was certain. But something was stopping him from telling the truth, something that might help us find her before it really was too late.

"You know," I said softly, "you can tell me anything. I can keep things between us."

He didn't answer. "Please," he said instead. "Please just *find* Lena."

I took that as my answer.

Back inside Brady's SUV, he shook his head. "Why wouldn't they tell us everything they know? They're obviously holding something back."

"That's my thought too," I said. "I'm going to make a call to some old friends at the FBI to see if they've heard anything about these families. Something that wouldn't show up in a standard background check."

Brady glanced at me. "You think they took Lena because of her family?"

"Maybe," I said. "They could be involved in some kind of illegal activity. Maybe they're not quite as shiny as the silver spoons they eat from."

25

LENA

I'D HARDLY SLEPT. Every time I closed my eyes, my thoughts spiraled back to Derek. What they'd done with him, and where they'd taken him. Had they taken other people too? Were there more rooms like this one? Would they bring him back, or was I going to be all alone forever?

Was this it? Was I just going to stay here, eating sandwiches and chips, until one day I didn't? All this time to think had led me to two conclusions.

First was that I might die here. I tried to make peace with that. If this was the end, I didn't regret my life. I had tried to be a good person. I loved hard and I lived hard. I hoped my family, Jason and my friends, would grieve and then move on. I hoped they would be there for each other. They could cry for a little while. A few weeks, maybe. Mom was already dying, for all I knew she'd already passed. That was the only part that broke me. She'd die never knowing what happened to me.

Dad would survive. He was a good dad. He worked a lot, but I never doubted that he loved me. Not like some of my friends whose parents didn't pay any attention to them as long as they upheld the family image. In our circle, it wasn't unusual to be left alone at ten years old with the housekeepers or nannies while parents traveled or worked nonstop. But when my parents were home, they showered us with love. Especially Dad.

And then there was Mark and Peter, my goofy brothers. Growing up with them had been fun and adventurous. They were protective and always watching out for me. I'd had a good life. I was only twenty-three years old, but I was grateful for all twenty-three of them. If this was how it ended, then this was how it was meant to be.

But then there was the second thought. If this wasn't the end, and it was just an obstacle I had to overcome, I had to think of a way to get out of this.

I thought back to Derek. About the plan we'd barely had time to form. About the quarter he'd hidden under the mattress when the doorknob turned. That second thought had me working on loosening the screw to my chain since he'd been taken. Slowly. Carefully. Leaning my body against the wall to hide what I was doing. My fingers were sore, my wrists aching, but I couldn't stop. If I did get free, what then? I'd fight them, but they were bigger. Stronger. Could I outsmart them? Blind them somehow?

The idea that came to me felt ridiculous. I could crumble bread from my sandwich, crush it into something like sand to throw into their eyes. Maybe it would be enough to distract them long enough for me to run. It wasn't a foolproof plan, but I couldn't just sit there anymore, waiting to die. I had to do something. I pressed harder against the screw. Nothing. Then...

It shifted. Barely. But it moved. My breath caught. My heartbeat kicked up a dozen levels. I twisted again. It turned. *Thank goodness!* It was working. Derek had been right.

My hands shook as I worked faster, panic and hope tangling together. I needed a plan. I needed a way to fight. A way out.

Footsteps.

My next meal. I shoved the screw back into place, my pulse racing, forcing myself to look small, and helpless.

And as if the universe had been listening, the door burst open. Derek stumbled inside. He had a black eye and fresh cuts on his face. "We have to go," he said, running toward me. I didn't hesitate. I yanked on my chain. He stared at it, stunned.

"You did that?"

I nodded.

"We have to go. Now." He grabbed my hand, and we ran down a dark hallway with my bare feet slapping against cold concrete. A latch flew open and suddenly he was shoving me forward. "Run!"

I ran. Branches scraped my arms, and pine needles stabbed my feet. The forest swallowed us as we fled. "Hurry! They're coming. Keep going!" Derek yelled.

And I did. Because, I was, in fact, running for my life.

26

MARTINA

I WALKED into the conference room at 7:30 a.m. sharp. The lights overhead cast a pale glow over several tired faces. The air smelled like burnt coffee and fast food. Selena, Val, and Brady were already seated, jackets draped over chair backs, laptops open. Vincent and Jerilyn, a member of the research team, sat across from them, shoulders slumped with fatigue. From what I understood, the research team had worked through the night in rotating shifts, digging into everyone connected to Lena's disappearance including Ethan, Jason, Tiffany, Jenna, the Sapphires, the Bucks, and Teresa McDonald.

"Morning," I said, closing the door behind me. The latch clicked louder than it should have. I took my seat and wrapped both hands around my coffee, letting the heat seep into my palms. A soft mumbling of "good mornings" were returned. I looked at Vincent, who had called the early morning meeting.

"So, what's up?"

"Well," he said, rubbing a hand over his jaw before offering a tired smile. "The team compiled everything that might be relevant on the subjects. Financial records, phone records, credit card activity. We looked for signs Lena bought a burner phone.

Spoiler—she didn't. At least not that we could find." He scrolled through his tablet. "There's been zero movement on her social media. We followed up with friends to see if she had any hidden or secondary social media accounts. She doesn't. There have been no sightings of Lena and no credible tips from the hotline. And no new activity on her phone."

That wasn't exactly surprising. It just confirmed what we already knew. He must have something else to have called the meeting.

He looked up. "So, we started looking into Teresa and the others' social media and backgrounds. None of them have a criminal history, and we didn't find anything suspicious in their social media except for one thing."

After giving him a look that conveyed very little patience, he said, "Ethan Buck *knew* Teresa McDonald."

Selena and I raised brows at one another. "How did they know each other?"

"We're unsure of their origin story," Vincent said. "But they are Instagram friends."

"How long ago did they become Insta friends?" Selena asked.

"Two years ago."

Selena said, "Any messages between them?"

"No DMs that we could find." He paused looking over at Val and Brady. I hadn't disclosed to them that sometimes we worked a bit outside of the law to get information we needed, but they seemed to understand, or at least they did now.

He continued, "But they liked each others' posts."

Selena said, "Could it be they were just suggested friends or friends of friends?"

Jerilyn said, "They share one mutual friend, Francesca Pinehurst. She went to the same high school as Lena and the rest of the group."

Selena frowned, tapping her pen against her notebook. "Ethan talked about Teresa's disappearance with glee... and he *knew* her. Who does that?"

"A Grade-A jerk," Jerilyn answered.

I tended to agree. "And he lied about ever hearing her name."

"What about the others?"

Vincent said, "Lena, Jenna, Jason, and Tiffany don't seem to have any connection to Teresa. Or Red Rose County. Just Ethan."

Selena leaned back. "Ethan sure is looking suspicious to me."

Val crossed her arms. "I want Ethan back in here."

Selena and I exchanged a look. "He told us any further questions should go through his lawyer."

Val eyed me. "So, he wants to play hard ball. Well, there's nothing stopping us from bumping into him."

I thought about Ethan, his plastered on smile, the way he deflected without seeming nervous. He could have set up Lena's abduction and killed Teresa. Or knew who did.

I turned to Val. "Have they found anything interesting from Teresa's crime scene like DNA or fingerprints that don't belong to her?"

"They're running tests now," she said. "But the body's badly degraded. Evidence may be limited."

Looking at Vincent, I said, "You've reviewed the background on Teresa McDonald's family?"

"Yes, but so far nothing stands out," Vincent said.

Selena said, "Maybe whoever did this wanted something from her family and didn't get it and that's why they killed her."

Val said, "The Sapphires know more than they're saying. Especially Joe. It's like he wants to talk, but something's stopping him. The McDonalds were heartbroken, but I didn't sense any deceit or holding back." She hesitated. "Last night, I called some of my FBI contacts to see if the Bucks, the Sapphires, or the McDonalds are into anything illegal, something that wouldn't show up in a standard background check or is off the record."

Brady's phone buzzed, sharp in the quiet room. He glanced at the screen, his expression tightening. "I need to take this."

The door closed behind him and that familiar unease crept in, the same feeling I'd had during our last kidnapping case. The slow realization that the people asking for help might be the reason someone was missing. And the question I couldn't shake was if Ethan was involved and if the Sapphires were hiding something, why hire me?

Vincent said, "If they're dirty or have a criminal past, maybe that's why they didn't want to report Lena's disappearance to law enforcement."

"As opposed to the lame story that their 'friend' said the cops wouldn't help?" Selena asked.

Val tipped her chin in agreement.

"When do you expect to hear back from the FBI?" I asked.

"Any time," she said. "Honestly I'm surprised I haven't already." Val stood up. "In the meantime, I want to talk to Ethan. And I want to talk to the mutual friend, Francesca Pinehurst, who connected him to Teresa."

Selena met my eyes. "Divide and conquer?"

"Yes," I said. "We'll talk to Francesca. Val, you and Brady can take Ethan. He's a bit tired of us."

Val agreed.

We needed answers, but one thing I was sure of was that someone, or more than one someone, was lying.

27

VAL

WE HAD A PLAN. A solid one. For the first time, it felt like the pieces were lining up, like the answers were finally pointing somewhere real. Toward the family. Toward Ethan. Martina's team worked faster than the sheriff's department ever could. Unlimited resources will do that, along with bending *a few* laws. Every person in the room was locked in, voices overlapping, hands moving, plans stacking on top of plans. Everyone hungry for answers. For Lena. For finding whoever had killed Teresa McDonald. I scanned the faces around the table, all focused, animated, and alive with momentum. Then Brady burst through the door. "You're never going to believe this."

The room went silent.

As the words left his mouth, the air seemed to vanish. Someone gasped. My pulse roared so loudly I barely heard anything else. I couldn't speak.

Martina recovered first. "We need to get back to Red Rose County. Immediately."

Heads nodded around the room.

She turned to Vincent. "The plans Val and I were working

on, I need for you to take point while we're gone. Use whatever resources you need. Time is of the essence."

"What about me?" Selena asked.

Martina hesitated, then said, "You're coming with me."

She looked back to Vincent. "You have the list. Talk to Francesca. Ethan. The friend group. Conduct the interviews. Backgrounds. Everything still outstanding. We stay in constant contact. I want updates in real time."

Vincent nodded. "You got it, Boss. Everything here will be handled."

She was already moving. "Thanks, Vincent." Turning to the rest of us, she commanded, "We need to go. Now."

The room snapped into motion. People grabbing files, phones, jackets. Martina's team mobilizing without a single question.

I was still reeling. Because what Brady had just told us... it changed everything.

28

MARTINA

YOU COULD'VE KNOCKED me over with a feather. Before me lay Lena Sapphire, sitting up in a hospital bed in Red Rose County. White sheets were tucked tightly around her thin frame, the steady beep of a heart monitor filling the room. She looked relatively unharmed, no bruises on her face, no visible cuts or scratches beyond a few faint marks along her arms. Her skin was grimy, her hair dull and tangled, as if she hadn't bathed in days. But for all intents and purposes, she was alive and well.

Deputy Baker, of the Red Rose County Sheriff's Office, had been tasked with watching over Lena until we were all sure she was safe. He said, "Now Lena, there are some folks here that have been looking for you and have some questions. Is that okay?"

Lena nodded.

"Hi, Lena," I said gently. "My name is Martina Monroe, and this is Selena Bailey. We're private investigators. Your father hired us to find you."

Val stepped forward. "And I'm Val Costa. This is Deputy Brady Tanner. We've been looking for you too."

"Thanks," Lena said weakly, her voice barely audible. "Is my dad here yet?"

"Not yet," I said. "We wanted to confirm it was you before notifying him."

Her eyes widened slightly. "Okay... can we call him now?"

I nodded, pulling my cell phone from my pocket, disbelief buzzing through me. I couldn't quite believe the words I was about to say. "Joe," I said when the line connected.

"Yes?" His voice sharpened instantly. "Martina, what is it?"

"We found her. Lena is alive. She's in Red Rose County. We're at Red Rose Hospital."

There was a sharp intake of breath on the other end of the line. "Who found her? How—"

"It appears she escaped. We haven't had a chance to speak with her yet. Would you like to talk to your daughter?"

"Yes, of course. Thank you. Thank you so much, Martina."

I handed the phone to Lena. Tears spilled from her eyes as she pressed it to her ear. "Dad," she whispered.

There were smiles. More tears. A raw, private moment that made my heart warm as I turned slightly away, giving them space, but still studying her from the corner of my eye. How had she escaped?

When she finally handed the phone back to me, her hands were shaking. With the phone pressed to my ear, I said, "Joe, is there anything else I can do for you?"

"No, but I'll be there as quick as I can. I have a friend with a private plane. We'll leave shortly."

"I'll see you when you get here." I ended the call and pulled a chair closer to the bed. "Lena, can you tell us what happened to you?"

She hesitated. "Again?"

"You've already spoken with officers, I presume."

She nodded.

"Well, your father hired me to find you, and I'd like to know who took you to make sure they don't try to get to you again. Do you understand?"

She nodded once more.

I glanced at Selena.

"You're so young," Lena said, studying her.

"Yep," Selena replied with a small smile.

That was when it hit me, Selena and Lena were almost the same age. This could've been Selena lying in that hospital bed. If anyone could escape a captor, it would be Selena, but even she hadn't managed it on her own when it happened to her in the past. Escapes like Lena's were rare. I leaned in, lowering my voice. "Can you tell me, from the very beginning, what happened?"

She let out a long breath, as if steadying her nerves. "I was outside Ethan's house. I was counting to myself to make the time pass. I was trying to prove that I wasn't scared of his stupid stories about kidnapping and missing women." She paused, her eyes dropping to the blanket. "I guess that's the last time I'm not afraid of that happening." She exhaled and went on. "Anyway, I was standing there, and all of a sudden I heard someone coming up behind me. I thought it was Ethan messing with me. He does that, he's such a jerk," she muttered under her breath. Then her shoulders stiffened. "I felt a prick in my neck, and then everything went dark." She shook her head. "No, that's not right. First I said, 'I know you're there, and I'm not afraid of you.' And then he said... that was my first mistake."

My stomach tightened.

"Then I felt a hand over my mouth. And a prick in my neck. After that, I don't remember anything." She swallowed. "Next thing I knew, I was in a room with cement walls with one window. Like a basement maybe. They had my ankle chained to the wall."

"And what happened while you were inside the room?"

"Honestly, not much," she said, almost confused by it. "It was really weird. I tried talking to them, asking what they wanted. At first I thought there was only one of them, but there were definitely two. They wore masks the whole time."

As we suspected. "Did they hurt you?"

She hesitated. "They fed me. They never really hurt me except for—"

She stopped.

"Except for what?" I asked.

"One of them burned me."

I raised my eyebrows. "They burned you?"

She slowly pushed herself upright, tugging the gown aside at her left shoulder. "You can take off the bandage to look."

Despite not wanting to mess up her recovery, I pulled back the tape and bandage. It took everything in me not to gasp. Selena and Val stepped closer, and our eyes met for a split second. The mark was unmistakable. It was a rose, just like the one on Teresa McDonald's body.

After reattaching the bandage, I said, "Did they tell you why they burned you?"

"He said it was punishment for being disrespectful."

"Did they hurt you in any other way?"

She shook her head. "No, not really. Honestly, the only other injury I have is a sprained ankle when I tripped over a log when we were running. That's why I'm here."

We? Did someone help her? "How did you escape?"

"I was able to unscrew the place where my chain was attached to the wall. I used a quarter that Derek gave me."

"Who is Derek?"

She explained about the second captive, another prisoner, and their plan for escape. "Where is Derek now?" I asked, turning to Deputy Baker.

"He's in another room being treated for minor injuries."

Lena said, "Can you have him come in here when he's done with the doctors?" Then, with a small smile, she said, "He's my hero. He saved me."

Deputy Baker said, "Of course. I'll go check on him."

Surely, two captives was unusual. I looked forward to hearing what Val thought about that. "What can you tell me about the people who took you?"

"Not much. Two men. That's all I ever saw. They wore masks. I could only see their eyes and lips."

"Do you remember what color eyes they had?"

"One had brown eyes. The other had blue. They were definitely Caucasian. Tallish, around six feet. Both of them looked like they worked out. They wore black clothes."

"Did they talk to you?"

"Not much. They were almost robotic. It was super weird."

"Was there anything distinguishing about them? Or something you can tell us that would help us identify him?"

"Not really. Except the one did know my name. Apparently he knew *all* about me."

She had been targeted, but why? "Did they tell you why they took you?"

"No. And I asked, a lot... until the punishment. The burn."

How awful. "Can you tell me about your escape?"

She said, "The day before, they took Derek away. I was terrified. Nothing made sense, and I thought something horrible had happened to him. But then this morning, the door burst open." Her eyes filled with tears. "He came back for me. Since I already had my chain undone, we ran. As fast as we could. Through the forest." She glanced down at her arms. "That's where I got the scratches. I tripped over a log and twisted my ankle, but he helped me up. We just kept running and running until we reached the road. We flagged down a car. They took us straight here."

I let a beat pass. "Do you remember anything about the inside of the building?"

"The room I was in had one window, but it was high up. I thought maybe it was a basement. But when we escaped, we only had to go up a few steps, down a long hallway and then it dropped us right into the forest."

"Did you look back and see what the building looked like from the outside?"

"No. I just ran as fast as I could."

"Do you know how long you were running?" Val asked.

Lena shrugged. "Probably an hour. I run pretty regularly and was going pretty fast until I tripped. Thankfully that happened right before we made it to the road."

"Is there anything else you can tell me that might help me find these people?" I asked. "So they don't take anyone else."

Lena frowned. "Have they taken someone else?"

"We believe they have."

"That's strange," she said, shaking her head.

"Why is that strange?"

She hesitated, searching for the words. "I kept having this feeling... like something else was coming. Like they were waiting for something. I don't know what."

A chill slid down my spine.

"At first, I thought it was money," she continued. "My family has money. That made sense. But then Derek was there, and Derek doesn't come from money. Not at all. The only thing we have in common is that we were kidnapped by the same people." She looked up at me, confusion and fear tangled in her expression. "What did they want with us?"

"It's a good question," I said. "We don't know, but we will get the answers. Because we're not going to let them hurt you, or anyone else, ever again."

She smiled faintly. "My dad says you're the best. He knew you'd find me."

"Technically, I didn't," I said.

"He said you would have, and that I could trust you."

I gave her my card, and said, "We're going to go talk to Derek, but if you need anything, you call me. I'll be back shortly. Selena will stay with you."

"Thank you."

Out in the hallway, away from Lena's room, Val stopped and lowered her voice. "It's the same people who killed Teresa McDonald. You saw the burn."

I nodded. "We need to stop these people. This job isn't done until we do."

Val met my gaze. "Agreed."

29

THE ARCHITECT

A TEXT MESSAGE flashed on the screen.

> The Ladybug has arrived.

A grin formed on my face as I texted back.

> It's showtime.

30

MARTINA

As we moved down the hallway to Derek's room, I was perplexed that there had been a second captive with Lena. How did that fit with our killers' MO?

"What do you think about there being a second captive?" Val asked.

"I don't know what to make of it. Especially the part about unscrewing the chain with a quarter. Have you ever heard of that?"

Brady said, "It's not impossible. If they didn't secure it well enough, it's possible."

"Well, then, I guess Derek really is her hero."

Val said, "I want to see if his story lines up with Lena's and to learn if he was taken the same way."

"Is it strange that of the three known victims there are two women and one man?"

Val tilted her head. "Some psychopaths don't care about gender. They just want victims."

"True."

We reached the room and quieted ourselves. Deputy Baker stood at the door and motioned for us to come in.

Inside sat a man in his early-to-mid twenties, with dark hair neatly combed back. His bright blue eyes lifted to meet ours immediately. There was bruising on his face, scratches along his arms, but he sat upright on the hospital bed, hands resting in his lap. He appeared alert and composed.

After introductions, we took seats across from him. "Do you mind if we ask you a few questions?" I asked. "We were hired to find Lena, and we want to find who did this, to her and to you, so they don't hurt anyone else."

"Of course," Derek said without hesitation.

"Would you mind telling us a little about yourself?" I asked. "Where are you from?"

"I already told the officers," he said with a hint of irritation. "But sure."

"We'd appreciate it," I said. "We're a different team. We're trying to stop whoever did this. It would help if we could hear it straight from you."

"Understood."

"Where are you from, Derek?"

"Modesto."

"And what do you do back home?"

"Handyman work. Woodworking. General repairs."

That explains the knowledge regarding the screw. "Do you enjoy it?"

"I do."

"Can you walk us through your abduction?" Val asked.

"Sure. I was leveling a door on the exterior of a house. Someone came up behind me. I assumed it was the home-owner." He spoke steadily, eyes forward. "When I turned, it was a man wearing a mask and dressed all in black. I fought him. He fought back." He gestured briefly to his face. Then lifted his shirt just enough to reveal a deep bruise along his side. "They kicked me when I was down.

Then I felt a prick. After that, I woke up in a room with Lena."

"That happened in Modesto?" I asked.

"Yes."

Modesto was nowhere near Red Rose County. Neither was Concord, where Teresa McDonald had been taken. All from different cities, but all had the same destination.

"And when you woke up?" I asked.

"I wanted out, immediately. I looked at how they'd attached me to the wall. I'm a handyman, I could tell they hadn't done a great job securing it."

"You noticed that right away?" Val asked.

"Yes. So, then, I checked my pockets and found a coin. Once I figured out a plan, I started loosening the screws."

"And you talked to Lena about escaping before they came in for you," I said.

"Yes. She'd been there longer. I felt bad for her, she was having a hard time and I knew we had to get out of there. When they came in, I tucked the quarter under the mattress. I hoped she'd find it. Thankfully, she did."

I studied him for a moment longer than necessary. Everything he said made sense. And somehow, that bothered me.

Val leaned forward. "What happened when they took you away from Lena?"

"They took me to another room. Just kind of threw me into a dark space. I figured they didn't want me in the same room as Lena anymore."

If they didn't want Lena in the same room, why had they installed chains in her room to restrain him? Was it psychological torture for Lena? Or perhaps they had set up the chains for their next victim.

"And when they put you in the room alone," she asked, "did they say anything to you?"

"No. They barely spoke at all." He shrugged slightly. "Anyway, when they came back for me, I was ready to fight to the death."

I studied him. "You fought them?"

"Yes. I knocked one of them out, took his knife and then was able to fight and stab the other."

Val's eyes sharpened. "Do you have any experience in boxing, or wrestling?"

"I wrestled in high school."

I exchanged a glance with Val. "You stabbed him," I said carefully.

"Yes. In the chest."

"Did you see either of their faces? Or any distinguishing features?"

"Unfortunately not."

"And then you went to look for Lena?"

"Yes, once I figured he was incapacitated, I started running down the hallway checking doors trying to find her. I had to open a few rooms before I found her. When I burst in, she'd already gotten the chain undone. I pulled her out and told her to run. We didn't stop until we hit the road. We flagged down a car. They brought us here."

Val watched him closely. Her expression wasn't sympathetic, it was measured like she was assessing the story.

"Is there anything else you can tell us that might help us locate the kidnappers?"

"I wish I could."

"Do you still have the knife?" Val asked.

"No," he said. "It was in the guy's chest when I ran."

I glanced down at his hands. They looked clean. Recently washed. Had they swabbed his hands before he cleaned them? "You saved Lena," I said. "And yourself. That's incredible."

He shrugged. "It was me versus them. I was going to choose

me. And Lena wasn't going to last much longer. She was having a rough time."

There was no emotion in his voice. "Thank you for speaking with us," I said. "One last thing, when you ran, did you see the outside of the building?"

"No. I didn't turn around. I just kept running. I had to make sure Lena was with me. We just needed to get out of there."

"And you only saw two people?" Val asked.

"Yes. Two."

The descriptions he gave matched Lena's almost exactly. Maybe we were only dealing with two men. Deputy Baker stepped forward. "Lena was hoping to see you again. She'd like you to come to her room, if you're up to it."

Derek gave a weak smile. "Of course."

He seemed to be doing very well, emotionally, considering the ordeal he had just been through. Brady and I handed him our cards. "If you remember anything else," I said, "or if you need us, call."

Deputy Baker escorted Derek down the hall toward Lena's room. I watched until they disappeared from view. Then I exhaled, slowly. "Does their story match your profile of how the killers would behave?"

"We assumed two kidnappers. This..." She trailed off, eyes distant. "I do believe it's the same people who murdered Teresa McDonald. But something doesn't fit."

"We're missing something," I said.

"Maybe we question them again tomorrow," Val suggested. "They could still be in shock and might remember something important after some rest."

"Agreed."

Before I could suggest going back to talk to Lena, my phone rang. I glanced at the screen and answered.

"Hey, Vincent. What's up?"

"I just finished interviewing Francesca, the mutual friend of Ethan and Teresa. They both knew Teresa because the three of them went to the same summer camp in sixth grade."

"All three. Including Ethan?"

"Yes."

Sixth grade. Twelve years old. They were in their early twenties now, so it had been ten years. Ten years wasn't *that* long. "It's possible Ethan doesn't remember her," I said, but didn't believe it.

"It's possible," Vincent said. "But we don't believe that's the case. He knew she was missing, they were Instagram friends and went to summer camp together. He *knew* her."

Agreed. "Did you find anything else?"

"She said she didn't think Ethan and Terry had any connection recently."

"Okay," I said. "What about Ethan's movements?"

"Surveillance says he's basically gone between home and work. That's it."

"Are you going to interview him?"

"I'm heading there now. Planning to surprise him at home, see if that throws him off. I'll bring backup."

"Good."

"Did you learn anything from Lena?"

After a brief update about the burn and Derek, I said, "We definitely think the kidnappers are the same people who killed Teresa."

There was a brief pause on the line.

"All right," Vincent said. "You need anything from me? You guys need backup out there? Anyone following you?"

"Not yet."

"Okay. Call if you need anything. I'll send people out if it changes."

"Thanks, Vincent."

I ended the call and relayed everything to Val.

"So not only did Ethan know about Teresa McDonald's missing persons case," she said slowly, "but he went to the same summer camp as her."

Brady exhaled. "That's not nothing."

No, it wasn't. And whatever we were missing, it was starting to circle back to the beginning with Ethan.

31

LENA

THE SIGHT of Derek warmed my heart. He saved me. If it hadn't been for him, who knows where I'd be right now. I knew he was just a handyman, but in my mind he was more than that. A hero. Someone who'd appeared when I needed him most. I wondered if Dad would be okay with helping him somehow, like giving him money, maybe a job. Something to thank him. Something to change his life the way he'd changed mine.

"How are you feeling, Lena?" Derek asked.

"Pretty good. They gave me something for my ankle, so it's not too bad. I'm just waiting for my dad to get here." I smiled at him. "I can't wait for you to meet him."

Selena stepped forward, and I noticed the way her eyes flicked to Derek, like she was studying him.

"I'm Selena," she said. "I work with Martina. I'm a private investigator."

"Oh," Derek said. "Nice to meet you. I just spoke with Martina and those other two."

Selena said, "You mean, the deputy and Val Costa. She's a former FBI profiler. They can be a little intimidating. Sorry if they were tough."

Derek's smile faded for just a second. "Not at all." Then it returned. "I was just talking to them about what happened. About how we got out."

"About how you saved me," I said with a grin.

"That's pretty amazing," Selena said.

She stepped aside then, and I realized, now that I wasn't chained to a wall, now that the fear had faded, I could really see him. Derek was good-looking. We'd talked for hours before they took him. About nothing. About everything. He made the time pass.

My thoughts drifted to Jason, my boyfriend, and guilt pricked at me. Why wasn't I thinking about him right now? Everything had been so crazy. I didn't have my phone and hadn't thought to call him. Before I could think too much about it, my father walked in, and the tears came instantly.

I'd never seen my dad cry before. Not once. And now here he was, eyes shining, his face tight with emotion.

"Lena," he said, coming straight to my bedside and wrapping his arms around me as best he could. He squeezed me carefully, like he was afraid I might break.

"I'm so sorry," he said. "That must hurt."

"I'm okay. It's really just my ankle. How's mom?"

"She's hanging in there. She's looking forward to seeing you."

And I was looking forward to seeing her. That had been the thing I worried about most, that I'd never see her again. Even now, rescued, I knew time was limited. She was so sick. Thinking about it made my chest hurt, but I pulled myself together. "Dad, I want you to meet someone. This is Derek. They kidnapped him too, but he helped me escape."

Dad looked at him. His expression was unreadable. "Thank you," he said. "I appreciate it."

That was it. Not a smile. Not relief. Just, *thanks*. Like Derek had held a door open instead of saving his only daughter. "He's a hero," I said with emphasis.

Dad's face shifted. He forced a smile. "You're right, honey. Truly, thank you, Derek."

They shook hands, and I wished Dad looked happier. I wanted to do something for Derek. I wanted to give him a token of appreciation, before he went back home to Modesto. I'd have to get Dad alone and talk to him about it.

"Did they say when you can leave?" Dad asked.

"The investigators want to talk to me a little more, but after that I'm free to go."

Dad turned to Derek. "How about you?"

"Thankfully. I'm just waiting for my family to arrive. They're taking me back home."

"And where are you from?"

"Modesto," I said for him. "He's a handyman. That's how he figured out how to get us free. It's like God brought him to me."

Dad's smile stayed in place as he said, "We're very grateful."

Selena stepped back. "I should probably go find Martina and Val."

Dad gave her a quick nod. Before they could say more, Martina, Val, and the deputy came back into the room.

Dad leaned down to me. "I'm going to step outside for a moment. I just want to talk to Martina."

"Okay," I said.

He left, and Derek pulled a chair closer to my bed and sat.

"How are you doing?" he asked.

"I'm okay. It's weird, though. I feel like I'm going to miss you, even though we didn't know each other for very long."

He smiled. "Yeah. I feel that too."

"I think we'll know each other for a long time," I said. "I really do. I feel like we were meant to meet."

Derek's smile deepened. "Absolutely."

32

MARTINA

JOE MOTIONED for us to head down the hall, and we hurried to be out of earshot of Lena's room. "What happened? What do you know about Derek?"

His demeanor read a lot more like anger and distrust than the joy of reuniting with his daughter. It was a little odd. Regardless, I filled him in on everything we had learned about her kidnapping, escape, and Derek.

"Any idea who took them?"

"Not yet," I said, not being entirely truthful. We did believe Ethan was involved, but it was too early to explain that to Joe. "We're heading to the scene where Lena and Derek were found by the good samaritan to see what we can learn. We will also continue to work with local law enforcement to find out who took Lena."

Joe paled.

I lowered my voice. "Lena is safe now. If there's anything you can tell us that might help us find these people, we'd appreciate it."

Joe looked at Val and Brady, then back at me. "I've said all I can say," he said. "Thank you again, but I don't need you to continue looking into this case. I'll make sure Lena is safe from here on out. I'll have payment sent to your office. Our business is finished."

Without another word, he turned and went back into his daughter's room.

Once he was out of earshot, Selena spoke up. "He doesn't want us looking into who took his daughter? Wouldn't you want answers?" She caught herself. "I mean, of course *you* would."

Val glanced down the hall. "There are definitely things he's not telling us. Do you get the feeling he knows who took her?"

If he knew, why not tell us? "Maybe."

Val reminded us, "Alice Sapphire's family has been friends with Ethan's family for generations."

I thought back to how Alice, Lena's mother, had told Val that Ethan was a good kid. "Do you think the Sapphires are protecting Ethan?"

"Maybe they're covering for him because of some kind of family allegiance." Val paused. "But if they were that close why would they let Ethan take Lena?"

Selena's eyes narrowed. "Maybe they didn't let him. Maybe he took her to get something from them."

Val cocked her head. "Something they don't want us to know about."

Selena turned to me. "Martina, you're not going to stop investigating just because he doesn't want you to, right?"

I looked at Val and Brady. They both gave me the same look.

"I don't think whatever this is, is over. There will be more victims if we don't find them first." I looked at Val and Brady. "I'd like to keep working the case, if the sheriff's department will cooperate."

Brady tipped his chin. "I can't speak for the sheriff, but we could definitely use all the help we can get. I agree with you, I don't think this is over."

"Neither do I," Val said.

There were nods all around. "All right," Val said. "Let's talk to the forensics team, then retrace where Lena and Derek ran from. If we can find where they were being held, there's a good chance we'll find enough evidence to identify the people who did this, and stop them."

My thoughts exactly.

33

VAL

WE MET the head of the CSI team, Brown, at a turnout on the side of the road. The spot was where Lena and Derek had been found by a good samaritan driving by, who had brought them to the hospital. The area was quiet, with only the intermittent hum of traffic drifting up from the highway. After brief introductions with Martina and Selena, I asked Brown about the evidence collection and his first impressions of our victims. "What was their overall condition when you met them at the hospital?"

"Lena was dirty," Brown said. "Hadn't showered, I'd guess, since she was abducted. She smelled like sweat and dirt. But relatively unharmed. Looks like a sprained ankle. We photographed the burn on her back."

He paused, watching my face.

Our eyes met. "We think it's the same too," I said, my mind flashing back to Lena and Teresa McDonald, both branded.

"And Derek?"

"Relatively clean," Brown said. "Probably hadn't showered in a day or two. No burns. But had bruising and abrasions to the ribs, chest, face, arms. He fought them, for sure."

Relatively clean? "What about his hands? Were they bloody?"

"No."

"Do you know if he washed his hands before you got there?" If Derek had stabbed someone, he most likely would have had blood on his hands and under his fingernails.

"Not that I'm aware of. It didn't look like he'd washed his hands recently. We swabbed his hands and took samples from under his fingernails. Since he fought the attackers, we're hoping to have captured some of their DNA."

"What about his clothing? What kind of shape was it in?"

"Dirty," Brown said. "Some dark brown spots on his shirt and pants, likely from when he busted his lip."

"No large quantities of blood?" Selena asked.

"No. Not that I could see. And honestly, the dark red I noticed could've been dirt. Hard to say until the lab tests it."

The four of us exchanged looks. No one spoke.

"What is it?" Brown asked.

"He says he stabbed one of the kidnappers," I said. "That's how they got away."

Brown took a moment, before he said, "If it was just one stab, it's possible he wouldn't have blood on his hands. Or if he wiped them on his pants. Anything's possible. I wouldn't rule it out completely. We photographed both Lena and Derek when they got here, swabbed their fingernails, and took their clothing into evidence. It's all with the lab now. You can talk to Jonathan when you get back to the station."

Jonathan was the head of the lab, and the husband of one of my best friends. I'd definitely be texting him as soon as we were done with the scene.

"Have you mapped possible locations of where Lena and Derek were held?" Martina asked Deputy Baker, who was the responding officer.

"Lena told us she'd been running for an hour and that she typically runs an eight-to-nine-minute mile. Probably faster for the escape, considering she was running for her life. We pulled records for all of the properties within a five-to-eight-mile radius based on that information, and have a few potential routes based on where they hit the road. We have teams being assembled to visit each property in the search area."

"Have you questioned the person who picked them up?" I asked.

"We got their statement. They told us everything they knew. They've gone home now."

Selena said, "You let them go?"

"It was four hours ago. We had no reason to hold them. We have their contact details if you want to talk to them."

"Anything strike you as odd about the situation?" I asked.

Deputy Baker hesitated, just long enough to notice. "Other than that they were able to escape?" he said. "It's not unheard of, I suppose. Especially since there were two of them."

"How was their demeanor?"

"They both seemed pretty shook up, and exhausted."

I looked back toward the dark tree line where the trail disappeared. Somewhere out there was the place Lena and Derek had escaped from. "Anything else you can tell us?"

"Not right now, but if we want to take one of the routes, the most likely route to where they were kept, we better get going while we still have daylight."

Turning to the group, I observed nods. "All right, let's get going."

As we started up the trail, the forest closed in around us. Tall pines and redwoods rose on either side. The air was cool with an earthy scent. The path was narrow, uneven, packed dirt broken by exposed roots and slick stones. It's not a surprise Lena had tripped and sprained her ankle.

"How's your mom doing?" Deputy Baker asked as we hiked in, falling into step beside him.

Deputy Baker had worked with my mother when she was still the sheriff. "She's enjoying her time living with Julie. They say they're becoming the Golden Girls. They're trying to get Diane to move in too, make it a trio. She's getting around okay, though. Thanks for asking."

My mother had suffered a stroke two years earlier. It was debilitating and she couldn't walk, and couldn't take care of herself. It was a tremendous blow, especially considering she'd always been the strongest, toughest person I'd ever known. Former sheriff and single mother to two headstrong daughters. But she fought and worked hard and willed herself back to self sufficiency. I'd never come right out and told my mother that she'd always been my hero, but I suspected she knew. It was no secret that I'd followed in her footsteps when I chose a career in law enforcement.

The trail steepened, forcing us to watch our footing. "And how are you and Brady getting along in the new house?"

"We love it. We've been decorating. It's just about perfect."

"You set a date yet?"

"Not yet. But I think we're getting close. Maybe after the case is closed."

Brady glanced back over his shoulder and smiled. Martina gave us a look, and I smiled too.

"Full disclosure. We're engaged."

"I caught that," Martina said. "Congratulations to you both."

"Thank you," I said.

"You work many cases together?" Martina asked as we pushed uphill, the trail winding tighter through the trees.

"A few, but we've known each other since we were kids. We both grew up in Red Rose County. We both left and started different lives. Him in the Bay Area, with a wife and kids. Me with the FBI on the East Coast with a husband and child. Then we both came back." A branch snapped underfoot somewhere ahead. "And suddenly," I said, "we were more than friends. We've solved a few tough investigations since I've been home. It's good working together."

"You're not working now?" Martina asked.

"Just occasional consultancy work for the sheriff's department."

"I used to contract with the CoCo County Sheriff's Department," Martina said, "mostly cold cases."

Selena piped up, stepping over a fallen log. "And in full disclosure for us, Martina married my dad when I was seventeen. That's how I know her. We've solved a lot of cases together too."

I glanced between them. They didn't look alike, but I had sensed there was something familiar there. The two had an ease and a closeness that was obvious. "And you work together now?"

"We do," Selena said. "I'm pretty lucky to have a stepmom like Martina."

"I can see that. I have a son a little younger than you. He's considering a career in the FBI now, despite my warning."

"You don't think it's a good option?" Selena asked as we continued deeper into the forest, the light thinning with every step. "I considered it for a moment or two," she said. "But I don't love rules."

Martina gave me a look and a nod telling me Selena's statement was absolutely accurate. I couldn't help but smile. "There are a lot of rules in the FBI. And to be honest, I broke a few when I was with them." The trail curved sharply, the ground dropping away to one side. "I don't regret many of them. But some had bigger consequences than others."

Much bigger consequences. I thought of being held captive

by the serial killer I was hunting, how I'd become the hunted instead. How I'd put everyone I loved in danger.

"What made you decide to retire from the FBI?" Selena asked.

"My mom got sick. She needed my help, and I was already on leave." I shrugged. "The timing felt right." A major understatement, even to my own ears. "I didn't want anyone else taking care of my mom," I continued. "I wanted to be here. She always took care of us growing up, even when it felt impossible."

We talked about our lives and cases we'd worked until we were pretty close to where we suspected the two had been held captive. The buzz in my pocket caught my attention. Pulling out my phone, I answered. "Hey Kieran, what's up? Did you find something?"

"Sort of," he said. "I haven't found any illegal activity, or even questionable activity, really. Some of them are involved in politics, others in business. On paper, they're clean."

I stopped hiking and looked at Martina, Selena, Brady, and Baker. "Clean?"

"Well," Kieran said, "officially, yeah. But it got me thinking. You said you've got a missing person and a dead body you believe are connected in Red Rose County?"

"Actually, three victims," I said. "Two kidnappings, one murder. The two kidnapping victims just escaped. We're on the trail now, looking for where they were held."

"They escaped? Can you walk me through it?"

Was he just curious or had something like this happened before? I explained the details about the captivity, the escape, and the burn.

"The burn?" he interrupted. "Is it like a brand?"

"Yes. Why?"

"Well," Kieran said, "like I said, on paper they're all clean. For people with that much money, I was suspicious. So I dug a little deeper and asked around." The forest seemed to go quiet around me as I listened. "Turns out there's been some whispers." As Kieran explained the rumors he'd heard, I processed them in real time, my thoughts racing ahead of his words. Could it be true? As he named names, the connections, and the associations, my heart rate picked up, thudding hard against my ribs.

A cold unease settled in my stomach. If these rumors were true, then not only were there more victims out there, but we could be walking straight into danger. Wealth didn't just hide secrets, it buried them and punished anyone who tried to dig them up.

34

MARTINA

OUR SMALL GROUP STOOD QUIETLY, as Val spoke on the phone with her FBI contact. No one said a word. Even the forest around us seemed to hold its breath.

Val's face tightened as she listened. Had they found something on the families? If I had to guess, based on the look in her eyes, I would say that they had.

My thoughts spiraled. Someone, or multiple someones, were plucking victims from across California and bringing them into Red Rose County to kidnap and kill. Two victims from the Bay Area. One from Modesto, further south. How many more victims were there that we hadn't found yet?

What disturbed me most wasn't just the pattern; it was the motive. We still didn't know why the victims had been taken. It didn't feel random. There had to be planning behind it. But if they were so well planned, how had Lena and Derek escaped?

Not to mention, Lena hadn't been taken by chance. She had been chosen for whatever this game was. So far, all she'd been able to tell us was that there were two people involved, confirmation of what we'd already suspected.

I hoped to God they'd pulled something usable from her and Derek. DNA. Fibers. Skin cells. *Anything.* Some trace evidence that could lead us back to who had held her, and why.

Now that we had three victims, thankfully, two of them alive, we might still have a chance to stop whoever was behind this before they hurt anyone else.

Val ended the call and shoved her phone into her back pocket with more force than necessary. She walked toward us, and said, "I don't know how credible this is, but my guy at the FBI says there are rumors. Nothing concrete."

"An organized crime ring?" I asked.

Val shook her head. "No. All of them are clean. No signs of illegal activity, but because of their wealth, it made Kieran dig deeper." She paused. "He says there are whispers. They could simply be an urban legend, but there's something called the Society. Or more specifically, the Society of the Rose."

The words sent a chill through me.

Rose. The burn on Terry McDonald. The burn on Lena.

"What does this Society of the Rose do?" Selena asked.

Val exhaled slowly. "It's a secret society, the kind you only know about if you're invited in. Old money. Legacies. Family lines. Rumor has it, it started at one of the Ivy League schools."

Selena folded her arms, eyes unfocused for a moment as she searched her memory. "I've heard of stuff like that," she said slowly. "A lot of Ivy League schools have secret societies. Invitation-only. You don't apply. You get tapped." She glanced up at us to make sure we were listening. "It's almost always legacies. Kids from donor families. Future politicians, judges, and CEOs. The kind of people who grow up knowing their last name opens doors long before they ever carn anything themselves. They don't usually meet on campus. That's intentional. They use private land like wooded properties owned by alumni or family trusts. Places with gates. No cell service. No cameras. No chance of anyone wandering in by accident."

Like Red Rose County.

She continued. "And from what I've heard, there are weird ceremonies. They wear uniforms, and sometimes hoods or masks. It strips away individuality and replaces it with rank inside the group. You're not supposed to feel like yourself, you're supposed to feel chosen and part of something bigger. Initiations are all about secrecy and control. Confessions. Humiliations. Symbolic acts. Things that bind everyone together because once you've crossed that line, you're all compromised the same way. No one can expose it without destroying themselves too. It looks ridiculous from the outside, but inside the circle it's *deadly* serious."

Her eyes flicked toward Val. Val looked interested, and Selena continued, "That's why people talk about Skull and Bones. It has members that became presidents, intelligence officials, and power brokers. That whole *Eyes Wide Shut* vibe with masked elites, rituals, and the unspoken understanding that wealth makes you untouchable. To outsiders, it looks like rich people playing dress-up in the woods. To insiders, it's a promise of protection and influence. Belong to us, and nothing touches you. And if you don't belong, or you threaten someone who does, you're a target."

Val eyed Selena. "Yes, and from what we understand, most of those societies are relatively harmless. But the Society of the Rose is *different*."

"How so?" I asked.

"Well, the rumor, because that's all it is, there's no hard evidence, is that it's made up of a group of extremely wealthy individuals. There's a hierarchy. And the way you move up is by completing certain acts of violence."

My stomach clenched. "Like?"

Val hesitated, as if choosing her words carefully. "They supposedly start small. Things like bar fights and then it levels up to kidnappings and eventually it escalates to murder, but not just any murder. They don't mean shooting someone and being done with it." She looked away briefly, eyes scanning the trees. "It's about proving yourself. They don't target just anyone. Early initiations target vulnerable victims, people less likely to be missed. The unhoused. Sex workers. And as you move up, it gets riskier. More difficult to get away with. If you succeed without being caught, you advance in the Society. Everything is sanctioned by a council, a group that approves the plan ahead of time. It's all tightly controlled by the group."

I swallowed. "So it's like a competition?"

"For lack of a better word. And the scariest part is that the competitors get help. They have support teams and help with logistics."

"And the families connected to Lena, are they supposedly involved with this?" I asked.

Val shrugged. "Like I said, this is all just rumor. One hundred percent speculation. To even be considered for an invitation, you'd have to have gone to a certain Ivy League school."

"But Lena didn't," I said. "Neither did her friends."

"Right," Val said. "Which means it could be someone they know. Someone from their past, perhaps someone from their private high school or a family connection."

"It's possible," I said. "What about the connection between Teresa McDonald and Ethan Buck, Francesca Pinehurst, did she go to an Ivy League?"

"We should check," Val said.

"Would it be unusual for the Society to take one of their own? Lena comes from a wealthy family. Wouldn't she be off-limits?" I asked.

"You'd think," Val said. "But maybe her family isn't part of the Society. Or maybe there's no connection at all."

I thought about Lena's words, how she'd kept saying it felt like something bigger was going on. How they'd held her, watched her, but hadn't hurt her. "Maybe it was someone's initiation," I said quietly. "Just a kidnapping. But Teresa McDonald... maybe that was something else. A different plan, a different killer. A different level in the Society."

Val didn't respond right away. "Maybe," she said finally. "And none of this is fact. It's lore. That's all."

"Do we know of anyone who's ever defected from the Society?" I asked.

"Not publicly. Kieran is finding us a contact for us to talk to. If we could get confirmation about this, it could help a lot. But the more I think about it, the more it fits." She eyed me. "Oh, and apparently all the victims get branded with a rose."

Selena and I exchanged a look.

Val said, "But it doesn't automatically mean they're responsible. It could be someone who knows about the Society and is trying to frame them."

"Or someone hurt by them, and wants revenge," I said.

Val nodded. "We need to check VICAP for any other bodies with a rose brand or burn. If there are more and they left any evidence behind, they could lead us to our killers."

She lifted her phone and said, "I'll call it in while I still have reception."

A moment later, a hollow whomp rolled through the ground, traveling up through my shoes and into my bones. Then the sound reached us. Branches snapped as I staggered, my instincts screaming one thing: *Bomb.*

Leaves and debris rained down, peppering the dirt around us.

For a split second, everything went eerily quiet.

Val froze, phone still in her hand, eyes locked in the direction of the blast. "That was a bomb. We must be close to where they held Lena and Derek."

And whatever evidence of that had likely just been destroyed.

35

MARTINA

THE FIRE DEPARTMENT had spent a considerable amount of time smothering the flames and protecting the surrounding forest. Had these people no shame? We all assumed the same thing— that this had been the kidnappers' hiding place and they destroyed it to erase evidence. In the process they easily could have started a massive uncontrollable forest fire. An entire county could have gone up in smoke.

Thankfully, the explosion had been reported immediately. We'd hurried back down to the road, both to get out of harm's way and to notify authorities. Fire crews worked throughout the night. In the gray light of morning, I stood staring at a cement foundation where a home used to stand. Nothing remained above ground. Just ash, twisted metal, and the sharp, chemical scent of burned accelerant lingering in the air.

A large man in a fire chief's uniform approached us, his boots crunching softly over debris. "Val, Brady," he said. "I hear this is connected to your case?"

"We believe so," Val said. "Chief, this is Martina Monroe and Selena Bailey. They're private investigators helping us on the case. They were originally tasked with finding Lena. Now we're trying to figure out who took her."

The chief nodded grimly. "Well, if this is where they held Lena, there's no evidence of it anymore."

That was exactly what I'd suspected. Still, sometimes the absence of evidence was evidence in itself. This was supposed to be a simple case. It had turned into anything but. Selena and I had been up half the night working through theories, coordinating with our team back home, trying to learn everything we could about the Society of the Rose. We tried to find every name, every connection, and anything linked to the group. And now we were standing in front of the physical remains of what we'd learned was a property owned by Tamara and Benjamin Bridgerton.

Once the fire department confirmed this was the residence that had been blown apart and incinerated, we dug into everything we could find on the family. We looked for any connection to Lena. There was nothing. Next, we went through Ethan Buck and the Bridgertons. Other than owning property in the same county, there was no other obvious connection, but we would keep digging. In my gut, I knew things had been set into motion by Ethan Buck. He had to have known the Bridgertons, or at least the people who were holding Lena and Derek at that house.

"Do we know how the fire started?" I asked as I stared at the foundation, the unease crawling up my spine. "It's very *clean*."

The fire chief followed my gaze. He didn't answer right away. Instead, he crouched, ran a gloved hand across the concrete, then straightened. "That's not an accident. It wasn't just a bomb." He gestured toward the slab. "To burn like this, down to bare concrete with almost nothing left, you're looking at a combination of high-explosive ignition and an accelerant designed to burn hot and long."

"What kind of accelerant?" I asked.

"Industrial-grade. Something that burns hotter than gasoline. Gas burns fast, it flashes, it moves. This stayed. My guess, it was a petroleum-based accelerant mixed with something like magnesium compounds or a gel fuel. Stuff that clings. Stuff that keeps burning even after the structure collapses."

Selena frowned. "That's not something you buy at a hardware store."

"No." He tapped the concrete with his boot. "They didn't just want destruction. They wanted sterilization. Anything organic, DNA, fibers, and bodily fluids, would've been incinerated."

My stomach dropped.

"Could the bomb have been remote detonated?" Selena asked.

He said, "Unlikely." He looked out toward the tree line, where the smoke had risen hours earlier. "This location is too remote. You wouldn't risk a signal failure. More likely it was on a timer. Simple and reliable. Mechanical or digital. Set hours, or even days, in advance."

"So no one had to be here to set it off," I said.

"Correct. Which means whoever planned this knew when there would be nothing left inside worth keeping."

"This wasn't a reaction," Val said, quietly. "It was scheduled. Perhaps once they knew Lena and Derek had escaped."

The fire chief looked at us pointedly. "You got lucky not being any closer than you were."

Had they destroyed the home just to eliminate evidence, or was it more than that? "I'm glad your team was able to put the fire out before it did more damage," I said, though my attention never left the concrete.

"If you hadn't called it in when you did, this could've been catastrophic for the county. No doubt about it. California already has enough problems with wildfire season. We don't need people setting off bombs to cover up kidnappings. I'll have my full report in a few days, but it was definitely arson."

I let that settle. If we'd been a tenth of a mile closer, we would've been blown to pieces. The thought made my stomach tighten. And yet, it almost felt like the explosion had been for us. The timing didn't feel coincidental. Lena and Derek had escaped eight hours earlier. Six hours before the blast. Why hadn't they set it off sooner? Did they need time to prepare? Or did they know, somehow, exactly when we'd come out to retrace their steps? I turned to Val. "What's your take on the timing of the blast?"

She didn't hesitate. "A little too close for comfort."

Selena stepped forward, her gaze moving from Val to me. "It's almost as if they knew we'd be here." She said what everyone else was thinking, but no one wanted to admit.

I studied Selena. "It's possible. But why? Even if they eliminated us, there are other resources on the case. Why would they go after *us*? Maybe they just wanted to destroy the site before we could get to it. Still—" I shook my head. "It was awfully close."

"The timing," Selena added. "It wasn't random. You know what they say about coincidences."

Val looked at Selena and then back to me. "Did you get the sense anyone followed you when you went back to the hotel last night?"

"No. We were careful. Did anyone follow you?"

"Not that I noticed," Val said.

"That doesn't mean someone isn't watching us," Selena said. "Or tracking the investigation. Trying to bury it so deep, we can't dig it up. Everything we've learned about this society, if that's what we're really dealing with, suggests these are wealthy and powerful people. It's not impossible someone in the sheriff's department has been compromised."

Val and Brady exchanged a look.

"Is it possible?" I asked.

Brady exhaled slowly. "I've worked with that sheriff's department for five years, there's no one I don't trust, but anything's possible."

"It could be that someone on the inside is being blackmailed for information. We need to run background checks on everyone with information about the case," Selena said. "Someone could have told them when we were coming to look for the site."

I felt a chill settle deep in my chest. "Perhaps there is someone trying to end the investigation."

"Or end us," Selena said.

"I can put in a request with our research team," Brady said.

Selena shook her head immediately. "I don't think that's a good idea."

We all turned to her.

"I think we need a roster of everyone with access to details about the case, then our team can run the background checks and start digging. We don't want people who might be suspects investigating themselves, right?"

The way she said it came off almost snarky, but I didn't think she meant it that way. She was stating a fact, not throwing an accusation. Still, I saw Brady stiffen. I hesitated, then said, "I think Selena has a point. If your team is researching their own department, they might be biased or it could get leaked that we think there's a mole."

Val glanced at Brady then to me. "I know the head of our research team. Lucy's one of my best friends. She would never compromise an investigation just because it's one of our own. She's loyal. Honest. And brilliant. If anyone can figure out who's leaking information, it's Lucy."

There was a note of indignation in her voice. "How about this," I said, stepping in before it escalated. "We split the workload and keep the investigation team tight. If Lucy is one of your best friends, I'm assuming discretion is something she can handle. This stays between the four of us and Lucy. No one else."

Val considered that, then said, "I think that's fair. I'll set up a meet with her. She'll understand the need for secrecy."

I turned to Selena. "Call it in to our team. And let's get a couple of our guys out here for security. Just because we haven't caught onto a tail doesn't mean we don't have one. Let's be extra cautious."

Selena gave a small smile. "You got it, boss," she said, punctuating it with a quick wink. That look, the confidence, and the energy, only came out when Selena felt sharp and fully in her element.

Someone was likely following us, or at least tracking the investigation. We'd come within ten minutes of being blown up. The job had just become a lot more dangerous. If Val hadn't gotten that call from the FBI, causing all of us to stop and wait while she spoke with her contact, we'd all be dead.

I looked at Val. We exchanged a glance, one of those looks that didn't need words. Either she'd just realized it, too, or she'd already been thinking it. Someone wasn't just trying to kill the investigation. They were trying to kill *us*.

36

LENA

As much as I wanted to be home, curled up in my own bed, the investigators asked us to stay in Red Rose County. Of course, Ethan's family offered to let us use their house, but I begged Dad to let us stay at a hotel. That was where I'd been kidnapped. I couldn't go back there. Not yet. Maybe not ever.

Dad reluctantly agreed. He bought out a floor at the local hotel just to make sure I was safe. A knock at the door brought a smile to my face. Derek had said he'd come by to check on me. I hated admitting how much I'd been thinking about him. The thought of him nearby made me feel... steadier. I opened the door, and my smile fell. *Jason.* I recovered quickly. "Jason! It's so good to see you," I said, wrapping my arms around him.

He hugged me tight. "I'm so glad you're okay, Lena."

"I am," I said, and I meant it. "I'm really glad you're here."

"I've been worried sick about you."

Another knock sounded.

Jason pulled back slightly. "Are you expecting someone else?"

"Maybe it's Dad," I said, though I didn't look through the

peephole. When I opened the door, my stomach fluttered. It was Derek. I don't know why he made me nervous.

I loved Jason, I did, but something felt different now. Maybe being kidnapped rewired something inside me. Maybe it was just the trauma. Or maybe it was that Derek had saved me. He'd gotten me out. He'd been there when everything else fell apart. Derek smiled. His face was still a patchwork of bruises, yellow and purple fading at different rates. "Come on in," I said. "Jason's here."

Derek stepped forward and held out his hand. "I'm Derek. Nice to meet you."

Jason shook it, then, unexpectedly, pulled Derek into a hug, pulling up the back of Derek's shirt and revealing a small tattoo on his right side. "Thank you for helping Lena. I'm really grateful."

Derek stiffened for just a second before returning it. "Of course. Anyone would've done the same."

Disappointment filled me that I'd only gotten a glimpse of Derek's tattoo. It was gone so quickly, I didn't have time to make out what it was. Why was I so drawn to Derek? Kicking out those thoughts, I said, "How's your hotel room?"

"It's great. It was very generous of your father."

Like us, Derek was asked to stay in town for another day as the cops were still investigating. "It's the least we could do. Does anyone feel like lunch? I'm starved." I'd skipped breakfast and my appetite had come back in full force.

Derek said, "Sounds good, as long as it's not sandwiches."

To my surprise, we both broke into giggles. I only stopped when I looked over at Jason who didn't understand our joke. He didn't know what we'd gone through. All I had eaten for five days straight were sandwiches and chips. If I never ate another sandwich for the rest of my life, that was just fine with me.

With my hand on Jason's arm, I said, "It's practically all they fed us."

Jason nodded while eying Derek suspiciously. Had he picked up on what I was feeling toward Derek? I didn't know if it was attraction. I didn't want to call it that. Maybe it was admiration. Gratitude. The cliché of the damsel rescued by the gallant warrior.

It would wear off, I told myself.

Less than a week ago, I'd been thinking Jason was the love of my life. That felt a little naïve now. I was only twenty-three; the likelihood Jason would be my one and only was so unlikely. Maybe it was too many fairytales told to me in my youth. I'd always imagined Jason as my knight and myself in a designer gown. But now all of that felt childish. I didn't want to be rescued. I wanted to be powerful and comfortable in my own skin. I wanted purpose. The opposite of how I felt all alone in that room with those sick men. The days of fantasizing about men saving me were officially over.

"Lena?" Jason's voice pulled me back.

"Oh, sorry. I was just thinking about food."

"I heard they have good pizza downtown," Derek said.

"Pizza sounds great," I said. I hadn't had pizza in forever. Jason nodded, though I could tell he didn't understand the easy rhythm between Derek and me. "Should I see if Dad wants to join us?"

They both nodded. I pulled out my new phone and texted him. He replied almost immediately.

"Yes. Be right out."

"Dad's coming with us," I said.

"Excellent," Derek said.

For a moment, I felt lucky. Not just because I'd been freed, because I had Jason, a man who'd loved me for a year. Derek, who'd saved me. And my father, who would've gone to the ends of the earth to find me.

Dad let himself into the room using the extra key. "Oh," he said, taking everyone in. "I see the whole group's here."

His eyes landed on Derek and stayed there a moment too long. I couldn't quite read the look he gave him. Distrust, maybe. Disapproval, for sure. Derek didn't come from our world. That shouldn't have mattered, Derek had saved his daughter. But Dad had always been particular about staying in our circles. But I didn't care. No matter what anyone thought, Derek would always be my hero.

37

VAL

LUCY'S EYES widened as I explained the situation, how we needed her to look into our own staff. *Quietly.* To see if anyone had been compromised. If anyone had been feeding out our location or details of the investigation.

"You got it," Lucy said. "I can work from home if that helps. That way no one's looking over my shoulder."

"I'd appreciate that."

Lucy exhaled. "I thought things were going to stay quiet in Red Rose County. I guess not."

I knew exactly what she meant. It had been quiet over the past year. Peaceful. Just like I remembered from my childhood. Now it felt like we'd stepped into some kind of sick game— *again.* "Work from home," I said. "And put your alarm on. I've got a feeling these people would do just about anything to keep their secrets hidden."

Lucy pushed up her glasses. "I understand. I'll let Jonathan know that I'm working on something top secret. I won't give him the details, but I'll tell him he needs to stay alert."

Jonathan, her husband, worked at the lab in Red Rose County. They'd met at work, the same way Brady and I had, *kind of*. I'd like to think working together is how we fell in love. That almost made it seem like the killers and criminals brought us together. Shaking the thoughts away, I said, "Good idea."

"I was actually about to suggest a night out," Lucy said. "But it seems like maybe you've got your hands full."

Me, Sally, and Lucy tried to get together at least once a week for some girl time. Well, medical examiner, top researcher, ex-FBI type of girl-time. Based on our professions, our topics of conversation varied from homicide investigations to toenail polish. There was *always* wine.

My phone buzzed in my pocket. It was Martina, I answered right away. "Hey," I said. "What's going on?"

"I have a bad feeling," Martina said. "If that bomb was meant to destroy evidence, or us, they may try to bury the entire investigation. Lena and Derek could still be in danger. I think we need to put them in protective custody."

"We don't really have that here in Red Rose County," I said. "What about your team?"

"We've got safe houses, just not out here. Maybe we do twenty-four-hour surveillance on them?"

"That could work," I said. "Or we keep them down at the station. It's not comfortable, but at least we'd have eyes on them."

"Unless they have someone on the inside," Martina said.

"Good point."

"Selena and I will head to their hotel. We'll talk to them and see if there's anything they can remember that could connect their kidnapping to the Society of the Rose. I won't say it outright. Just feel it out."

"Good idea. How are you and Selena doing?"

"We just got back to the hotel a few hours ago. We had a chance to regroup with the team back home. But the timing of that blast doesn't sit right with me."

"It doesn't with me either." And it didn't. If I hadn't taken that call from Kieran, we would've been at the site when it went off. We would all be dead. Which meant Martina was right. If they were willing to do that, Lena and Derek were still targets. I lowered the phone and relayed everything to Lucy.

To Martina, I said, "I'm heading over there too. I'll bring Brady."

With the call ended, Lucy studied me. "After what happened at that house, you should be watching your back too. Maybe *you* need twenty-four-hour surveillance."

"I've got Brady," I said lightly.

She gave me a look. "Don't be ridiculous."

"You're right."

"What about Martina and Selena?"

"They've got some of their security detail on the way."

Lucy tipped her chin. "Smart."

Point taken. "I'm heading to the hotel. Do you need anything else from me?"

"No. I've got it," Lucy said. "Be safe out there, Val."

I stopped by Brady's cubicle and leaned in, whispering where I was headed and asking if he could come with me. Without a word, he grabbed his keys and we hurried out of the sheriff's station.

While Brady drove to the hotel, I called Lena to ask which room she was in. She gave it to me immediately. When I asked if she knew what room Derek was in, she gave me that too. She seemed quite attached to him. I supposed it made sense; she had been held with him, and he ultimately saved her.

To be honest, I was looking forward to a second interview. Not to step on Martina's toes, but sometimes hearing the same story from different angles brought things into focus for me. Considering it was possible we were dealing with a bunch of murdering billionaires, it would be good to know if there were details that would align with the Society's previous acts. Assuming we could get a contact to tell us more about that.

Martina pulled up shortly after. I waved, and my phone vibrated again, in my hand. I recognized the name and number instantly. "Did you find me someone?" I asked.

"I did," Kieran said. "But this has to be handled carefully. No one can know he's talking to you."

"Understood."

He gave me the details. I slipped the phone back into my pocket, already moving. Turning to Brady, I said, "We have to go meet a source. I'll tell Martina."

After a quick jog over to her, I told her the latest. She told me to be careful, and I ran back over to Brady's SUV and climbed in. With the address of the meet put into the navigation, we tore out of the hotel parking lot. There was no time to lose, because whatever we were up against wasn't waiting, and neither could I.

38

MARTINA

After a swift knock on the door to Lena's hotel room and announcing that it was us, the door opened and there she stood. My first thought was that Lena was a miracle. The fact she stood there alive was incredible. She looked to be feeling better since we met at the hospital. She'd likely had a shower and was feeling more normal.

With a warm smile, she said, "Hi, Martina. Hi, Selena."

"May we come in?"

"Yes, of course. Please come in."

She stepped aside. "This is my boyfriend, Jason."

With a small wave, I acknowledged him although we'd already met. The room was relatively small, definitely not a luxury suite. Red Rose County didn't have those. Two double beds, a narrow desk, and warn carpet.

"Please, sit," Lena said.

She took the chair by the desk while Selena and I perched on the edge of one of the beds.

"So," Lena said, folding her hands together, "what did you want to talk about?"

"We just have a few follow-up questions about what

happened," I said. "I'm not sure if you want Jason here for that conversation."

Jason turned to Lena. "It's up to you."

Lena hesitated. "Do you mind stepping out for a minute? I'm sorry, it's just... I guess I'm not ready for an audience yet."

With a reassuring smile, he said, "It's okay. I get it."

"Maybe you could go hang out with Dad if he's not working," Lena said. "Or you could go for a walk—"

I interjected. "Why don't you go to Joe's room? It's best to stay here at the hotel. We have reason to believe Lena could still be in danger, and that could put you at risk as well."

Jason froze. "Oh. Well...."

Lena shook her head. "Stay, Jason. I'm sorry. It's fine. This is all so new and strange."

Jason hesitated, then nodded and sat on the other bed, facing Lena.

"As I said," I continued, "we have reason to believe you could still be in danger."

"Why?" Lena asked. "What happened?"

"We believe the house where you were held was destroyed by a fire. They just finished putting it out. The sheriff's department and our team visited the scene. It's gone now."

Selena added, "We think they did it to destroy evidence."

"And that means you and Derek could still be at risk."

Lena's eyes widened. "Should we go get him?"

"We'll talk to him in a minute," I said. "But first, we believe the people who took you were sophisticated."

Lena nodded slowly. "Yeah. They were... methodical. Almost robotic. Everything felt planned. Like they had strict procedures. Only one of them lost control, when I taunted him. He *didn't* appreciate that."

"When you say you taunted them, what did you say?"

"That he probably lives in his mother's basement and girls

teased him in school. Questioning his manhood, that kind of stuff. He didn't like that."

"How did he respond?"

"He burned me."

"Do you know what he used to do that?"

Lena hesitated. "It was something on a chain," she said. "It happened fast. He heated it right in front of me, but it was too far away for me to see clearly. Some kind of round-ish metal object. Then he pressed it to my back."

"I'm so sorry that happened to you." I glanced at Jason. I wasn't sure how much he knew about what had been done to Lena. His brow furrowed and his hands were clenched.

"Now that you've had some rest," Selena said, "can you remember anything else? Anything that might help us identify them?"

"No. I wish I did. It was all so strange."

"You said they were dressed in black," I said.

"Yes."

"And you never saw their faces clearly?"

"No."

"Did you notice if they had cell phones?" Selena asked. "Or if they were communicating with someone other than the two you saw?"

"I don't remember that. If they did, it wasn't in front of me."

"What about the room?" I asked. "Any markings? Anything distinctive?"

"It was dark-ish with only a single light and window. Cement walls. Pretty clean, actually. Except for the bucket. And the mattress on the floor."

"Anything else you can remember?" Selena asked.

"No. But maybe you should go check on Derek. I don't want anything to happen to him. I'd be devastated if anything happened to him."

Irritation flickered across Jason's face, quick, but unmistakable. "We'll check on him now," I said. "Thank you, Lena. Please stay put."

"We're going to have surveillance on your hotel room," Selena said. "Don't leave for any reason. If you need anything at all, call us or Val. We'll bring it to you until we're sure you're safe."

"Absolutely," Lena said. "I'm just worried about Derek now."

Jason cleared his throat. "Is it okay if I stay here with her?"

"Of course," I said, looking to Lena.

"Yes," she said. "Of course."

"Good to see you, Jason," I said as we stood.

He nodded.

Selena and I stepped out into the hallway, the door closing softly behind us. Two doors down, I knocked on room 721. No answer. Selena and I exchanged a look. "Maybe he's sleeping," she said. "Or went for a walk."

"Let's call him. I'll go down to the front desk and have them connect me to his room. You stay here."

Selena nodded and remained outside the door.

Down in the hotel lobby, I asked the clerk to call the room. He obliged and handed me the receiver. I pressed it to my ear. It rang. And rang. And rang. No answer. I returned the receiver to the desk.

"Is everything okay?" the clerk asked.

"Actually, I'm trying to reach one of your guests. Derek Dunn, in room 721. I'm part of an investigation in collaboration with the sheriff's department, and we're trying to ensure his safety."

"Oh, okay. Is there something else I can help you with?"

"Is there any way you could let me into his room?"

"I'm sorry," he said immediately. "I can't do that."

"That's fine. Thank you for your help."

I headed back upstairs. Selena was standing outside Derek's door, crouched slightly, as if trying to hear through the wall. She hurried toward me before I could approach.

"I've been listening," she whispered. "He's definitely inside. I thought I heard his phone vibrating, and then he spoke to someone but I couldn't make out what he said."

My gut stirred. "Why wouldn't he answer the door or answer my call?"

"I don't know."

Maybe he knew he was in danger. Maybe he didn't want to open the door to just anyone. Or maybe something else was wrong. I knocked again. "Derek. It's Martina and Selena. We'd like to speak with you."

There was a pause. Shuffling sounds inside. Then the door opened and Derek stood shirtless, only wearing a pair of jeans. He was fit, but the bruises from his attack were difficult to look at. "Oh, hi. Is everything okay?"

"We're just checking on you," I said. "Do you mind if we come in?"

He stood back and gestured for us to enter. He didn't offer us a seat, not that there was one other than the beds. "I wanted to notify you that we're putting twenty-four-hour surveillance on your hotel room. And we're asking that you not leave the hotel until we can ensure your safety. We've also notified Lena."

"I understand."

"And we have a few follow-up questions," I continued.

"Shoot."

If I didn't know better, I'd say Derek was recovering very well. "While you were being held, you saw two men, correct?"

"That's right."

"Did either of them have a cell phone? Did it seem like they were communicating with anyone else that might indicate there was a third person involved?"

"No, I don't remember that."

"When you escaped," I asked, "when you stabbed one of them and fought off the other, did it seem like more people were coming? Did you hear other footsteps or an alarm?"

"No. As far as I could tell, it was just the two of them."

Nothing in his story changed. "Is there anything else you've remembered that might help us find who did this to you?"

He shook his head.

"If you need anything at all," I said, "call me, Val, or the sheriff's department. We know they took your phone. Do you want us to get you a new one?"

"Oh, no," he said. "That's okay. I actually picked one up."

"When?" I asked, surprised.

"We went to lunch today. While we were downtown getting pizza, I stopped into a shop and bought a prepaid." He hesitated. "Actually, Lena bought it for me. She's very generous. So is her father."

"Understood," I said. "Do you mind if I get the number?"

"Of course."

He gave it to us. Selena typed it into her phone.

"Please stay in your room until we give you the all-clear," I said.

"Can I visit Lena?"

"Yes," I said. "Absolutely. Actually, just don't leave the hotel."

With the tilt of his head, he said, "Hopefully this will all be resolved soon."

"I hope so too."

Derek turned his back to us and picked up a t-shirt from the bed, and that's when I saw it. A small tattoo, just above the hem of his jeans, nearly hidden. The image made my heart pound. He turned back quickly and slipped the shirt on. "Is there anything else I can do for you?"

"No," I said trying to remain calm. "That's it. If you need food, clothes, or anything at all, let us know."

"I appreciate it," he said with a smile.

Selena and I stepped out and closed the door.

Once we reached the parking lot, I turned to her. "Did you see the tattoo?"

With brows raised, she said, "Yes, I did."

We both stood, a bit stunned at the revelation. Finally, I said, "We shouldn't leave the hotel until the surveillance team gets here. I don't want him out of my sight."

39

VAL

WE ARRIVED in the parking lot of an abandoned shopping center in the East Bay, on the far edge of the Bay Area. As Brady slowed the SUV, I scanned the empty rows of cracked asphalt, wondering how much information we'd get from the source. I hoped it would be enough to find out where these people were, and enough to stop them.

Brady had driven, but the instruction from the source was that he would only meet with me. I had to go in alone. Parked, I leaned over and kissed Brady. He squeezed my hand, as he locked eyes with me. "Be careful."

"Will do."

I climbed out of the car and adjusted the weight of the weapon at my side and the bulletproof vest beneath my jacket. I didn't know what I was walking into, and if this was a setup, I was going to be ready. My life was too good to throw it away.

Without further ado, I headed across the parking lot and walked to what looked like an abandoned grocery store. The paint was peeling from the walls, and the windows were boarded up. The faint outline of the store's old name lingered above the entrance, letters so sun-bleached I couldn't quite make them out.

It was quiet, unnaturally so.

Despite the eerie vibe, I rounded the corner to the back of the building where a loading dock must have once been. That's when I spotted a black sedan, shiny and new, unmistakably expensive. Definitely, out of place.

Perhaps my source was still an active member of the Society. From what Kieran had told me, once you were in, you didn't leave. Even if you wanted to. Like a gang, there was only one way out. I moved toward the sedan as a figure stepped out from behind it.

He was tall, in his fifties, with dark hair and a tailored suit that probably cost more than my monthly mortgage. I didn't know what I'd expected, but it wasn't a businessman driving a Mercedes. I approached cautiously. "I'm Val. Thank you for meeting me."

He nodded. He didn't offer his name or offer his hand. He just stood there as he scanned the lot. His gaze met mine. "This meeting could get me killed. And make no mistake, if I was murdered by them, nobody would ever find my body or learn who was responsible."

"Understood," I said, and I did. "This stays between us. Any information you give me will be shared with my team, but not your physical description or the details of our meeting, per your request."

He nodded once.

"I was hoping you would be able to confirm a few details," I said and then told him everything I had learned about the Society of the Rose. As I spoke, he listened, his expression unreadable.

When I finished, he gave another short nod. "That's fairly accurate," he said. "There's initiation, and then there are levels within the organization. A lot like a corporation. In order to move up the levels, there are a defined set of acts to qualify for the promotion. The higher the risk, the higher the reward."

"How do the participants prove they have completed the task to get promoted?"

His eyes swept across the parking lot before he said, "Video."

A sick feeling filled my gut. "Where are the videos kept?"

"I'm afraid I can't tell you that."

"Self incrimination?" I asked, with a brow raised.

He gave a slight nod.

"What's the purpose of the group? Why do people want to join?"

He let out a quiet breath that almost sounded like a laugh. "People with too much money and nothing else to do. But mostly it's about power. Taking someone's independence and their life, is the ultimate power trip." His eyes flicked toward the empty lot, then back to me. "They feed on power and the fear of others. It's a game to them. A way to make themselves feel bigger."

"And you're not like them?" I asked with a hint of skepticism.

He studied me for a moment. "Call me reformed."

"Do you know who the active members are? How many there are? We're trying to find a connection to Lena Sapphire."

He smiled then, but there was nothing warm about it. "There is a connection," he said. "But I'm not going to tell you what it is. If I give away members, I compromise myself. You must understand that, Agent Costa."

The silence that followed felt heavier than the vest beneath my jacket. So he wasn't going to give me names. *Great.* "Is there anything about the members that makes them stand out? What gets them chosen to be part of the Society?"

"Mostly family ties and wealth. It used to be that you had to attend a certain Ivy League school. It's expanded now. But more than that, it's about how much money you have and your family connections. And of course, the proclivity for such activities."

I instantly thought of Ethan Buck and his generational wealth. "If I asked you about a specific member," I said carefully, "would you be able to tell me if they were involved?"

"I'd really prefer not to."

I thought about Lena, his reaction when I'd mentioned her name earlier. "My team and I find it peculiar that they might have taken Lena. It seems like she'd be off-limits, considering she's likely within the circle of those involved."

"By design," he said. "Higher risk, higher reward."

"Was the intention to kill Lena?"

"It could've gone that way, but it wasn't supposed to," he said with zero emotion.

"But she escaped."

He smirked again.

"Are you saying she didn't escape? Did they let her go?"

"No," he said. "That's not what I'm saying. I'm saying it was by design."

I frowned. "I'm not following. She was held captive for five days. Disappeared from Ethan Buck's home, which I believe he orchestrated the abduction, or at least he helped facilitate it. Was Ethan Buck involved?"

He shrugged.

"She was relatively unharmed. Aside from the brand. Why?"

He lifted a finger, signaling for me to wait.

Then, without another word, he turned his back to me and began unbuttoning his dress shirt. My pulse spiked as he lifted the fabric just enough to expose the skin above the waistband of his trousers.

There it was. A small rose tattoo. He turned back around. "She belongs to us."

I stared at him, my stomach twisting. "I'm not sure I understand. All the victims, do they all become yours and therefore get the brand of the rose?" I didn't recall Derek having been branded. Maybe they hadn't held him long enough for them to get the chance.

"Some belong to us more than others," he said. "But typically, yes."

He spoke in riddles, like someone who'd lived inside the Society for too long, like he was speaking a language only they fully understood.

My thoughts went back to Lena. Her kidnapping. Her captivity. Her escape. None of it sat right. "Okay, She belongs to them. Then why keep her for five days? Well fed. Unharmed. Why bring in a second prisoner?"

With dead eyes, he said, "Lena wasn't the target."

"Then what was she?"

"Bait."

My chest tightened.

He continued, "She was bait for a higher-value target. Worthy of the ultimate prize."

"What's the ultimate prize?"

"To become the Crown."

I shook my head. "I'm sorry, I'm not following."

"To become the Crown," he said. "The head of the Society. The one everyone answers to."

I stayed silent.

"It isn't inherited," he continued. "It's earned. When the seat opens, which it will soon, there's a competition. Three are chosen to compete in the hunt. The winner becomes the Crown."

"What do they hunt?"

"A living trophy," he said. "Someone whose capture proves you can outmaneuver law enforcement, and create fear without consequences."

All I could think was how incredibly sick all of this was.

He continued. "Whoever delivers the high-value target and takes their life, becomes the Crown."

My skin prickled. "Was Derek the high-value target?"

He shook his head. "Lena was the bait," he said. "The high-value target is... much more valuable."

"Like a celebrity?" I guessed.

"Of sorts."

"But who?" I pressed.

"That, I can't say."

He stepped toward the driver's side door. "But if you find the Crown, you'll get your answers."

"You can't even tell me how the target was chosen?" I asked.

"I cannot give any names," he said without turning back. "Remember what I told you—high-value bait, high-value target. The goal is to become the next Crown. I can say no more."

He climbed into the sedan. All I could do was stand there and watch as he drove away, the sound of the engine fading into the quiet of the abandoned lot.

A sense of dread settled deep in my chest as the pieces of the investigation clicked into place. Lena's disappearance, the family not contacting law enforcement, the hiring of Martina, the location, the Society, and the obsession with status and spectacle. As for who the high-value target was, only *one* name came to mind. And I needed to warn her, before it was too late.

40

THE ARCHITECT

"Do you have eyes on the Ladybug?" The name was not an endearment. It never had been. Ladybugs are symbols of protection, good fortune, and innocence. I looked forward to squashing those attributes.

"Yes, sir," he said. "She's in the parking lot sitting in her car. How do you want me to proceed?"

"Cautiously. The Ladybug is most vulnerable when she doesn't realize she's been marked." As the hunt grew near, I was growing a bit impatient. It was as if I could feel her heartbeat and smell the metallic scent of her blood. "What's the latest update on the investigation?"

"They believe *Derek* and Lena are still in danger," he said. "They haven't realized she was never meant any harm."

"That's very good."

"One thing that could hinder our plans is that law enforcement is planning to assign twenty-four-hour surveillance on our hotel."

A minor inconvenience. "I see how that could become a challenge, but it's not prohibitive."

"I have contingencies. If I can get the Ladybug to the location before they mobilize, your plan is safe."

"That's a bit risky now. I have a new idea." As I explained, my little helper's interest grew. That was good, because I couldn't do it alone. I finished with, "As the new Crown, there will be an open seat beside me. Follow my instructions and the seat is yours."

"Are there any rules regarding the Ladybug?"

There were always rules. "Just one. You can't kill her. That's for me, and me alone."

41

MARTINA

WE'D BEEN SITTING in the car for three hours, while we watched Derek's room and while Steve and Otto watched us. Our bodyguards had just arrived, but were likely as bored as we were. A stakeout was my least favorite activity as a private investigator. But until I got word that we were all clear, I wasn't leaving this to local law enforcement. I was sure they were good at their jobs, but they had to work within the confines of the law. I didn't. What I *did* need to do was protect Lena, and whoever else they might hurt next.

Selena handed me a protein bar. I took it, unwrapped it, and took a bite. I barely tasted it as I stared out at the hotel entrance and its rooms.

My phone buzzed, and I was grateful. "Hi, Vincent. What did you find on Derek Dunn?"

"I've got his driver's license photo. It looks like the guy. His work history checks out. Everything lines up."

That didn't feel right. "But you haven't talked to his coworkers, family, or friends to verify who he says he is, have you?

"No. Just records."

"Something's not right here. Maybe we need to take a trip to Modesto and start asking around."

There was a pause. "That's a five-hour drive, Martina."

And? I didn't respond. He said, "But we can send a team."

"Do it," I said. "Something's wrong here, I can feel it."

"Got it."

"I've got another call," I added. "I'll get back to you." I disconnected and immediately answered the incoming call. "Hi, Val."

"Hey, I just got back into town," Val said. "I'm at the station with Lucy and Sally."

"Did you find someone compromised within the sheriff's department?"

"No, but I met with the source, and he told me some interesting things."

My pulse started to race. "I'm in the car with Selena. I'm going to put you on speaker."

"I'll tell you everything, but where are you right now?"

"We're outside the hotel. We didn't want to leave until I was sure we had eyes on Derek and Lena."

"Has your team arrived yet?"

"Yes, they got here about ten minutes ago."

Val said, "Good."

"Why? How did your meet go?"

"Well, I didn't get a ton of information, but I know he's a member. And he showed me a tattoo he had on his right side. A small rose. It's barely noticeable, but unmistakable."

Selena sucked in a sharp breath. "Like Derek's," she said. "He has one. We saw it briefly in the hotel room. We thought it was suspicious."

Val said, "We know. I'm here with the medical examiner. She showed me the photographs of all the injuries and that's when I saw Derek's tattoo. He's one of them."

I straightened in my seat. "If he's a member, why would he help Lena escape?"

Val said, "Lena was bait for the real target."

Selena and I listened as Val explained the hierarchy, the structure, and the ultimate prize to become the head of the Society.

"Do you understand what that means, Martina?" Val asked.

Selena gasped again before I could answer. "Martina," she said, her voice trembling, "you're the high-value target. Think about it. That's why Joe Sapphire insisted it had to be you!"

My stomach dropped. "But why? I don't know any of them."

Selena said, "Because you make a lot of headlines."

It was true. Hirsch, my firm, and I had solved some tough and very public cases, making my identity a bit too known for my comfort. It attracted deranged killers, and now it seems, a secret society of killers.

Selena cheeks turned an angry red. "Joe hired you, knowing what they were planning *to try* to do to you! He insisted on you taking the case and wouldn't settle for *anyone* else."

The memory slammed into me. I'd relented and told him I'd think about it, but that I wanted some time to make a decision. Before I could, he had showed up in the parking lot at my car door, begging. It didn't make sense why he wanted me on the case, but unfortunately it was now very clear. My grip tightened on the steering wheel.

"He said you had to be the one to find her," Selena went on. "That's why he didn't go to law enforcement, instead he went to you. They used Lena. And maybe the only way Lena was ever going to be released was if they delivered you."

"Maybe he didn't know he was walking me into a trap?" Did Joe Sapphire know the intention was to kidnap and kill me? Or was he innocent? Maybe someone contacted him and said not to go to law enforcement and knew he'd go to my firm? It was a stretch. My gut was telling me he knew. But who had contacted him? Val and I both thought he knew more than he was telling us. It had now been confirmed.

Whether he knew all the details or not, it was clear this wasn't an investigation. It was a hunt, and I was in the crosshairs. I sat there, stunned.

When I took the case, I certainly didn't think I would be hunted so a group of rich nutjobs could decide who got to be the head of their billionaire psychopaths club.

Selena fumed. "He knew. And he's going to pay!"

"Hold on. Let's just stay calm. What else did you learn, Val?" I didn't want Selena losing her cool now, endangering herself and everyone else.

"Martina, it gets worse." Val's voice was steady, but I could hear the weight behind it. "My source said there are three teams in the competition. Whoever Derek is working with is only one of the hunters. Derek may be involved, but he's not acting alone."

My mind could barely comprehend what that meant. Three teams were after me? "But why let Lena go? And how does Teresa McDonald play into this?"

"We're not sure, but if you think about the timing, when we found Teresa's body, you were in the Bay Area and rushed back. And then you were back in the Bay Area and Lena escaped. I think it was all to get you back to Red Rose County."

The words landed like a kick to the chest.

"Martina," Selena said, her voice shaking now. "These people have deep pockets. Unlimited resources. This is seriously dangerous."

There was a brief pause before Val added, "Selena is right. We think you should go into protective custody."

My stomach twisted. "I'm not hiding," I said immediately.

"Especially not from a bunch of sick people who think taking lives is a game."

"Listen," Val said. "My source said if we find the current Crown, we'll have the answers we need. But until then, we keep you alive. That means putting you in a safe house."

I snapped. "I'm usually the one protecting everyone else."

"I know," Selena said softly. "But they want you here, to trap you, which means we need to move you. Take you back to the Bay Area. One phone call to Stavros and you'll be in the most secure location possible. Somewhere no one can get to you."

I let out a sharp breath. "So what, you want me holed up in hiding while these psychopaths run around trying to capture me?"

"Martina." Selena, calmer now, met my eyes. "No case is worth dying over. You've told me that a hundred times."

I sat back, the weight of it all pressing down on my chest. It wasn't paranoia or theory. It was real, and it was already in motion. "What do we do about Derek?" I asked.

"We'll take care of Derek," Val said. "We'll pick him up and bring him back to station. We'll try to get him to talk, tell us who he's working with."

Selena said, "I think we should take a crack at him first. We're not bound by red tape. Our interrogation may be... more effective."

There was a pause on the line. "I'm going to pretend I didn't hear that," Val said. "But perhaps we'll let you folks talk to him first, if that's what you're requesting. We'll be there in fifteen minutes."

"We'll see you when you get here."

Val said, "We need to get you out of there, Martina."

"I'll leave when you have him in cuffs." I shoved my phone into my pocket, my fingers moving on muscle memory alone. Outside the car, I popped the trunk and pulled out my gear. The

Kevlar vest slid over my head, the straps biting into my ribs as I secured them tight. Weapon secured, I was ready for *Derek*.

Selena stared at me, startled. I gave her a short nod. "Let's go," and waved to Steve and Otto to follow.

The hotel hallway smelled like stale carpet cleaner and recycled air. My shoes echoed too loudly as I marched down the corridor, adrenaline roaring in my ears. I didn't hesitate, I slammed my fist against Derek's door.

"Martina?" he said when he opened it, blinking. "Is something wrong?"

"Oh yeah," I said, shoving him backward hard enough that he stumbled and fell onto the bed. "Something's very wrong. How about you tell me a little about the Society of the Rose?"

"The—what?" he said, too fast, too rehearsed. "I don't know what you're talking about."

I climbed onto the bed, forcing him flat on his back. "Who are you working with?"

"I don't know what you're talking about," he cried, his face crumpling as he started to sob. "They took me too."

The tears were sloppy. Convincing, if you didn't know what real fear looked like. I glanced at Selena.

She shook her head once. "Wrong answer."

I pressed my knee into his chest, feeling his breath hitch beneath my weight as I took a pair of cuffs off my belt and secured him. Selena rifled through his pockets, fast and efficient, until she pulled out a phone.

With a nod, I pulled Derek up and sat him down in the chair near the desk. "Who sent you?"

"I don't know what you're talking about."

Fists on hips, I said, "We know you're one of them. Are you the one who thinks you'll kidnap and kill me to become the next Crown? Or are you just a little helper?"

Derek paled.

"Who are you really?"

Derek looked away.

"We saw the tattoo. We know you're one of them. Why did you help Lena escape?"

Derek glared at me, "I don't know what you're talking about. I'm a victim."

"He's not going to talk to us. I think we should find out who Derek has been talking to." Selena tapped the screen on his phone. "One number," she murmured. "Let's start there." Selena hit send and raised the phone to her ear.

Derek started to protest, panic breaking through his act, so I clamped my hand over his mouth. "Be quiet," I snapped.

"Hello," Selena said. "This is Selena. Who is this?"

After a beat, she said, "A friend gave it to me."

Selena eyed me, "I'm handing the phone to my friend now."

I took the phone. "This is Martina Monroe. I hear you've been looking for me."

There was no hesitation. "Yes," the voice said. "And I can't wait to meet you in person."

A chill slid down my spine.

The voice said, "See you soon." And the call ended.

"Call Vincent," I said. "Now." Vincent would find the location of the caller. And I would find *him*. If he was looking for the ultimate challenge, then he'd just hit the jackpot.

42

MARTINA

A SHARP KNOCK at the door pulled my attention away from Derek. "Selena, get that," I said, without taking my eyes off him.

She opened the door to find Val, Brady, and several uniformed deputies standing in the hallway. The sight of them should have brought relief, but it didn't. "I've already cuffed him."

Val's gaze flicked to Derek, then back to me. "Did he say anything?"

"No. Nothing useful." Should I tell her I'd spoken to one of them? That I'd heard the voice of someone hunting me? We'd given the phone number to Vincent to trace. We hadn't heard back yet. It would take time, but I knew they'd move heaven and earth to find the location. Still, time felt like a luxury we didn't have. What had started as a missing person case had turned into something else entirely, a game. A deadly one. And the end goal for the killer wasn't Lena. *It was me.*

People like this shouldn't be free. They shouldn't get to sip champagne at country clubs while deciding who lived and who died. The Society of the Rose needed to end, for good.

I'd taken down criminal organizations before. Trafficking

rings and murderers who thought they were untouchable. But this was different. These people lived in the shadows and were insulated by their power and wealth.

But I had the best people in the world at my firm, and we would find them. And we would make sure they spent the rest of their lives in prison instead of planning their next kill.

"We got his phone," I said. "We talked to one of them."

Val's raised a brow. "We'll take it from here, Martina. We need to get you somewhere safe."

I glanced at Selena. Her face was rigid with anger, hands clenched at her sides.

"Yes. But there's someone I need to talk to first."

Val followed my gaze. "Joe Sapphire."

"Exactly."

I turned back to Derek and stepped close enough that he flinched. "This isn't the end," I said. "You'll know when it is."

His eyes darted away.

"Those bracelets I put on you? That's just the beginning," I continued, my voice cold. "You will never be free again. I will make it my mission, if it's the last thing I ever do, to make sure you spend the rest of your life in prison."

I didn't wait for a response. I stormed out, Selena right behind me, my pulse hammering as we moved three doors down to Joe Sapphire's room. I knocked hard. Movement on the other side. Shuffling. A pause. Finally, the door opened.

"Martina? Selena?" Joe said, forcing a weak smile. "Is everything okay? I was just on a call—"

"No," I snapped. "Everything is *not* okay."

His shoulders sagged immediately.

"May we come in?"

"Sure," he said, stepping aside.

Selena shut the door behind us with a solid click. Joe stood there, suddenly smaller than I remembered. His eyes were bloodshot. His hands trembled. Glaring at him, I said, "It's time to tell the truth."

"I don't know what you're talking about," he said, though his voice cracked halfway through the sentence.

"We know about the Society. We know Lena was bait. We know the goal was to kidnap me—and ultimately—kill me. It's why *you* hired me."

His face drained of color.

"You're part of this. You always were."

He opened his mouth, but Selena cut him off. "Save it," she commanded. "We know you're involved. Now, we want details. We want names. This ends *now*."

Joe staggered back, collapsing into the chair like his legs had finally given out. He buried his face in his hands. "You don't understand. You have no idea what they're capable of."

Selena moved in closer. "Oh, we understand just fine. And if you don't start talking, you're going to see what *I'm* capable of."

He shook in his chair.

My anger burned hot. This man had played on my heart-strings. He'd looked me in the eye and talked about his missing daughter, knowing I'd lived that nightmare myself. That wasn't desperation. That was manipulation. "Who contacted you about Lena's disappearance?" I asked. "Or were you part of the entire game from the beginning? Are you one of them?"

"I'm so sorry. I couldn't let them hurt Lena." He looked away, staring at the wall, then back at me, his eyes hollow. "I didn't know what the plan was. All I knew was that I had to hire you to find her. I swear that's all I knew. I didn't know what they were going to do."

"And if you had known? Would it have been okay with you if they killed me to save your daughter?"

He bowed his head, shame pouring off him in waves.

The silence pressed in around us.

It made me wonder, briefly, what I would do for my own daughter. For Selena. The answer came fast. I would find her and I would save her. I would never sacrifice an innocent person to do it.

"Who contacted you?" I demanded. "Who told you to hire me?"

Joe shook his head again, a single tear slipping from the corner of his eye. "I'm so sorry."

Selena leaned in, her rage sharp enough to cut. "We know everything, Joe. We know about the Society of the Rose. We know the Crown is up for grabs. We know people are competing for it, and that killing Martina is the target."

Joe flinched.

"Are you a member?"

He shook his head.

Selena demanded, "Let me see your lower back."

He stood and lifted the back of his polo shirt, without questioning why. *Because he knew why.* "I'm not one of them."

Confirmed by the fact he didn't have the rose tattoo. How did he know that's what we were looking for? "How do you know about the Society?"

He looked away. He had to know some members to know what we were looking for. But who? From what we understood, they're highly secretive.

Selena stepped closer to Joe, her voice rising in anger. "We want to know who told you to hire Martina. And don't bother trying to protect them, because every single one of them is going down. This isn't something we'll back away from. Now that we know they exist, we won't stop until they're all locked up."

I watched Joe crumble under her words. His shoulders sagged. His breathing became uneven. Selena was fiercely protective, and I appreciated every second of it.

Part of me was still in a state of shock that all of this was happening. That the entire investigation was a ruse to trap and murder me. "Who told you to hire me?" I asked again.

He sniffled, defeated. "My wife."

The words hit like a gunshot. "Who told your wife to hire me?"

Joe looked at me, with eyes full of regret and shame. The expression made my stomach drop. "No," I said quietly. "She's not—"

He nodded.

And then buried his face in his hands.

My mind swirled as the pieces of the puzzle came into view. There was going to be a vacancy for the Crown. His wife was terminally ill. I stepped back, the room suddenly too small. The Crown's position was coming open because the current Crown had stage 4 breast cancer with only days or weeks to live.

"She's the Crown," I said incredulously.

Joe lifted his head and nodded once more.

The truth settled over me, practically suffocating me. Lena's own mother had approved her kidnapping and green-lit my abduction, and my murder, in order to secure her successor before she died. Not to mention, the lives she must have taken to achieve her position as the Crown.

Selena and I exchanged a look. "Well," Selena said grimly, "I know exactly who I'd like to pay a visit to."

"She can't know I told you," Joe said, desperately. "Please."

"How long have you known?"

"I didn't," he sobbed. "Not until she got sick. Not until she told me what was going to happen to Lena."

His body shook as the weight of it crushed him. But my sympathy was gone. He'd made his choice, and it sealed his fate. But the Crown had made a much more foolish choice. Alice Sapphire's decision to target me had marked the beginning of the Society's end.

43

MARTINA

FILLED with rage and disbelief and sadness, I stood quietly in the hallway as Selena paced back and forth, her footsteps soft but restless. "What are we going to do, Martina?"

I shook my head slowly. There were too many things we needed to do, and no clear place to start. Was Lena safe? That was the question that mattered most. I supposed we could ask her mother. *She would know.* My gut said Lena was out of danger's way, but considering her own mother set the whole thing up, it was anyone's guess.

Down the hall, Val stepped out of Derek's room. When she saw us, she walked over, her expression guarded. "He's on his way to the station."

"Good." Hopefully, his incarceration was permanent.

"How did things go with Joe?"

I filled her in on the entire conversation, including the revelation that his wife was the Crown. Val stood there, either processing or too stunned to speak. I wasn't sure which.

"We haven't talked to Lena yet," Selena said. "We don't know what she knows, or if she was in on the whole thing from the beginning."

She looked at Val, then at me.

I hadn't suspected Lena of being involved. If she were, I doubted they would've sent Derek in to help her escape. And she'd been so visibly shaken by the ordeal. But then again, she could simply be a great actress.

"We should talk to her," Selena said.

"I agree. But I think we need to get you out of Red Rose County," Val said, eyeing me.

"I'm definitely leaving," I said. "That's for sure. What are you going to do with Joe?"

"I'm not sure yet. Why don't you go talk to Lena, and I'll talk to Joe. I don't want him running back to the Bay Area and telling his wife we're onto them. If we want to catch these people, it's better if they don't know we're looking for them."

"Agreed," I said. "I'll talk to Lena. Jason's in there too. We'll see what we can find out."

Val nodded, still stoic. She hadn't commented on the fact that Lena's mother was the Crown. The one who had approved this entire operation *from her deathbed*. How cold did you have to be to do something like that? As your last dying act, to have your own daughter kidnapped just to lure out a renowned private investigator to be captured and killed? What was *wrong* with these people?

"All right," Val said. "We'll check back in."

We knocked. The door opened shortly after, Jason standing there. Lena sat in the background, perched on a chair near the desk, her shoulders slumped, her face pale. "Come in," Jason said.

He shut the door behind us, and Selena and I perched once again on the edge of the bed across from Lena. "There have been some developments."

"Oh?"

"We know who's behind your kidnapping."

Her eyes widened. "You know who did this to me? Is Derek okay? Have they found him?"

"We actually believe he was involved with your abduction and that the escape was planned."

She scrunched up her face. "I don't understand. He was with the kidnappers?"

"Yes. It was all staged," I said. "You were never intended to be hurt."

Her face paled and tears welled in her eyes.

Calmly, I said, "Did you know they were going to take you that night?"

"No," she said, shaking her head furiously. "No. I would have never agreed to that. I would never have agreed to be burned and chained up. Are you sure Derek's one of them? He seemed so genuine."

"We're 100% sure," Selena answered.

With widened eyes, she said, "So there was three of them?"

Studying her face, I believed she was genuinely surprised. I said, "There are more than three." Glancing over at Jason, I wondered if he was part of the Society. "Jason, do you have a tattoo?"

"No." He said, looking a bit puzzled.

"Can you lift the back of your shirt, please?" Selena asked.

He did without hesitation. There were no marks. He wasn't one of them. If that were true, he probably didn't know the Society existed. I turned back to him. "Do you know if any of your friends have a tattoo of a rose on their back or side?"

Jason frowned, clearly confused. "None that I know of. My male friends—"

"Or female," Selena added.

"No, I don't think so."

He'd known Ethan since childhood, and should know if he had a tattoo, but not necessarily. Especially if Ethan had gotten the tattoo recently. Or he didn't have one. If Ethan wasn't a member of this Society, was it really possible that his setup at the house hadn't actually been connected to the kidnapping? It felt like too much of a coincidence for that to ring true.

Looking at Lena, I said, "You're sure you didn't know about any of this? This wasn't one of your pranks?"

"No," she said firmly.

I nodded.

"Wait," she said. "Does that mean I was never really in danger? But Derek, his face was bruised—"

"He took a few hits to play the part," Selena said matter-of-factly.

Lena looked like she was going to cry. "Does Dad know that this was all for—" Her voice cracked. "Wait. If I wasn't in danger, then why did they take me?"

Meeting her gaze, I said, "It's my understanding it was to get to me."

"To get to you? So they took me because of you, not because of me?"

"Yes."

Lena looked beyond perplexed. I glanced over at Selena, and she gave me a quick nod. We were in agreement. Lena didn't know about the kidnapping. She wasn't involved. And she would probably be devastated if she ever learned the truth about her father, and her mother. *Her mother.* Cold. Calculating. Murderous. The thought made my stomach twist.

"It's likely you're safe to go back to the Bay Area, but let me speak with Val and see if she still needs you here."

"Okay."

"We'll let you know what we find out. Just sit tight for now."

As we stepped out into the hall, my heart broke a little more for Lena. She'd been through a life-altering ordeal and to add insult to injury, it was at the hands of her own *mother.*

Out in the hall, Selena and I waited. Voices echoed down the corridor, raised voices. Val's voice, unmistakable. She was furious. Whatever Joe Sapphire had said hadn't gone over well. A few minutes later, Val emerged, her face flushed red, her body tense. "Unbelievable."

That was my thought too.

"Unfortunately, we don't really have anything to charge him with," Val said. "But we don't want him going back and alerting his wife. And like I said, I don't think you're safe here."

With a quick nod, I said, "We're leaving now."

"How did things go with Lena?"

"Well, we spoke. I don't think she's involved or knew anything about the plan. I don't think Jason did either. We checked, he doesn't have the tattoo. He said none of his friends have one either, which means Ethan doesn't have one, if he's telling us the truth."

Val went quiet, thinking. She ran her fingers through her shoulder-length dark hair. "Then why would Ethan create the perfect setting for her to be abducted?"

"Maybe a favor for someone?" Selena offered.

"A favor," Val repeated. "When I questioned Mrs. Sapphire, I asked her about Ethan—whether they got along. She said he was a good kid. I thought that was strange at the time, because... well, nobody else described him that way."

Selena and I nodded. "Maybe she asked him for a favor. Maybe she lied and told him it was a surprise for her or something like that. Or maybe she was blackmailing him and didn't tell him any details of the plan."

"We won't know until we ask her, and him," Val said. "We need to get back to the Bay Area."

"Agreed."

"Let me talk to Brady," Val said. "We'll either try to keep Joe here to silence him or we'll have to release him. But maybe we can bring him down to the station for official statements. Either way, I'll buy you some time to get out of here. Your company has a safe house set up?"

"We do."

Val said, "Where's your team?"

I turned to where Otto and Steve, my bodyguards, stood. *Bodyguards.* I couldn't believe it. I'd sworn I wasn't taking another dangerous case, and here I was, surrounded by my own security detail. "They've been watching us this whole time. They can't get to me."

"Good."

"We're going head out now. Let's keep in touch."

"Will do," Val said. "Be safe, Martina."

"I will."

I glanced back at Steve and Otto, two of our toughest body-guards, and headed down the stairs toward the parking lot.

The wind moved through the trees, rustling leaves that had kept dark secrets for decades. How many victims had there been? All hidden in the woods, nature itself almost laughing like a cruel joke, beauty and ugliness intertwined. It felt good to be getting the heck out of there.

Inside my car, I pressed the button to start the engine.

Click.

That was odd. Maybe I'd left a light on and killed the battery. I tried again.

Click.

Selena screamed, "Get out of the car!"

And then it hit me, too late to think, and only time to move.

I shoved the door open and ran.

The impact slammed into my chest like a solid wall, knocking the air from my lungs. There was no sound at first, just a crushing pressure, like the world folding inward. I was airborne for a split second, and then I crashed into the ground. I hit hard. Everything went white. Then black. Then nothing at all. I lay there, stunned, my ears ringing, or maybe not ringing at all. I couldn't tell. I couldn't hear anything. Smoke burned my throat. Heat pressed against my back. I tried to move and didn't understand why my body wouldn't listen. *Selena.* The thought cut through the haze like a blade. Where was Selena?

44

MARTINA

PANIC FILLED every cell in my body. Quickly, I tried to roll onto my side. Gravel bit into my cheek as I tried to push myself up onto my knees. I was only moderately successful. My body didn't seem to understand what I was asking it to do. I scanned the parking lot, searching for Selena. It was quiet, too quiet. I'd lost my hearing. The high-pitched whine was distant and wrong, like it belonged to someone else. Then my ears rang as sound rushed back in all at once. There was shouting, and boots pounding the pavement. Someone was yelling my name.

"Martina!"

I wanted to answer, but it felt like it would take too much energy. Energy I didn't have. Hands were suddenly on me, steadying me, helping me upright. It was Otto. "Are you okay? Can you hear me?"

I just stared at him.

"Blink if you can hear me."

I blinked once. Then a second time.

"Good," he said. "We're going to get you to the hospital."

"Selena," I said, using every ounce of strength I had left.

Otto turned, and my eyes followed his.

Steve was on the ground, kneeling. I saw an outstretched hand. *Selena.* I tried to move toward her.

"Hold on," Otto said, practically carrying me as we crossed the pavement.

As we approached, Steve was helping Selena sit up. "Are you okay?" I asked. It felt like I was shouting, but I knew it was barely more than a whisper.

She looked up at me and nodded.

My legs gave out. Otto caught me, lowering me gently back onto the ground.

"Okay," he said calmly. "Let's take it easy. We're staying put. Okay, Martina?"

I complied.

More voices. More feet. Shoes running on pavement.

I glanced up and saw Val and Brady. "Are you all right?" Val asked, her head tilting slightly.

She turned to Selena, who raised her hand weakly. We were both still on the ground.

Brady pulled out his radio, calling in an ambulance, and alerting them to what had happened.

Someone handed me a bottle of water. I drank, the coolness soothing my throat. I took slow, deep breaths, forcing my nerves to settle. It was the second bomb detonated in my presence in Red Rose County. Somebody liked blowing things up. One of the contestants?

No one spoke after that. Just the shuffle of movement as Selena and I were carried away from the scene. Probably a precaution in case there was a secondary explosion planned.

These people wanted me dead so badly it didn't matter who I was with or who else got hurt. Anyone around me was at risk. Which meant I couldn't go home. I couldn't be with Charlie or anyone I cared about. I couldn't be with anyone at all. I had to be vigilant. Check everything. I hadn't expected a car bomb. I'd thought there would be a kidnapping first. But thinking back to the Bridgerton house, the one that exploded just before we arrived, I should have known better.

With three different killers coming after me, it made sense they'd use different tactics. One wanted me blown up wherever I stood. Another wanted me kidnapped and killed quietly. Or maybe the game was escalating because someone knew we were onto them. Or maybe they'd simply decided to end it once and for all. Stop the questions. Stop the investigation. And they knew there was only one way to do that. Take me out. No ceremony. No pomp. No circumstance. Just end me. All for some sick, twisted club. More than ever, I knew I had to take them down, one by one, starting with the Crown.

45

MARTINA

With a heaviness settling deep in my chest, I ended the call. The sound of Charlie's voice had warmed me, but it only sharpened the sadness that followed, knowing I couldn't go home to him. What I wouldn't give to be snuggled next to him on the couch, our little dog Barney curled up on my lap, eating popcorn and watching a movie. Why had I taken this case? Why hadn't I just said no?

My half of the hospital room was quiet now. The hallway lights were dimmed, everything washed in a pale, faded glow. No windows. Just a sad little corner of a hospital emergency room, cut off from the world.

The curtain pulled back, and a nurse in rose-colored scrubs beside a doctor in a white coat approached. The doctor asked, "How are you feeling?"

"Like I was just thrown to the ground and run over," I said, trying, and failing, to make a joke.

The nurse smiled politely and slipped a blood pressure cuff around my arm. It tightened, squeezing until my fingers tingled.

"So Doc, what's the verdict?" I'd already gone in for X-ray and a CT scan. They'd taken enough blood to run all the tests.

"Well, you've got a mild concussion and some bruising," the doctor said. "But the good news is, there doesn't appear to be any internal bleeding."

"When can I go home?"

"Because of the concussion, we recommend you stay overnight for monitoring."

That certainly wasn't going to happen. "This isn't my first mild concussion."

Across the bay, I heard Selena's voice. If I didn't know any better, I'd say she was feeling okay. She was talking adamantly, complaining that she wanted a Sprite instead of 7-Up.

I could have cried happy tears. She'd be fine. *Thank the Lord.*

The doctor, with her shiny spectacles, studied me for a moment. "Do you have someone who can stay with you overnight? Someone to check on you?"

"I have a whole team, Doc."

She hesitated. "I can't make you stay if you want to go."

"I want to go."

She nodded slowly. "There's no medical reason you can't. Everything looks okay, aside from the concussion. But your body's been through a traumatic event. You need rest."

I'll rest when this is over. "Can you pull back the curtain so I can see Selena?"

"Of course," the nurse said, hurrying to do so.

The curtain slid back, and there she was. My bonus daughter. Seeing her sitting up, animated, very much herself again, sent a wave of relief through me so strong it made my heart swell. She was okay. And for now, that was enough.

"How are you feeling?" she asked apprehensively.

"I'm fine. They're going to have to try harder than that to keep me down."

She smirked. "No doubt. Martina, were you talking to Dad?"

"Yeah. I talked to him. He sends his love and asks for you to call him."

She nodded, then her expression shifted. "We're headed home after this, right? Like... we're getting out of here?"

"We are."

The doctor said, "You do need to take it easy, Martina."

Selena snorted. "She doesn't know the meaning of such a thing. But I'll keep an eye on her."

The confidence in her voice was incredible. She had bruising on her face, little cuts and scratches, but she was clearly doing just fine. *To be young again.* To be able to bounce back like that. If I were being honest, I felt every bruise and scrape along with the massive headache.

On the other side of Selena's bed, Steve and Otto stood quietly, watchful as ever.

The doctor said, "We'll give you some space. But you take care of yourself Martina. You too, Selena."

"Thank you."

Selena waved as the nurse and doctor left.

Once we were alone, I looked at Otto. "What's the plan?"

"Well, as you can imagine, we can't completely confirm your safety here. They saw you in the parking lot. They could have eyes inside the hospital."

My stomach flip-flopped.

"We want to move you right away. You and Selena both."

Selena said, "All right. Let's go."

She started climbing out of the hospital bed, still wearing a white gown covered in little blue flowers. She paused, looked down at herself, then back up at me.

"Well," she said, "after we get dressed, of course."

I shook my head, unable to stop myself from smiling. Despite the darkness that weighed heavy, there was always a reason to smile. Sometimes you had to look for it, and sometimes it was standing right in front of you, stubborn and bruised.

"We talked to Stavros," Otto said. "We're putting you in one of our top-level security spots. Nobody will find you."

I thought about that for a moment. Stavros was the one who'd pushed Joe Sapphire onto me. I highly doubted he knew about any of this, but did he understand what was really going on? I hadn't spoken to him since we arrived. "Did you tell Stavros what was happening?"

"Just that there was an attempt on your life," Otto said.

"I'll talk to him later."

Selena hurriedly pulled on her jeans and threw on a top, not bothering with modesty. Not that Steve or Otto would be looking.

There was a knock on the door. Steve rushed over to check, then turned back. "It's Val."

I said, "Let her in."

Selena was still hooked up to an IV, so she hopped back onto the bed, fully dressed. I swear that girl had nine lives, like a cat.

Val stepped inside, her expression all business. "How are you two holding up?"

"Well enough."

She got straight to it. "The fire chief and his team did a sweep around the car. No secondary devices. No obvious trigger point. Whoever did this wasn't nearby. They were watching from a distance."

"We figured as much."

"Our bomb experts are still investigating. They're hoping to find some sort of signature, anything that connects it to the explosion at the Bridgerton house and other bombings that could help us find who's behind it. It's possible they're not in the Society and they just do freelance work for them."

Those unlimited resources could go a long way. "Okay."

She shifted, lowering her voice. "We also pulled security footage from the hotel parking lot and the surrounding area."

My chest tightened. "How far did you look?"

"We pulled traffic cams within a two-mile radius, but all the feeds were dark for about an hour before and after the explosion."

"Dark how?"

"Looped," Val said. "Pre-recorded footage. Same thing with the hotel cameras. Clean splice. Whoever did this knew exactly which cameras mattered."

"They planned it," I said. "And they've been watching."

"It's easy to do," Selena added, "when you've got a lot of money and a sick mind."

Val didn't disagree.

"Where are Joe and Lena?" I asked.

"We brought them down to the station. We're taking official statements and holding them until we're comfortable releasing them back to the Bay Area. And the two of you, when are you heading to the safe house?"

"As soon as we get dressed and they take out the IVs."

"We'll keep this going while you're away. Don't worry, we've got this. I'm bringing in some of my pals at the FBI since they found some unsolved cases with the rose branding in both California and Nevada."

There was no way I was just sitting back and letting someone else take over the case. I might be going into hiding, but I wasn't handing over the investigation. Not now. Not after this. Val must have sensed my hesitation.

"We can handle this, Martina. We'll question Alice Sapphire. We'll get to the bottom of it. You don't need to worry. You need to get rest and stay safe."

"I *am* worried."

"Look. They didn't just try to kill you. They nearly killed

Selena and Brady and me too. They don't care who's near you when they strike, everyone else is just collateral damage. So if you don't care about yourself, care about the people around you."

"That's exactly why we're being careful."

Val looked me straight in the eyes. "We have leads, and we're following them. We'll keep in touch throughout the investigation. I'll give you the number to an encrypted phone so you can reach me. I'm guessing you'll have one too."

"Of course. I'll pick mine up when we head back to the Bay Area. I'll let you know when we arrive."

"Take care of yourself, Martina. You too, Selena."

I waved.

Steve and Otto were already moving. "We'll be right outside," Otto said. "Let us know when you're ready. We've got a van and we're ready to move."

I agreed, but as I gathered myself, one thought cut through everything else. Before we went to the safe house, there was one stop we needed to make.

46

THE ARCHITECT

WITH THE STATE of the competition, it wasn't a surprise the Crown had called a meeting. She was still with us, therefore still the ultimate authority. Succession was a fragile thing, and discretion mattered now more than ever. One misstep, one poorly chosen act, and the scales could tip against us.

We stood in a line beside her hospital bed. Her second-in-command, the Bishop, stood at her side like a shadow.

The Crown turned her head slightly toward me, her movements slow. Her eyes were glassy, but sharp. "What is the status of the task?"

I glanced at my two competitors before answering. "There have been two direct attempts," I said with confidence. "Both aimed at completing the game. Both failed. And both were similar in nature. That means a pattern. A pattern that could be traced back to us if this continues." After a brief pause, I said, "I believe competitor number three should be eliminated from the competition."

Her gaze shifted to my rival. The one who had outsourced the task. The one responsible for the attempted bombings on the Ladybug. It was sloppy and reeked of cowardice. I preferred to be face-to-face. Hand to hand. That was true power. And that was exactly how I intended to claim the win.

My competitor cleared his throat. "True," he said, forcing calm into his voice. "It wasn't the best tactic. I admit that a third attempt might give law enforcement too much to work with." He turned his head slightly, meeting my eyes. "And you," he added. "You still believe it's feasible to attain the target?"

The second competitor spoke before I could. "Yes. We think she's headed back to the Bay Area. She could already be back. We believe they're putting her in hiding. She knows she's the target."

The Crown's brow furrowed slightly. "How on earth would she know that?"

It was a fair question. One we didn't have a solid answer for. "I don't know," I admitted. "She must have figured it out somehow. Perhaps the two attempts made her realize she was the common denominator. Or someone is talking to her and warning her that she's the target."

The Crown shifted against the pillows, irritation flashing across her pale face. "Where is my husband?"

"He's in Red Rose County," I said. "With Lena."

Her eyes narrowed. "Why are they still there?"

"We aren't sure. Apparently, they need them for questioning. And our Pursuer has been arrested."

"Why?"

"We're unsure."

The Crown shook her head slowly, disgust curling her lip. "Are any of you capable of completing this task?" Her gaze cut sharply to the competitor who had outsourced the attempt and back to us. "And you two. I have seen nothing from either of you. What exactly have you been doing? Perhaps none of you shall ascend to the throne." Then she turned to the Bishop. "Perhaps the competition should be eliminated entirely. And the Bishop shall rise to the Crown."

Outrageous. I reminded her, "It's never been done that way."

Her head snapped toward me. "I *am* the Crown," she said, her voice hard despite its weakness. "And I shall decide. I can rewrite the rules if I choose. It is not worth my legacy, or our society, to continue this foolishness. You've had plenty of time to complete the competition. And you have *all* failed."

My pulse hammered in my ears. "I have someone watching her."

"Really?" the Crown asked. "Where is she right now?"

"As of the last report, I've been told she's back in the Bay Area. Still en route to her destination. We believe they're moving her to a secure location."

"And you have a car following them?"

"I do," I assured her.

Out of the corner of my eye, I saw competitor number two stiffen. Surprise flickered across his face. I would win and I would be the next Crown. "I will achieve this goal," I said firmly. "I will not be caught. I will not tarnish your legacy, or the reputation of our society. You have my word."

The Crown studied me for a long moment and then turned to my competitor. "Competitor Three, you are no longer in the running. You may leave."

His face fell, shoulders sunk. He bowed his head and exited. He deserved to be eliminated, he'd acted like an amateur.

"As for the two of you, you have three days to complete the competition," she said. "If, by the end of three days, the Ladybug still walks this earth, none of you will ever ascend to the Crown. Do you understand?"

She broke into a fit of coughing, the words rasping out as her body betrayed her. She didn't look well. Not at all. And yet, the spite and fire in her eyes remained untouched.

"Understood," I said.

"Understood," my remaining competitor echoed.

"Good," the Crown said weakly. "Then I need my rest. I expect full reports daily. You may go."

We nodded in unison.

And then, a crash sounded down the hall. It was as if someone had slammed a door wide open.

"What was that?" the Crown demanded.

All eyes turned to the Bishop. "I'll go see," he said, moving toward the door.

The Crown said, "If needed, execute the protocol."

"Understood, ma'am." But before he reached the door, shouting erupted, footsteps pounding down the hall. Then the door to the Crown's room burst open.

47

MARTINA

OUR EYES LOCKED from across the room. There lay the woman who had sanctioned my kidnapping and murder. I stood with my bodyguards and Selena beside me, the weight of the moment pressing into my chest. Then I stepped forward, crossing the threshold into the room.

Three men surrounded her. I didn't recognize any of them. The oldest stood closest to the bed, his posture protective. "Can I help you?" he asked.

"I'm here to speak with Mrs. Sapphire."

He turned to her. A small smile curved her lips. "It's fine," she said. To the men, she said, "We'll speak later. Leave us."

The men hesitated, their eyes never leaving me as they filed out, each one clearly sizing me up. I wondered, briefly, if they were part of the Society. If they already knew exactly who, and what, I was standing in front of.

Alice Sapphire shifted, already sitting upright in the hospital bed, pale but composed. With a small smile, she said, "I'm so glad you're here. I want to thank you for all the work you've done to find Lena. I hear she's safe and sound in Red Rose County."

She tilted her head. "Do you know when she'll be coming back home?"

I closed my eyes for a moment, then opened them. "She's safe and sound in Red Rose County because I have people protecting her," I said with an accusatory tone.

She glanced toward the door where the men had exited, then back to me. "Well, that's good to hear," she said calmly. "Is there anything else I can do for you? I'm very tired. I'm not well."

"Yes, I understand that, Mrs. Sapphire. And yet you still put your daughter through the trauma of being kidnapped. Being held captive, terrified and alone. Burned and branded with your society's mark." My voice hardened. "She'll never be the same. And knowing her own mother was responsible—"

"I don't know what you're talking about," she interrupted. "I think you're confused."

"I'm not confused. I know you are the Crown, the head of the Society of the Rose. I know you orchestrated your daughter's kidnapping so that your husband would hire me in order to lure me to Red Rose County."

Her smile didn't waver.

"So that three of your underlings could compete for the Crown and ascend to the top after your death. The winner being the one who kidnapped and killed me first." I moved closer. "What kind of person does that? What kind of mother?" Now inches from her face, I said "You. *That's who.*"

Her eyes flickered.

"We know everything," I said. "You're going down. And not only that, your daughter is going to know what you did. What your husband did."

"You can't prove anything, Miss Monroe," she said coolly.

Shaking my head, I said, "But I can. But what I don't understand is how you got Ethan to set up the kidnapping. To shut off the security cameras. To lure her outside with some stupid prank."

She smirked then. Her eyes darkened, her true nature slipping through the cracks. "I don't know what you mean. Ethan's a good boy." She leaned back against the pillows. "You're out of your league, Miss Monroe. Now, if you don't mind, I'd appreciate you leaving. I'm very tired."

"I want names. I'm taking down the organization once and for all."

Her voice dropped to a gravelly whisper. "You don't know what you're dealing with. If you were smart, you'd leave now and watch your back." She smiled. "They're not finished with you."

Selena walked up to Alice. "And we're not finished with you!" She lifted her phone, the screen glowing. "I've been recording this entire conversation. Everyone is going to know who and what you really are."

The satisfaction drained from Alice Sapphire's face. In an instant, she morphed back into the sick, dying woman in the hospital bed. "What are you going to do? If you haven't noticed, I'm dying and have nothing left to lose."

"Is that right?" I held her gaze. "You don't care about your family name? Your legacy?"

With a gaze that could set a forest fire, she said, "Please leave."

"Not until you call it off. It's *over*. This little competition is over and so is the Society of the Rose."

Her true self reemerged and a devilish grin appeared on her face. "Good luck, Ms. Monroe."

Before I could protest, a tight boom sounded beneath us and the floor shuddered. Otto was already moving, sprinting to my side. "We need to get you out of here. Now."

As he pulled me toward the door, I glanced back at the

Crown. She was smiling. Not startled. Not confused. *Satisfied.* The blast hadn't been meant for us. Somewhere below, something had just been wiped clean, and I had a bad feeling that it was evidence that could have helped us take them down.

48

VAL

As I RUSHED toward the station, I thought, *What a week.* Checking the time again, I was late and didn't want to miss the meeting. But I had to step out when I received the phone call from Martina. She had gone to the Sapphire house to confront Alice Sapphire, only to be dragged out when what sounded like a small explosive detonated inside. The blast hadn't been big enough to damage much of the house, but it had been enough to convince her the conversation was over.

Martina theorized the explosion hadn't actually put her in danger. I wasn't so sure. The only comfort I held was that Martina and Selena were finally in the safe house.

Even so, I worried about her. The more I learned about the Society of the Rose, the more disturbing it became. Once I told the FBI we had intel, that we knew who the Crown was, they assembled a task force and requested a meeting in Red Rose County. Apparently, the Society had been on their radar for a while. Mostly rumors that never quite solidified into proof. But now we had something concrete. The branding. The rose. The one consistent indicator that our victim had died at the hands of the Society. It was a trail to follow.

My contact and former supervisor at the FBI, Kieran Fox, explained that investigations had been initiated in the past but had been quickly shut down. Every time with the same unspoken implication. That the heads of organizations, directors of the FBI, members of the CIA, the president, members of Congress, senators, and powerful people, had ties to the Society. Or worse, were part of it. And not a single one wanted the members to be exposed.

Kieran warned me this was dangerous territory. That we should back down and let the FBI handle it from there. Ignoring that advice, as I'm sure Kieran expected, I decided to hear them out and see what their plan was.

With or without them, I would keep investigating and try to put together a case. One little problem though, we didn't have a killer's name tied directly to Teresa McDonald's body, or who actually took Lena.

But if we could prove the Crown was the head of this organization, it wasn't any different from organized crime. All we had to show was that the Crown approved it, and that she and her members were complicit. The trouble was, she didn't have long to live and prosecuting just her wasn't going to be enough.

In my head, I kept picturing people in cloaks, chanting around a fire in the middle of a forest. Primitive and ritualistic. But I didn't actually know what they did behind closed doors. I was hoping the FBI could finally shine a light into what they were really like. Lucy jogged up to me, breathless. "They're here."

Lucy was joining me in the meeting, along with Brady. Lucy had found a few cold cases that she thought could be connected to the Society. Unfortunately, none of them were recent, but it could show a pattern of crimes by the organization. Some of the murders were thirty, forty, and even fifty years old. Going through the autopsy photos had been grueling. Bodies laid out on stainless steel tables, grainy images yellowed with time. But all of them had one thing in common, a rose burned into their flesh. The most peculiar thing was that the only new victim in the past two decades was Teresa McDonald. Maybe they'd learned a few decades back that it was easier to get away with murder when there was no body to examine.

Inside the conference room, Brady was already seated. Lucy and I were the latecomers. I gave a quick wave and took the empty chair next to Brady, Lucy settling in on my left. Kieran looked over at me with a familiar smirk. "You're not very good at being retired, Val."

I shrugged. "Hey, the serial killers come to me now, I don't go looking for them."

He grinned. "You are quite the killer magnet."

Low chuckles rippled around the table, before Kieran continued, "Val, let's start with what you know, and then we'll get into what the FBI has and what the plan is."

With a nod, I said, "We know of one kidnapping victim, Lena Sapphire, was the bait for the current target, Martina Monroe. And we have the body of Teresa McDonald. Lucy's also found a few others, decades old, we believe are connected. We have one presumed member in custody, and we have identified the head, or the Crown of the Society, Alice Sapphire."

Kieran nodded. "That's a lot to learn in a week. Now, lets's hand this over to Guy Mortenson. He's heading the task force, but I'll be here for moral support."

He gave me an encouraging wink. I suspected he'd really come to check on me as opposed to getting his hands dirty. He knew I didn't always play by the rules, something that had been difficult when I was a federal agent. Now I was just a citizen working with the sheriff's department, trying to convince the FBI to let me help for, at least, as long as it took to take the organization down.

Guy cleared his throat. "Yeah, we found a few, thanks to your team's investigative skills, including Ms. Monroe's." He paused. "I understand she's not able to be here."

"She's in a secure location," I said. "We've been communicating through encrypted phones. They're actively going after her. From what we understand, there are three different assassin-type members vying for the top spot. To get there, they have to kill Martina. So she's under lock and key."

Guy nodded grimly. "Good. These aren't people you want to mess with. If they want her dead, they're not going to stop trying, especially if killing her is the price of ascension."

"What do you know about them? What should we expect? All we have is this case and some older ones we believe are connected. Is this literally just some twisted fraternity, or sorority, killing people because they have nothing better to do with their money and time?"

Guy didn't hesitate. "It goes deeper than that. We believe the Society of the Rose started over a hundred years ago. We've spoken to a few former members, people who managed to get out. They've told us what they were told over the years, by other members. It's as close to fact as we can get at this point. These aren't people who keep records. The only thing they do record is their crimes. They're used as evidence for promotion. We've been told they're destroyed after they are viewed by the group." He paused, letting that sink in. "They're stealth. Invisible when they want to be. So keep in mind, some of this is lore, some of it is fact. We're not one hundred percent sure which is which."

"Understood."

"Okay," Guy continued. "The Society of the Rose started over a hundred years ago on the East Coast, at an Ivy League school. From there, it eventually moved west to Red Rose County."

I let out a small gasp before I could stop myself. They'd been there the whole time. How had nobody known?

"Apparently," Guy went on, "this is where they conduct their meetings. And it appears some of their kidnappings and killings."

He gestured vaguely, as if mapping it out in the air. "The thinking is that this area became a haven for those that settled into metropolitan areas on the west coast: California, Nevada, Washington, and Oregon. They vacation here in their second, third, or fourth homes. It's nobody's primary residence."

"It's a perfect spot if you want privacy."

"Exactly. It's remote with plenty of places to hide bodies. Plenty of places for secrecy. When they started the organization, they built a hierarchy. Five levels."

The room went still.

"The first level is the Initiate. New members. Invited by a current member. Sometimes by family members. Legacies get preferential treatment. It includes men and women. Equal opportunity psychopaths."

A few uneasy shifts around the table.

"Once an initiate commits their first violent act, sometimes something as minor as a bar fight, beating someone in the street and getting away with it, they rise to level two: the Blooded."

Lucy's pen paused mid-note.

"At that level, they participate in a kill, but they're not the actual killer. They're being trained. Taught how to hunt. How to clean up. How to disappear. Think of them as apprentices. They don't have much power yet within the Society. After assisting a higher-level member, they move to level three. They become the Pursuers. At that level they're given tasks. It's basically like, we showed you how to do it, now go do it according to the plan."

The concept made my stomach churn.

"If they succeed, they rise to level four and they become an Architect. These are the designers. They plan the kills. They can execute themselves or delegate down to the Pursuers. Level four is the highest rank before the Crown."

He looked around the table for comprehension. "Architects can choose to kill or not kill. If they have retired from the acts, they can take a seat on the board. They're like a governing body. At the top of it all, is the Crown. The Crown chooses a confidant, or right hand. They're given the title of the Bishop."

My mind processed. *The Initiate. The Blooded. The Pursuers. The Architects. The Crown. The Bishop. The Board.*

"With the current situation," Guy continued. "Alice Sapphire, the Crown, is on her deathbed. She doesn't have long. That seat needs to be filled. But only once a competitor has completed the task. Only Architects are eligible. The Architects, along with the Crown and the board, design the game. Three Architects are chosen. Whoever reaches the target first becomes the new Crown."

Lucy looked up. "So that's where we are right now."

"That's exactly where we are," Guy said.

Lucy hesitated, then asked, "Do they have all the cloak-and-dagger stuff too? Chanting in the forest?"

"They're very ritualistic," Guy said. "Very hierarchical. But they don't meet out in the forest. It's usually inside one of the homes here in Red Rose County, one of the grand ones up in the hills. You can imagine which ones."

I could, and it made me ill.

"They have underground spaces, like fancy basements. There's a dress code. Cloaks, from what we understand. Symbolic jewelry to denote rank. These people are murderers and psychopaths, but these aren't reckless kids. These are serious, powerful, and wealthy individuals. And they only become more wealthy and more powerful through the organization. Therefore, they will protect it at all costs."

He glanced at me. "Now, it seems you have one of them in

custody. Codename Derek Dunn. Good fake identity. His real name is Oakley Patterson."

My stomach sank.

"We believe he's a member. Likely Blooded or a Pursuer, assisting an Architect currently in the competition."

"He's not talking," I said. "Not to us. Not to Martina. Not to anyone."

Guy nodded. "If he talks, the Society won't be happy. And they won't hesitate to eliminate him. We'll keep him in custody for now. Maybe relocate him. Maybe offer a deal. We'll see if we need him." He sat back. "We want to take them down for good and we believe that with a thorough review of the murders that we can attribute to the Society, we can at least prove the crimes belong to the group." He paused, eyes serious. "But the tricky part is proving the group exists before we get shut down."

"So, what's the plan?"

"We have to keep it quiet," Guy said, "quiet enough that the powerful people who may be part of it don't catch on. We don't have a roster. We know who the Crown is, and that's pretty much it. For all we know, we could be working alongside people within our own organizations who are involved."

Letting that sink in, I said, "So you need people on the outside. People you can trust."

"Yes, and we believe there is a way to identify members, to ensure those we let in on the operation aren't members."

I raised a brow. "The rose tattoo."

"Correct," Guy said. "Now, we're obviously not going to walk around the FBI or local law enforcement asking everyone to lift their shirts. But if we're suspicious, we can try to get a look. You know what I'm saying."

I did.

"Which is why we need to keep this extremely tight. Only

reach out to people we believe can actually help the operation. And even then, only give them limited details."

I crossed my arms. "And how do you suppose we take these people down? I'd think you'd need more people, not fewer."

"True, but right now, because there hasn't been a handover of leadership yet and the current Crown is very sick, the organization is vulnerable. They're at a weak point. If we exploit that, we might be able to identify members, put surveillance on them, collect evidence, and eventually tie them to the murders."

It was a decent plan. Just not a fast one. "Eventually? Martina is currently in a safe house. How long do you expect her to stay there?" And what about her family and friends? Her life? How do they protect someone indefinitely? Witness protection? I don't think Martina would go for that.

"Well," Guy said, "we may only need to protect her for as long as Alice Sapphire is alive. Once she dies, the organization loses its leader. That puts them in a tricky position. That's where we think we'll get the most traction."

I nodded slowly. "How long do we think she has?"

Kieran said, "From what we can tell? Maybe a week or two. She's pretty sick. But you never know."

A week or two. That was a long time when someone was being hunted.

"And we think we have a way to generate a list of potential members," Guy said before explaining the FBI's plan to monitor the Sapphire estate. Watch who came and went, with the assumption that members would show up to pay their respects before Alice Sapphire died, and then build a suspect list from that intel. It was a good plan. But I wasn't someone who just sat around waiting for someone to die, and I had a feeling Martina wasn't either.

49

THE ARCHITECT

I STARED at the empty chair where the Crown should have been sitting and couldn't help but imagine myself there. It would be natural. *The right thing.*

The Bishop struck the gavel against the table, the sharp crack echoing through the chamber and pulling my attention back to the room. The board sat elevated above us, literally, while I sat beside the remaining competitor for the Crown. Behind us, the rest of the organization filled the room in orderly rows, cloaked and silent.

This was an emergency meeting, convened at the Crown's request. The Bishop stood in for her, as she was too weak to attend herself. The Bishop surveyed the room before speaking. "Thank you for convening so quickly. As you all know, the clock is ticking. Time is running out for the Crown."

Low murmurs rippled through the chamber.

"However, we have encountered a problem."

The murmurs grew louder until the Bishop raised his hand. "Silence."

The room obeyed.

"As all of you know, there has been a competition underway

to fill the Crown's seat. In the course of completing this competition, law enforcement has become aware of our organization. They know the Crown's identity. They have one of our members in custody. And they appear to know not only that we exist, but that we are actively targeting the Ladybug."

Low mumblings could be heard throughout the room.

"It has also been brought to our attention that multiple law enforcement agencies are now coordinating efforts to dismantle us."

Gasps followed.

Hadn't they been paying attention? Or were they all too busy tracking stock returns, climbing ladders, and polishing reputations. We had been issuing updates. We all knew the failures and the risks that came with them.

Two bombing attempts and two failures. In my opinion, even one failure was too many. It hadn't even been twenty-four hours since the Crown disqualified the third competitor for his incompetence. He had brought scrutiny to the Society, that should have been means for elimination as opposed to a measly disqualification. Although, his failures didn't explain how law enforcement had uncovered the Crown's identity. Someone talked, someone who should have been silent. But who?

"Because of this scrutiny," the Bishop said, "the Crown and I have conferred. I have presented the matter to the board. It is the decision of the Crown and the board that the competition for ascension will be halted. There will be no further attempts on the Ladybug," he said. "Is that clear?"

He scanned the chamber.

Several members nodded. One rose to his feet. "I agree," he said. "This is the smartest course of action. No one wants this level of attention. They cannot be allowed to fully uncover our Society or its members."

"They already have," I said. "Why stop now?"

The Bishop's gaze snapped to me, sharp and cold. "Because if you continue, you risk bringing us all down with you. And that is *unacceptable*. Do you understand?"

"I understand." That didn't mean I agreed.

"In the unlikely event that the Crown passes before a new competition can be safely initiated, I will serve as acting Crown until such time as conditions allow us to proceed. Please know, we have no intention of abandoning our traditions. This is merely a suspension. A strategic pause that will serve all our interests."

A moment later, he stared out at us. "It is said."

"It is said," the group repeated.

"You are dismissed."

Muffled shuffling sounded as members rose. The meeting had dissolved into quiet obedience. As I moved toward the exit, I kept my expression neutral. As far as I was concerned, they could suspend the competition if they wanted, but I had no intention of doing so. I would be the Crown.

Not because it was granted, but because I earned it. Let the others retreat to their glass houses and locked gates, pretending fear was wisdom. Not I. *I finish what I start.*

50

MARTINA

PACING the living room of the safe house, I couldn't stop thinking about how wrong all of this felt. I'd said *no more dangerous cases*. I said it more times than I could count. And yet here I was locked down with Selena, both of us having nearly been killed twice, while billionaire psychopaths hunted me. *Hunted us.* Anyone near me was in danger. Selena. Val. My family. I knew the safe houses and I knew the protocols. I knew no one could reach us here, not with armed guards posted outside and layers of security in place.

Still, I'd be lying if I said I didn't want to be at home with Charlie and Barney. Snuggled up with Charlie and watching our dog, Barney, spin in excited circles when he knew it was time for a walk. That wiggly tail. Those big brown eyes staring up at me, begging for just one more treat. That was home. *This wasn't.*

Before we left Red Rose County, I'd warned Charlie that where I was going would have to remain secret until it was safe and that he needed to keep the home security system armed and to be vigilant. And I wanted so badly to call Zoey. To hear her voice and absorb that bubbly energy of hers. Heck, what I wouldn't give for a burger with Hirsch. He'd eye me as I stole a few fries off his plate, and then say, "You know you can order your own, right?"

Lord, why was it so hard to say no to an investigation?

Why couldn't I just back down? Accept a peaceful, quiet life behind a desk, hiking during the week, playing with my dog, and watching movies with my husband. Trips to Oregon to visit Zoey and Henry. Gym sessions with Selena. I could have all of that. Yet, I kept running toward danger.

Maybe there was no fighting it, it's just who I am down to my core. *I am Martina Monroe and I fight for justice.* Truthfully, sometimes I wished I were someone else. Someone who didn't put herself or the people she loved in danger. Life could be so simple and carefree.

But the truth was, we don't get to choose who we are. Pretending to be someone we're not is *exhausting.* Painful. No one should have to live a life that wasn't true to who they are on the inside.

One thing was for sure, I could never stand on the sidelines while groups like the Society of the Rose killed for sport. I supposed it was time to stop fighting with myself. The sound of the phone made me jump. I answered immediately. "Hey, Val."

"Hi, Martina. How are you feeling?"

"Like a caged animal."

"I completely understand. We had our meeting with the FBI."

"And?"

"They have a plan to get a roster..." She detailed the meeting and the FBI's plan. She ended with, "They want us to stand down until they can build their case."

Silence stretched between us.

I had a feeling Val wasn't someone who waited around while other people crossed T's and dotted I's. And neither was I. "So what's our plan?"

"That's exactly what I wanted to talk to you about." I heard a vibration and then she said, "Sorry, I need to put you on hold, Martina."

As I waited, I thought about the FBI's plan. Solid for a long-term investigation. But from experience, surveillance, evidence gathering, compiling a roster, and building a prosecutable case could take years. *Years.*

We couldn't let them keep operating that long. There had to be another way to expose them and make it clear that no amount of money or power put you above the law.

Selena walked into the room, a towel wrapped around her, water still beading on her shoulders. "Who are you talking to?"

"Val. She put me on hold..." I relayed what Val told me about her meeting and the FBI's plan.

Selena scrunched her face. "Great. By the time they finish, the Society will have changed everything. New tactics. Better body disposal. They'll vanish."

She wasn't wrong. Sure, a roster might expose them and ruin reputations and maybe crumble a few companies. It could save a few future victims, but that wasn't enough. I didn't want them retired on the beaches of Tahiti. I wanted their views to include bars and concrete walls.

"You still on hold?"

"Yeah. Not sure what's going on."

The line clicked. "Sorry," Val said. "There's been some breaking news. My source, the one still active in the Society, just called."

My pulse spiked.

"The competition, it's off. You're no longer a target."

I froze. "Are you sure? Is this credible?"

"Yes. They held an emergency meeting, they somehow found out we're on to them and that we know the identity of the Crown. They don't want the scrutiny. It's off."

"So they're just not killing anymore?"

"Not exactly. They're pausing. Planning a new competition once it's safe."

"So this reprieve could be temporary."

"I think so. But they're not stupid. Going after you again would make them the top suspects."

I exhaled.

Selena stood with one hand on her hip, towel clutched in the other. I lowered the phone. "Competition's off. I'm no longer a target."

Selena cocked her head. "Just like that?"

"They don't want to be caught."

Back on the phone, I said, "That's good news. I hope the FBI keeps digging."

"Oh, they will. These people have destroyed too many lives. I'm not letting this go."

"I'm not either."

She chuckled softly. "I thought so. I'm heading to the Bay Area later today. Maybe we meet tomorrow morning to come up with a plan."

"Aren't you working with the FBI?"

"They can run their long-term strategy, but I think you and I can do better. Are you in?"

I smiled. "I'm in." I ended the call and looked at Selena. "Let's pack. We're leaving."

Selena didn't move. "You really believe it's safe?"

I grabbed my bag. "I want to believe it. But part of me knows that people like this don't just stop. I also know that if they come for me, I'll be ready."

51

MARTINA

THE NEXT MORNING, I dressed to meet Val, still thinking about the night before, about coming home. Charlie had squeezed me so tightly I could barely breathe. I almost didn't want him to let go. It had only been a few days since I'd seen him, but it felt like a lifetime. All the things we could have lost. The life we'd built together. I felt a nudge at my ankles. "Oh, hi, Barney." I crouched down and scratched his neck as his tail wagged furiously.

"We both missed you," Charlie said.

"Well, I missed the two of you quite a bit," I said, smiling. "I've never been so happy to see two creatures in my whole life."

"Have you talked to Zoey yet?"

"I called her on the way home." Of course, she had no idea anything had been wrong. I never told her when I was working a dangerous case. She had enough to focus on with school. We talked a few times a week, but I protected her from the scariest parts of my life.

Selena had agreed to stay the night but had said she'd feel better getting back to her routine the next morning. Selena was solitary by nature, an introvert. She needed space to process, and I understood that. What feels right for one person doesn't always feel right for another. And that's okay. What makes us different makes us special.

"This is all over now?"

I clenched my teeth. "Not quite."

He raised his brows. "You still have to put the bad guys in jail."

"That's right. Val and I are meeting to come up with a plan."

"And you're sure it's safe now?"

I shrugged. "The official word is that it is. But you know me. I'm always on guard."

"Yes, you are."

I wasn't convinced the threat was gone, but I'd slept well for the first time in days. Dressed and fed with a kiss goodbye from Charlie, I hopped into the car to meet Val at a coffee shop near the office. Somewhere public yet quiet enough to talk privately before looping in the rest of the team.

I decided that I wasn't fighting who I was anymore. I was done pretending I wanted a quiet life behind a desk. It just isn't who I am.

The coffee shop was one I'd gone to for years. I'd go there when I needed a break, or when I met with Hirsch. I planned to arrive early, snag the most private table to make sure no one overheard us. The last thing we needed was to scare civilians.

As I drove, I glanced in the rearview mirror. A dark sedan was behind me. No front license plate, but it was a newer car. I continued driving, thinking about how Val's FBI experience and profiling skills, combined with my firm, could move faster than the Bureau's timeline.

I turned onto the highway. The sedan followed. Coincidence, I told myself. There were plenty of black sedans in the neighborhood. I took my exit. So did the sedan. My senses piqued. Someone was following me. I stayed calm and pulled into the coffee shop parking lot. The sedan parked right next to me. *That was awfully bold.*

Out of the car, I leaned against my driver's door ready for whatever came next.

The driver stepped out of his car. He was mid-to-late forties and well-dressed in a pale, blue cashmere sweater and dark trousers. Ordinary enough to blend in anywhere. His eyes were dark, and cold. His gaze met mine as he walked right toward me. He smiled.

"Do I know you?" I asked.

And then it hit me. *I did know him.* He was in Alice Sapphire's room. One of the three men standing there until she dismissed them like servants. He walked over to face me. "I believe we've seen each other in passing."

"They told me you called it off."

In an amusing tone, he said, "*They* did."

"You're one of them."

His head tilted slightly. "Why don't you and I have a conversation."

My pulse stayed steady. "Are you the source?"

He smirked. "Hardly."

And just like that, I knew the competition was *not* off, at least not for this guy. This man, this killer, wasn't ready for the game to be over. "You're one of the Architects."

"I think you know too much."

And before I could fully register what was happening, he was beside me and had something hard pressed into my side. Likely a firearm.

He leaned in so close I could feel his breath in my ear. "I think you should come with me, Martina."

Keeping cool, I said, "I'd love to, but I have plans. I'm meeting a friend for coffee."

"You already had breakfast," he said. "Eggs. Sausage. Looked good. It must be nice to have a husband that cooks for you."

Cold spread through my chest. He'd been watching me *inside* my house. I just hoped my home surveillance system had captured his image. Whatever this man thought he was doing, he wasn't getting away with it. "I'm not going anywhere with you."

"Come now, or you'll be sorry."

"Sorry pal. You'll have to try to kill me right here, in broad daylight. Good luck getting away with that." I forced my breathing to stay steady. "To ascend to the Crown, you have to get away with the crime, right? Otherwise, you end up disgraced and in prison. So then, what's the point?"

The weapon pressed harder into my ribs.

"You're right. I suppose I'll need to do something to compel you. How about, you leave with me now, or the first person who walks out that door, I shoot them in the face. *I don't care who they are.* And then you come with me. And if you don't, I'll kill the next one and the next one, until you agree."

My heart pounded. "You'll never get away with this."

"Oh, but I will. It's a stranger killing. No motive and no suspect. All they'll be able to say is, 'it's so tragic, so sad.'" He made a soft, mocking whine.

Something clicked into place then. This man was unhinged and wanted nothing more than to kill me, and had no issue killing others in the process. How long would it take Val to realize I had been taken.? Did she know what type of car I drove? Would she figure out what happened before it was too late?

"Fine."

He stiffened, just a fraction before the creepy grin returned. "Let's go."

He turned toward his car, pulling me by the arm. As soon as I was inside, he strapped on my seatbelt before he hurried to the driver's side. As he drove out of the lot, I said a silent prayer.

52

MARTINA

HE DROVE with his left hand, the weapon steady in his right, angled toward my ribs with a grin on his face. If boldness was what pleased the Society, he certainly had it.

"You know this ends only one way," I said. "The Society of the Rose is finished."

"If I go down, Martina, I'll go down in history."

"And where exactly are you taking me?"

"Oh." He turned onto a winding road. "I just thought we'd get out of the city and return to nature. My friends have a little farm not far from here." He gestured vaguely ahead.

He might have been rich, connected, and powerful but he was also seriously deranged. And that was dangerous. I ran through my options. Simply overpowering him while driving could be too risky. If I tried to take control of the vehicle or inca-pacitated him, at his current speed, the vehicle could spin out or rollover and we'd both be dead. I had no Kevlar and no margin for error. To buy some time, and gain information I hoped to use later, I said, "What's your name?"

"Ashton."

"How'd you get into the Society?" I asked. "School friends?"

"My father was a member. It was nepotism, really. I'm a nepo baby, as they say."

"And the Society matters so much to you that you're willing to kill me despite their orders? Why?"

"At first, it felt good to be part of the Society. I liked the feeling of belonging and being among like-minded people who were powerful and strong. I couldn't stand the idea of blending in with all the sad sheep that surrounds us." He sighed. "But it just isn't what it used to be."

"When did you realize that?"

"When the Crown got sick. She should have stepped down. Started the competition immediately. Instead, she clung to power." He scoffed. "And they all just followed her. Like sheep."

"But you're not a sheep."

His lips curled. "Exactly."

"And that's why they called off the competition?"

"Yes."

"So what does killing me prove?"

He finally looked at me. "I want to do what they couldn't. I don't need to be the Crown, but I want to show them I think for myself, and that we all should. Naturally they'll see I'm better than them."

"Are you?"

His cheeks flushed. "Yes."

"Won't they be upset you defied orders?"

"Orders," he spat. "I no longer take orders. To be honest, they all sicken me."

"So, you're done with them but still want me?"

"Yes. I knew you'd be a great challenge, and I love a challenge. No aging dinosaur is going to tell me I can't fulfill my destiny."

"Why not just shoot me in the parking lot?"

He laughed darkly. "Where's the fun in that? You think I

don't know you're armed and ready to fight?" He glanced at my coat. "If all I wanted was a quick kill, I could've killed you several times already. For instance, I could have shot you with a rifle this morning while you were enjoying your eggs. But, no. There's an art to this. It's not just about ending someone's life. It's about the hunt." The road narrowed and trees closed in. "It'll be you versus me. Best hunter wins." He smiled. "How does that sound?"

It sounded *insane*. I whispered another prayer under my breath, then met his gaze. "Sounds like fun."

He threw his head back and laughed, it was loud, and manic. And I knew one thing for certain. I needed a plan, or I wouldn't make it out of this alive.

53

VAL

I PULLED up to the coffee shop looking forward to finally sitting down with Martina and building a real strategy. The Society needed to become history, a lesson law enforcement studied after the fact. A reminder that monsters don't always look like monsters. Sometimes they hide behind polished smiles and fancy houses, and you don't know what's underneath until it's too late. I pushed open the door and stepped inside. Surveying the cafe, I didn't see Martina. I glanced at my watch. I was two minutes early. Martina was usually early too. Maybe she'd hit traffic or was running late.

I went to the counter and ordered a caramel latte and then took a seat at an empty table near the window. I pulled out my phone and checked for messages. None.

A few minutes later, my coffee was ready. I took a sip. Caramel. Surprisingly good. Still, something tightened in my gut. I looked through the windows. No sign of Martina.

She was only a few minutes late, but that wasn't like her. Not today. Not after everything. Maybe she was caught up at the office. I called her cell phone, but it went to voicemail, next I tried her office. "Drakos Monroe Security & Investigations. How can I direct your call?"

"Yes, can you put me through to Martina Monroe?"

"She's unavailable at the moment. Can I take a message?"

"Is there someone else on her team I can speak with? Is Selena Bailey available?"

"Who is calling?"

"Val Costa."

"Yes, one moment."

A moment later, I heard, "Hey Val, What's up?"

"Have you talked to Martina this morning?"

Selena hesitated. "When I left the house this morning. Why?"

"She was meeting me for coffee, but she's not here. I might be overreacting. She's only five minutes late."

Selena didn't reassure me. "Which coffee shop?"

"Battle Grounds."

A beat.

"I'll call my dad. See if she's still at the house. I'll call you right back."

I ended the call and scanned the shop again. I told myself I was being paranoid. That happens when the person you're meeting was recently the target of three killers.

I took another sip of coffee and immediately regretted it. My nerves were already humming. My phone buzzed, and I answered immediately. "She left a while ago. She should've been there by now. Have you tried calling her?"

"I did. No answer. What kind of car does she drive?"

"A Subaru Outback. Dark metallic blue."

I walked outside, my eyes sweeping the parking lot. There was a blue SUV. "Do you know her license plate number?"

"No, but I could look it up."

"Does she have anything distinctive on or in her car? A decal or license plate frame?"

"Her car is usually super clean, no trash."

I moved closer and looked through the window. The car was immaculate. My stomach clenched. "Give me a sec," I said and rushed back into the coffee shop. I called out, "Is anyone here the owner of the blue Subaru Outback parked outside?"

Heads shook. A few confused looks. No one spoke up. I was already moving back outside. "Selena, I think Martina's car is here. She's not."

Silence on the line.

I had been told the competition was paused and that Martina was safe. I strolled around the vehicle, searching for signs of a struggle. There were none. But I felt it. "I think she's been taken."

"We can find her," Selena said immediately. "I can get her location if she has her phone. Dad and she share their locations. I'll call you back."

The call ended.

Surveying the area, there was no sign of which way she could have gone. No cameras outside the coffee shop. My phone sounded. Selena rattled off the coordinates and then said, "I'm putting a team together. We're heading out now. ETA is twenty-seven minutes."

Rushing toward my car, I said, "I'll meet you there."

My heart pounded so hard it felt like I might crack my ribs. I'd told Martina she was safe. She wasn't. And wherever she was, I knew she wasn't there by choice. If she died, it would be my fault.

54

MARTINA

HE STOPPED the car in front of a ranch-style home surrounded by nature. At first glance, it was idyllic with its low roofline, wide front porch, and weathered wood. Mature trees surrounded the property, their branches heavy, shrubs and thick hedges hemming the house on all sides. No neighboring homes. No road noise. Just the whisper of wind through leaves. It was quiet, isolated, and *hidden*.

How long before Val would realize I'd been taken? Would she know to call my office and ask if anyone has seen me? I had to pray that she did, otherwise I wasn't sure how I was going to survive this. But I knew that if I could stay alive long enough for them to find me, I'd make it. If not, I'd have to try to kill him. I wasn't opposed to the idea.

With glee in his voice, he said, "We're here." The gun never wavered as he gestured it in my direction.

"Don't get any funny ideas. I want this to be fair."

Fair?

"Get out of the car. Slowly."

I did, keeping my movements controlled. He exited too, circling fast, the gun still trained on me. I didn't have a shot without risking he could pull his trigger faster. He was already moving, anticipating me.

"Okay, here's the game. I'll give you a one-minute head start."

My pulse thudded in my ears.

"And then, I'll hunt you."

The way he said hunt made my skin crawl. "Any rules?"

He smiled. "That's it." His gaze flicked over me. "You've got one minute to go as far and fast as you can. I've seen you run at the gym. It'll hardly be a challenge for you."

How long had he been watching me?

"Let's go," he said, almost giddy.

He escorted me to the edge of the front deck. The land dropped away into uneven terrain. There were trees, fallen branches, and dense undergrowth. No clear paths with plenty of places to trip. He raised the gun and fired into the air. The sound cracked through the trees.

"Go!"

He didn't need to tell me twice. I tore forward without hesitation, pulling my firearm from my jacket as I sprinted. I zigzagged, searching the area for wide trees or low shrubs where I could take cover.

When the minute was up, a gunshot split the air behind me.

I dove behind a thick pine, chest heaving. With a quick glance, I could see his shape moving through the trees. He was fast. *Dang it.* And he knew it. I didn't know the land well, but running blind wasn't enough. I needed help, *now*. I pulled out my phone to call 911.

No reception.

Shoving the phone back into my pocket, I took a second to decide my next move.

He called my name, his voice drifting through the trees, taunting me. Another shot slammed into the trunk inches from my head, and bark exploded.

I bolted from my hiding spot. As I ran, branches tore at my arms. Thorns snagged my clothes. My breath rasped loud in my ears as I pushed deeper into the woods.

Suddenly, I was transported back to my Army training days. Like combat, this was a fight to the death. I glanced over my shoulder and saw his silhouette closing in. I aimed and fired. *And I missed.*

It was difficult to hit a moving target. Therefore, I needed to keep moving. He was right, I was fit. But I'd have to pray that they found me before I ran out of steam or made it to the road and could flag someone down.

Another crack off a nearby tree.

Staring ahead, I studied the trees, mostly skinny. Too skinny to hide behind. Some with pock marks that looked like bullet holes. My heart skipped a beat. *This isn't his first hunt.*

55

VAL

SPEEDING DOWN THE HIGHWAY, I was closer to where he'd taken her than Selena's team was. Glancing at the clock, I couldn't help but feel that every second a door could be closing. What was he doing to her? Torturing her? Branding her? Or something worse? My phone rang. "Val, are you there yet?" Selena asked.

"I'm about two minutes out. Any word?"

There was still a thin sliver of hope that Martina was safe and sound. But I knew better. She had been taken. The question wasn't if, but by whom. My money was on the Society. Someone who couldn't tolerate that they'd called off the competition. An Architect who had been close enough to taste power and couldn't stand being told to wait.

These weren't people who de-escalated. They didn't accept loss. They didn't retreat. They proved, rebelled, and escalated. The competition being called off wasn't a deterrent, it was an insult. And insults like that don't make men like him safer. They make him dangerous.

"Do you mind keeping your phone on when you get there?" Selena asked. "You can mute it. I just want to listen."

I understood what she was really asking. If something happened, she wanted to hear it.

"I'll keep it on, but muted."

"We're a few minutes behind you. We have to make sure she's okay. Nothing bad can happen to Martina. Do you understand?"

The panic in her voice came through loud and clear. "I do."

The GPS chirped as I reached the last known ping from Martina's phone. It was a road. There were no houses or buildings, just trees. Unmuting the phone, I said, "Selena, I'm here. There's just a road. No sign of a vehicle."

"Cell reception might be bad. Is there a turnoff?"

I scanned ahead. A narrow gravel drive disappeared into the trees. "Yeah. There's a driveway. I'm heading down it."

"If you lose signal—"

"You'll know why."

As I drove down the gravel road, my phone chimed once, and that was it. The signal was lost.

Martina had been missing at least thirty minutes. Probably more. Forty-five, if she'd left earlier. A lot could happen in forty-five minutes.

The road opened into a clearing. A ranch-style house came into view, unremarkable, mid-century. Not grand. Not flashy. Just a bit hidden and isolated. Trees and bushes wrapped around it like a wall.

In the driveway sat a dark Mercedes sedan. *They were here.* I shut off the engine and opened my door slowly, listening.

I pulled my extra Glock from the glove compartment. It was possible I'd need both of my weapons. I moved toward the house, staying low, peering through windows as I passed. There weren't any lights on or signs of movement or a struggle.

Then I heard it. A gunshot cracking through the trees. Dread slammed into me, as I realized he wasn't just holding her, he was hunting her. I raised my weapon and ran toward the sound.

I thought, *Please, Martina. Hold on, I'm coming.*

56

MARTINA

WHITE-HOT PAIN tore through my arm. I switched my gun to my other hand. I could shoot left-handed, but I wasn't quite as precise. Blood soaked my sleeve, warm and slick. It wasn't just a graze. Adrenaline soaring, I turned, scanning for him. He wasn't in my line of sight. Hopefully that meant if I couldn't see him, he couldn't see me.

I hit a wall of brush, a thicket dense enough to hide me if I lie low. Quietly, I climbed down and pressed flat, heart hammering, I forced my breathing to quiet.

This was combat now.

Footsteps crunched closer.

Branches snapped.

"Martina," he called, almost kindly. "Hope that didn't hurt too bad."

Rage surged, but I crushed it down and listened. Counted steps. Waited. *This was my moment.*

Five seconds. Ten. His shadow crossed the brush line, and I fired.

A grunt, then a string of curses, and the woods exploded with return fire. By the grace of God, I didn't take another hit. I rolled and ran. Bullets chewed bark behind me. I slid behind the widest pine I could find, cut sideways, and came up firing.

This time I caught him, hard, in the arm. His weapon clattered to the ground. I charged.

He lunged for the gun. I kicked it away, felt a jolt up my leg, and he slammed into me. We hit the ground hard. He clawed for my weapon. I drove my knee into him and rolled free. He staggered up, searching.

I had a clean shot. I aimed for his thigh and fired. He dove, scrabbling, somehow grabbing the fallen weapon as he went. He started to raise it up, but I stepped in, squared up, and aimed for center mass. The shot landed. His hands went slack. The gun fell from his grip. He fell.

I stood over him, chest heaving, arm screaming, and with my weapon steady and positioned on him. Blood soaked the ground between us.

Footsteps pounded in from my right. I glanced over. *Val.*

She took in the scene in a heartbeat, eyes flicking from me to Ashton, who was gasping. "Are you okay?"

With a quick look at my arm, I said, "I'm fine. I think."

She studied me. "There's no cell reception. I'm going to run back to the road to call for an ambulance. Selena's team should be here any minute. You got this?"

Tears burned hot and sudden as they streaked down my cheeks. "I got it... Thanks for coming for me."

She gave me a small grin. "Looks like you didn't need me." She then turned and ran.

I dropped beside Ashton, after kicking his weapon farther away, and pressed down on the wound in his chest. Blood bubbled at his lips. "Well played," he mumbled. A moment later, his body went slack and I lifted my bloodied hands.

He was gone.

57

MARTINA

MY EYES FLUTTERED open and for a moment I didn't know where I was. Then the hospital smells hit me, and the steady beep of a monitor pulled everything into focus. A hospital bed. White walls. My arm wrapped tight, and immobilized. The doctor's words came back to me in fragments. "The bullet hit an artery. If you hadn't gotten here when you did, you might have lost it. Or worse." I let out a slow breath and turned my head.

Charlie sat in the chair beside the bed, a book open in his lap, a cup of coffee resting on the table next to him. He looked up immediately, eyes searching my face.

What a wonderful thing to wake up to. "Morning," I said, my voice rough.

"Good morning. How are you feeling?"

"Tired."

He smiled faintly. "That's normal."

I reached for him with my left hand. He took it instantly, squeezing like he was afraid to let go. "I don't say it enough... but I love you."

He said it plenty, but I never got tired of hearing it. "I love you, too."

His eyes filled, and for a second his voice failed him. "I'm not sure I've ever been so scared."

"I'm okay. I'm here."

He nodded, but I could tell he wasn't convinced. "You almost weren't."

"I know."

There were a dozen conversations hovering between us about danger, about choices, and about me giving up the job. We both knew how that one would end. I understood his worry, I worried about Selena, about my team, and about everyone who stood near me.

Selena stepped in carrying her own cup of coffee, her gaze flicking immediately between us. "Everything okay?"

"We're good," I said, trying to sound convincing.

Her shoulders relaxed. "No issues overnight?"

I glanced toward the door. Steve and Otto stood outside, unmistakable even through the glass. They didn't know who else might come after me. I thought I was probably fine. The one person who wanted me dead was already gone. But Charlie and Selena had insisted. Val had agreed it wasn't a bad idea.

"Nope."

"How are you feeling? Ready to get back out there?" She gave me a wink.

With a half-hearted smile, I said, "I think I'll take a break for a while. The doctors say I'll be here a few days."

"Smart. I talked to Zoey," she said. "She wants to hear your voice. And asked me to have you call her as soon as you were awake."

"I will."

Her phone buzzed. Selena glanced at the screen.

"That's Val," she said. "I'm going to take it. Call Zoey."

She stepped out of the room quickly, the door swinging shut behind her. I leaned back against the pillow, still holding Charlie's hand, knowing, without being told, that whatever Val had to say would change the quiet all over again.

Charlie handed me my phone; it was already calling Zoey.

"Hi, Mom. Are you okay?"

"Yes, honey. I'm just fine." It wasn't the first time I'd been shot. If we were keeping tabs, it was the third. Maybe I was like a cat, like Selena, with nine lives. Three bullets down. I suppose that meant I had six more left. Not that I was hoping for more. Still, it felt like a testament to something bigger. I'd come close to death so many times, and every time, God had pulled me back. I had people looking out for me and my prayers had been answered on multiple occasions. I couldn't ignore that.

"How are you and Henry doing? How is the clinic?"

"We're all good here," Zoey said, "but you gave us quite a scare, Mom."

I smiled faintly. "You know one silly psychopath isn't going to take me out."

"Oh boy," she said. "You sound like Uncle August."

Uncle August, my former partner, August Hirsch. My mother and Zoey always preferred to call him by his first name.

"Well," Zoey said, "I'm just heading off to the clinic. Can I call you later?"

"Of course. I love you, honey."

"Love you too, Mom."

I handed the phone back just as Selena hurried into the room, eyes wide, barely containing herself. "Martina, you're never going to believe this."

I braced myself. "What?"

"Well, on our way here there were some updates."

"Updates?"

"Yeah. Apparently when the police searched Ashton Edina's car, the Architect who was trying to become the Crown and kidnapped you, they found a manifesto."

My pulse sped up.

"He called the Society of the Rose *sheep*," Selena continued. "He listed names of members and victims that died at their hands."

"You're kidding,"

"Nope. And as soon as Val saw it, she took photos. She said she didn't know who they could trust with a list like that. These people have ties everywhere."

"Where's the list now?"

Selena shrugged. "You know how Vincent has his connections to the media?"

I smiled. "Oh yes. I do know about Vincent's ties to the media."

"Well," she said, "according to Vincent, the manifesto is about to go live. Social media. Traditional news outlets. Everywhere. It's about to blow up."

Good. "Hopefully that will be the end of them."

"Yeah. Ashton basically buried the Society of the Rose. It's going to die right along with him."

The members would be furious. Angry enough to come after me? Or Val or anyone associated with its demise? Not that I'd outed them; it was Ashton, but they could feel it was because of me he snapped. I couldn't think about that. That would be another battle for another day.

But then I thought about his rants, the way he'd spoken about the Society calling them sheep who couldn't think for themselves. It wasn't surprising that he'd decided to expose them for the world to see. He was an Architect, after all. Control mattered to him, even in death. I could already imagine the media storm that was coming and I just hoped they kept my name out of it. I was done being famous. I still wanted to do my job, get justice and find the missing, but I didn't want the attention. I didn't want people reaching out to me to spread their message or recruit me into some sick little club. *No, thank you.*

"I hope it saves lives."

"Me too." Selena hesitated, then added, "Val said she's working on getting more details about Lena's kidnapping, because some of it still doesn't make sense. Ethan Buck's role and who actually took Lena. Why they had her escape. Why Teresa McDonald's body was left on the trail. Val said she'll update you when she's got answers."

A few answers would be nice. "Is Lena back home yet?"

"Val says Lena and her father are home now."

"Is she okay? She went through a traumatic event."

"The Red Rose County deputies told Val that Lena seems to be holding up okay. But she doesn't know yet that her parents were involved in her kidnapping, or that the Society exists and her mom is their leader."

That information was possibly going to be more traumatic than her kidnapping. Pushing that aside for the moment, I glanced at Selena's coffee cup, then at Charlie's.

Charlie smiled. "I'd bet you'd love a cup of coffee and some breakfast."

I nodded. "Just a little."

"You got it."

I leaned back against the pillows, suddenly aware of how good it felt just to be there. To be surrounded by Selena and Charlie, by people who cared whether I lived or died. I was still curious about Val. We hadn't had much time to get to know each other, but I could already tell we had a lot in common. She might be a retired FBI agent, but she couldn't back down from the work any more than I could. We were the same that way.

I looked forward to her visit, and even more, to seeing what law enforcement and the FBI were willing to do to make sure the Society of the Rose died, never to be resurrected.

58

MARTINA

Seated at the coffee shop, I waited for Val. I wasn't sure if I was trying to prove something to myself, or to the universe. That I could sit there, on the edge of the place where I'd been taken, hunted, and nearly killed. That I was tough. That I wasn't afraid. Or maybe it was simpler than that. They had the best coffee in town.

Or maybe I wanted neutral ground when Val filled me in on the case. She'd promised a full update, and I was looking forward to hearing it. We'd been texting over the past two weeks. She'd checked in on my recovery, and I'd asked how things were progressing. Today was the first time we'd meet face-to-face since I was shot.

The bell over the door jingled. Val walked in wearing jeans and a light sweater, hair loose, lip gloss catching the light. No armor. Just her. I waved, and she spotted me immediately.

"How are you feeling?" she asked as she slid into the chair.

"Almost as good as new."

"That's good to hear."

I nudged the caramel latte toward her. "I ordered for you. I remembered that's what you said you liked."

She smiled. "Thanks."

"And... thanks for helping save my life."

She shrugged. "Equal trade." After a sip, she said, "That's so good."

"This place used to be one of my favorites," I said. "Now I have some mixed feelings."

She smiled faintly. "I was surprised this is where you wanted to meet."

"I wasn't about to let some deranged individual take my favorite coffee spot from me."

With a playful smirk, she said, "I completely understand."

"How are things back in Red Rose County?"

"Quiet again. Although it's a little eerie, knowing a secret society operated there for nearly a century. All those years growing up there, I never would've guessed."

"Well," I said, "most people don't assume something like that is happening in their own backyard. Hopefully, it's stopped now."

She gave a small laugh. "Me too. Nobody likes being taken by a deranged killer. Trust me."

"You've been abducted?"

"Twice," she said dryly. "Zero stars. *Would not recommend.*"

With a chuckle, I said, "I wouldn't either."

She sat back. "You want to hear the latest?"

I'd been at home, out of the office for the past two weeks, and hated it. "Yes, please."

"Well, with the manifesto going public including the names and the victims, law enforcement across California and Nevada are reopening cold cases. Suspects are being questioned. Known members of the Society are scrambling to explain their involvement. Ashton didn't give us the locations of the bodies, so we're still trying to find them and bring closure to families. We've already located a few, but there's a lot more out there."

"That's something."

"The FBI's undertaking is massive. Their attempt to hold all those accountable could take years, but it's being fast-tracked."

"I'm glad."

"And more specifically," Val said, "we finally have answers about Lena's kidnapping. All the parts that never made sense."

I leaned in.

"With the list public, we were able to apply pressure. We re-questioned Oakley Patterson, AKA Derek, and Ethan, along with Jason, Tiffany, and Jenna. From what we can tell, Jason, Tiffany, and Jenna had no idea what was really happening. Ethan did set it up. He planned the prank to get Lena alone, away from cameras. Lena's mother asked him to do it, but he didn't know the real plan or that the Society existed. He only stayed silent before at Alice Sapphire's request. So, not likely a murderer, but still a creep."

"That tracks."

"Two Society members actually took Lena," Val said. "They drugged her and held her in Red Rose County. When you went back to the Bay Area, the plan shifted. They needed you back."

My jaw tightened.

"So they dug up Teresa McDonald's body and left it on the trail to pull you back to town."

"And the connection between Teresa and Ethan?"

"It's a little unclear, but what we think is that they chose Teresa's body to keep Ethan quiet. But it's a little murky. We don't think he's involved in her death."

"Any new forensic leads on Teresa?"

"No," Val said. "But it strengthens the conspiracy case. The feds are trying to charge the Society as a whole. RICO might apply, it's complicated, but they're pushing."

"And Derek?"

"After Teresa's body was found and you returned to Red Rose

County, they staged the escape. They beat up Derek for authenticity and then he helped Lena 'escape.' She was never meant to be held that long. It was supposed to be three days max. Alice Sapphire wasn't pleased when it dragged on."

"So everything was designed to move me."

"Exactly."

I shook my head. "No offense, Val, but if I never go back to Red Rose County, don't hold it against me."

"No offense taken. Though I have a feeling, it wouldn't scare you off forever."

"Well," I said, "it sounds like the Society may actually be finished."

"Let's hope so," she said. Then her smile faded. "There's one more thing."

I waited.

"Rumors," she said. "Whispers. This was the Society of the Rose, specific to Red Rose County. But there may be others. Similar groups. Elsewhere."

"That's disturbing."

"It is. The FBI's forming a task force to look for signs of others."

I made a silent note to say a prayer that it was only a rumor.

We finished our coffees. The conversation drifted, from work to life. When we stood to leave, I realized we'd ended not just as colleagues, but as friends. People who understood each other. As we said goodbye and promised to stay in touch, I had the distinct sense this wasn't the last time our paths would cross. Because we were two warriors who couldn't, and wouldn't, *ever* back down from a fight.

ALSO BY H.K. CHRISTIE

The Martina Monroe Series —a nail-biting crime thriller series starring PI Martina Monroe and her unofficial partner Detective August Hirsch of the Cold Case Squad. If you like high-stakes games, jaw-dropping twists, and suspense that will keep you on the edge of your seat, then you'll love the Martina Monroe crime thriller series.

The Val Costa Series —a gripping crime thriller with heart-pounding suspense. If you love Martina, you'll love Val.

The Neighbor Two Doors Down —a dark and witty psychological thriller. If you like unpredictable twists, page-turning suspense, and unreliable narrators, then you'll love *The Neighbor Two Doors Down*.

The Selena Bailey Series (1 - 5) —a suspenseful series featuring a young Selena Bailey and her turbulent path to becoming a top-notch private investigator as led by her mentor, Martina Monroe.

A Permanent Mark A heartless killer. Weeks without answers. Can she move on when a murderer walks free? If you like riveting suspense and gripping mysteries, then you'll love *A Permanent Mark* - starring a grown up Selena Bailey.

Please Don't Go She thought she left the past behind. Until a long-buried secret pulled her back—and turned her into a killer. A fast paced and addictive revenge thriller.

For H.K. Christie's full catalog go to: **www.authorhkchristie.com**

At **www.authorhkchristie.com** you can also sign up for the H.K. Christie reader club where you'll be the first to hear about upcoming novels, new releases, giveaways, promotions, and a **free e-copy of the prequel to the Martina Monroe Series, *Crashing Down*!**

ABOUT THE AUTHOR

H. K. Christie watched horror films far too early in life. Inspired by the likes of Stephen King, Jodi Picoult, true crime podcasts, and a vivid imagination she now writes suspenseful thrillers.

She found her passion for writing when she embarked on a one-woman habit breaking experiment. Although she didn't break her habit she did discover a love of writing and has been at it ever since.

When not working on her latest novel, H.K. Christie can be found eating & drinking with friends, walking around the lakes, or playing with her favorite furry pal.

She is a native and current resident of the San Francisco Bay Area.

To learn more about H.K. Christie and her books, or simply to say, "hello", go to **www.authorhkchristie.com**.

At **www.authorhkchristie.com** you can also sign up for the H.K. Christie reader club where you'll be the first to hear about upcoming novels, new releases, giveaways, promotions, and a free e-copy of the prequel to the Martina Monroe Series, *Crashing Down*!

ACKNOWLEDGMENTS

My sincere thanks to my incredible Advanced Reader Team. Your willingness to dive into my stories early, catch those pesky typos, and share your thoughtful reviews and support means more than you know. Your enthusiasm helps bring these books to life.

To my editor, Ryan Mahan, thank you for your sharp eye, thoughtful suggestions, and dedication to making each story stronger. I'm grateful for your careful edits and insight.

To my talented cover designer, Odile, thank you for your creativity, guidance, and the beautiful covers that help my books stand out.

To my best writing buddy (also known as the boss), Charlie, thank you for the constant encouragement—and the reminders that it's time to step away from the keyboard. Without you, I'd probably spend the entire day locked in my office instead of tending to your very important needs: snuggles, scratches, treats, and long, wandering walks.

To the mister, thank you—as always—for standing by my side and supporting this dream.

And finally, to my readers: thank you from the bottom of my heart. Because of you, I get to live the dream of writing stories for a living.

Made in United States
North Haven, CT
08 April 2026

91111953R00174